STEVE ERICKSON'S
RUBICON BEACH

"One of the most notable books of the year . . . In his second novel, *Rubicon Beach*, Steve Erickson has shunned the strictures of realistic fiction to create a highly imaginative work whose true subject is the imagination itself. . . . Part science fiction, part surrealist love story, part political fable, *Rubicon Beach* combines all these elements into something whose overall impact is curiously close to that of opera. The strong passages attain a stirring lyrical intensity. . . . There is no question that he is a young writer to be watched."
—THE NEW YORK TIMES BOOK REVIEW

"The dark, ever-reaching beauty of *Rubicon Beach* is the very image and echo of the empty garden of our time. . . . A courageous author. A great book."
—EAST VILLAGE EYE

"An original vision, rendered concisely and bravely . . . an adventurous intelligence ranging free."
—L.A. STYLE

D0775697

BOOKS BY STEVE ERICKSON

DAYS BETWEEN STATIONS
RUBICON BEACH

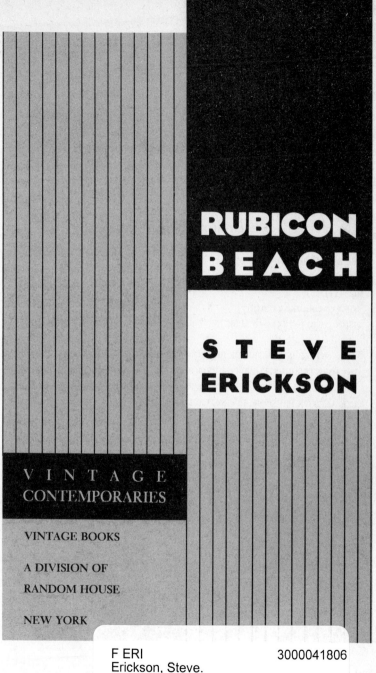

RUBICON BEACH

STEVE ERICKSON

VINTAGE
CONTEMPORARIES

VINTAGE BOOKS

A DIVISION OF
RANDOM HOUSE

NEW YORK

FIRST VINTAGE CONTEMPORARIES EDITION, SEPTEMBER 1987

LIBRARY OF CONGRESS CATALOGING-IN-PUBLICATION DATA
ERICKSON, STEVE.
RUBICON BEACH.
(VINTAGE CONTEMPORARIES)
I. TITLE.
[PS3555.R47R83 1987]   813'.54   87-40069
ISBN 0-394-75513-8 (PBK.)

DISPLAY TYPOGRAPHY BY JESSICA SHATAN

AUTHOR PHOTO COPYRIGHT © 1987 BY ALISON COBB

MANUFACTURED IN THE UNITED STATES OF AMERICA
10 9 8 7 6 5 4 3 2 1

ONE

I GOT OUT late winter. I was off on the exact day by thirty-some hours, which is not bad calculations. I made the decision when I went in to keep track of the days, for the simple reason that it was the intention of my jailers to jettison my sense of time and place. They brought you in a metal truck with no windows and took you out in the same truck or one damned similar. The rumor was that Bell Federal Penitentiary was somewhere in the plains of the Montana-Saskatchewan annex. The sight from my cell would not have refuted this. The white of the snow and sky filled my eyes like the sheet pulled over the head of a dead man. If it was not Montana-Saskatchewan, then it was the North Pole, or the moon. It was a signal to anyone who's ever doubted the terror of an idea that almost all of us in this prison that had no time or place were utterly guiltless of a violent act, unless one counts the violence of tongues.

I wasn't one of them. Maybe I should have been. I wasn't one of any of them; probably I should have been. Ben Jarry asked me once, How long you think you can be neither one nor the other? and I said, As long as I choose. Because I chose to be neither, it never occurred to me that anything I did could have ramifications. One day I told some guy a joke and the next day they hung Ben Jarry with it. Then they let me go, not because they appreciated my sense of humor but because they understood it was the worst thing they could do to me. They knew I'd tell that joke in my sleep forever. Virtually every moment of the two years and four months I sat in Bell

Pen I imagined what it would be like to be out, I imagined the ride out the iron gates in a metal truck with no windows. I was so innocent that it never occurred to me there might never be such a ride. I waited for it. I kept track of the days. Then I told some guy a joke and stopped counting the days, at which point I got the ride in the metal truck. Some time in this period, between the joke and the ride, I lost those thirty-some hours. My jailers were ironic people.

The metal truck took me to Seattle. We got there around one in the afternoon. The door of the truck opened and there was a pier; the glitter of the sea was like glass in my eyes. I just sat in the back of the truck until someone said, Move. I stepped into the street, the guard slammed the door, and the truck rolled off, leaving me there with the clothes on my back. Then someone in a brown suit walked up to me and said, Are you Cale? He saw the look on my face and watched me watch the truck and said, Follow me. I said to him, I had this feeling I was going to be on my own; he could see I was relieved. Not a chance, he answered; what, you think we're not going to keep track of you? We're going to keep track of you. The two of us walked back toward this little corrugated shack on the pier. Maybe, I said to him, I'll just slip away sometime, what's to stop me from doing that? We got to the door and he opened it and turned to me and said, And where you going to go, Cale? Besides, he said, you're on our side now. Have you forgotten? You nailed Ben Jarry for us, re-member? I said to him, It was just a joke; and he said, Yeah old Ben would laugh his head off right now, if he could get a little breathing room around the neck.

And he said that to me, and I knew from there on out everything was going to be a windowless metal truck, wher-ever I went and for as long as I lived. And they got me on this boat going down the coast to Los Angeles, and not a soul to be seen on shore for five days and fifteen hundred miles except a soldier here and there, the guards at the Northwest-Mendocino frontier. We came into L.A. middusk. Behind us the sky was yellow and black and the city was blue and orange. It took two hours sailing in, past the blank smoky moors of the Hollywood Peninsula to our north, navigating our way through the outlying swamps where the Hancock Park mansions loomed in ruin, sea water rolling in and out of the porticoes around the doors. Sometimes in the upper floors of a couple of the big houses you could catch a light burning, which would suddenly go out as our boat neared—squatters hushing their fires because they thought we were the feds. On an island to the south stood a large empty hotel. We crossed the rest of the lagoon into Downtown and then up the main canal. I could see the smaller canals trickling off between the buildings which were black like the mansions behind us, and there was a sound from the Chinese storefronts along the water. It was like bubbling music. What's that sound, I said to someone on board, who did not answer; some guy was calling to him from the dock something about the cargo, and the one on board called back glancing my way. I was the cargo. I realized why we'd kept our distance from the peninsula, they figured I'd jump ship and swim to the cliffs, or maybe take a jump over the side back in the swamps and make for one of the houses. They did not understand, or else did not believe I understood, the concept of absolution. When the guy pulled me up onto the dock I saw the look in his eyes. Didn't matter whether he knew Ben Jarry or not, or whether he believed the things Ben believed. If I'd hung Jarry myself or even slit his throat, these people couldn't have had greater contempt for me; that would only have been murder, a lesser sin than treachery. And I realized why we'd sailed as near the cliffs as we had: I'd never have made it alive, but they wouldn't have minded my trying.

❧

I was set up in the Downtown library to live and work, even paid a small wage for doing it. It was one of the conditions of the parole. The library was a hundred-foot tower with a point at the top and the bottom running off in four directions like the wax of a tall gray candle—catacombs of words and dust, manuscripts that nobody read stacked in corners. The library and hall of records were consolidated to serve the urban L.A. population, such as it was. Running the library, I was guaranteed to have contact with almost nobody. I don't think it was intended I should like it in the high tower of the Downtown library. I think someone figured it would seem a bit like jail. I liked it quite a bit; after all, it seemed a bit like jail. A narrow circular stairway led up to a small white room where a narrow uncompromising bed waited in the corner. Beside the bed was a small table. There was a desk, which I had not had at Bell, at the window, and the sight from this cell was an improvement as well, no doubt of that—not the wastes of the annex but the harbor four blocks north where I came in, and to the west in the distance the swamps and the angry blare of the sun muttering through the trees. In the spring and summer I heard the prostitutes lived out there and had their men on the banks, and the vines of the lagoon glistened with the sap of women's legs.

My duties were threefold. The first was to make sure that in the files of the library all entries beginning with the letter A always preceded those beginning with B. The second was to make sure those doors that were now locked remained locked except to guys in suits with keys. Every once in a while a guy in a suit with a key would show up at the library and unlock a door and disappear inside. Sometimes I caught a glimpse of the books on high shelves. It should go without saying that I did not have any important keys myself, at least not yet. The third duty was to vacate the premises of squatters every night. In my first three weeks I found only one woman with a red sack that I suspect contained a small human being. I left both

the woman and her sack alone. "But in the morning," I said
to her, "you have to be gone."

~

I never closed up the building when I went out in the evenings; I wasn't expected to. As I said, I had no keys. It didn't
bother me that I was followed; I knew it was routine. The
feds weren't trying to fool me, they were out in the open. I
wondered why they followed me since there wasn't any place
to go; a few guards at the canal gates and bridges would have
kept me in town. It was possible, I guess, that someone could
vanish into the cracks of Los Angeles and drop out of sight.
But you still weren't going anywhere. You still had to come
out somewhere in Los Angeles. I hadn't been in town long
before I noticed that music was everywhere, the music I
heard out of Chinatown that first night. It came out of the
buildings, a distinct and different melody out of each one.
The few people you did run into hummed a lot. The ad-
dresses of the doors were scratched and defaced; there were
no signs on the street corners. Ask someone how to get to this
place or that and he'd sing you the directions.

I kept asking people where the sound came from and finally someone explained, The sea, the sound was the sea,
seeping in under the city and forming subterranean wells and
rivers. The rivers made a sound that came up through the
empty buildings, and the echoes of the buildings made a
music that came out into the streets. One day you'd see a
building standing upright and the next day it was entirely
collapsed, the earth caved in around it, the music turning into
a hiss from out of the rubble. In Chinatown they called the
shops along the water the Weeping Storefronts; at night you
could hear them gurgling and howling in the dark all the way
from the library tower. I went there one night after checking
out an isolated hardware store for a radio. The clerk asked if I

was a cop. I'm no cop, I said. He thought about it a moment and looked me over and then said, No radios here. I'm a law-abiding citizen, he said. He said, You new around here or what? and I said, Sort of, and he said, Check out Chinatown, bub, but watch it. I went to two merchants in Chinatown before the third led me into a back room and asked for the fifth time if I was a cop and sold me a transistor radio. He wrapped it in paper and had me put it in my coat pocket and let me out the back door. By now I knew there was something wrong. But I had the radio and didn't notice anyone following me for a change, so after walking briskly along the wharf toward home I decided maybe I wasn't in such a hurry.

Staring into the sun from the harbor, I saw before the shadowmansions of the lagoon something like a black mountain rising from the water, alive with insects; not until it blocked out the sun entirely could I tell it was a boat. Its dark wood hull was blotched with oil and slime, and a cloud of soot hovered over the deck. The deck was swarming with voices, Asian and Spanish and Portuguese and German, to the dull percussion of the tide and the sobbing of the storefronts at my back. The vessel glided past the first dock where I had originally disembarked and then headed into the canal gate, its engines cut and the whole hulk of the thing slipping along soundlessly. The silence of it snuffed the yammering of the people. Just a lot of faces, old Chinese women in scarves and bareheaded Latinos and their wives and here and there a child, all watching from the edge of the boat—or so I thought. When they got right next to me about thirty feet away I saw, in the fast groan of the last sun and the few nagging lights of Chinatown, the nullified blaze of all their dead eyes; every one of them was blind. A towering wooden crate of blind people drifting the waterways of East L.A. I turned around and took my radio home.

At the library I closed the doors and slid the bolt without checking for squatters first. If there were squatters tonight, room and board was on me. I read at my desk awhile and went to bed. Not long after turning out the light there was a dull thud in the distance, so quiet I might not have noticed but for the way the tower shook. It lasted only a few seconds but I lay there half an hour gripping the sides of the bed so hard I could have broken my hands. Then I got up and took a shot of brandy and got back in bed and read some more and tried to fall asleep. There was the sound of sirens and shouting. Finally the music put me out—the city music, not my radio—and I noticed it was different music, the sound of the buildings in the distance had changed. The last thing I thought of was all those blind people watching me across the water.

~

Two or three nights later I was sitting at my desk and looked up and there was someone in the doorway. He was huge black man, a little under six and a half feet tall; a few more inches of him on each side and he wouldn't have fitted the space in the wall. His hair was cut close to his head and speckled with gray, and his flat face looked as if it were pressed against a window, except there was no window. There was a step up into my room and he took it. He made no apologies for his sudden appearance, even though I'd been visibly startled. His voice was much softer than I would have thought. Are you Cale? he said. He might have been there to kill me for all I knew; that was a serious possibility. I was a little relieved that it mattered to me much. By now I thought I didn't care who killed me; it had been months since I cared about being free or being alive enough to know freedom. Now, seeing this black monster, I cared a little, at least until the scare in me died. Then I didn't care again. Let's assume I am, I said, then what happens?

"Then," said the monster, "I come in and have a seat."

"You've already done half that."

His head barely cleared the low ceiling of the tower. He admired the view of the harbor. He took in the bed and the desk and the small radio I'd gotten in Chinatown and then me. He sat on the bed and the mattress wheezed under him. "Mister Cale," he said in this distant voice, "my name is Jon Wade. I'm a federal inspector. Would you like to see my credentials?"

"Sure."

He took credentials out of his coat and handed them to me and I handed them back. "I came in from the seaboard last night," he said, putting the credentials away, "on a special assignment. I thought that while I was here, we should get to know each other."

"What for?"

"I will be seeing you and you will be seeing me. It's an empty little town and we're bound to run into each other. The police, as I think you're aware, have you under surveillance. Personally I would rather use them for other things. My understanding of your case is such as to lead me to conclude surveillance isn't especially necessary. My understanding of your case is such as to lead me to conclude you're not going anywhere. I believe you're a man who takes his prison with him—I think you follow me. But for me to take these officers off your detail requires you and I getting our signals straight. Because as I think you know, or as you should know, part of that surveillance is not just keeping you on a long tether—"

"Not that long."

"Not that long, all right, part of that surveillance is not just keeping you on a tether, but also making sure that, for the time being, for as long as the government chooses to keep you on parole out here in the territories, you do not get your brains smeared across any random urban edifice."

"Does the government really care?" I said.

"Well, Mister Cale," he said, sinking across the width of the bed into the wall, "it does and it doesn't, you know. It does and it doesn't. At some point it's not going to give a good God damn where your brains are; the public-relations value of their whereabouts is short-lived. But for the moment the government thinks you're a fine example. It likes the idea of a man who sells out his compatriots." He stopped and waited for me to react. He shrugged. "My own understanding of your case is such as to lead me to conclude that the government cares more about your welfare than you do yourself."

"If I'm ready to let someone blow my brains out, there's not much you can do about it."

"Exactly my own feelings," Wade said. He laboriously unfolded himself from the bed, standing in midroom and fairly filling it. "But my superiors still want you alive for a while, and I don't want to expend the energies of the local officials keeping my superiors happy. So I'm asking you to be a little careful, not embarrass me either by getting yourself taken out or by violating any of the local ordinances. For instance," he said, watching the radio on my desk, "there is a local ordinance against radios. A misdemeanor of course, but in the case of a felon on parole even a misdemeanor is a lot of incrimination."

"I didn't know about the ordinance," I started to say.

Wade raised his hand. "Don't." Watching the radio he said, "I'm sure you've broken no laws. If I knew you had broken any laws I'd have to arrest you, and it's tedious. I have other things. If I knew you had a radio I'd have to take you in. Please, don't. I know that I can assure my subordinates that your excursion into Chinatown the other night had nothing to do with any radio. If you had bought a radio," he said, still staring at it, "by now you would have known enough to deep-six it in a canal somewhere. That makes life easier for me and for you."

"It's silly," I said.

"We live in silly times," he said. "In a town where music is the topographical map, radios are compasses of anarchy. The music of the earth is legal and the music of men is not. I don't make the fucking laws." He said, "Get rid of the radio, Cale." Then he turned and went to the door. He said, "It's enough I have to deal with guys messing with the music of the earth. You feel the shaking the other night?"

"I thought it was a quake."

"That's fine," he said, "we'd as soon everyone thought it was a quake. Someone set off an underground explosion a couple miles northwest of here out on the peninsula. Redirected one of the underground rivers. Now the whole section of town other side of the harbor's got a new melody. It's a genuine subversive fuck-up. You want to tell me about silly? Of course my superiors on the seaboard think it's political, because they think everything's political. Because everything *is* political. So they wonder about you, of course. You're not setting off underground explosions, are you Mister Cale?"

"Not lately."

"Not of the geological sort anyway," said Wade. "Well, all right. Consider yourself grilled and interrogated on the matter. My own understanding of your case is such as to lead me to believe it will suffice." He paused a moment, looked at me sideways and nodded a bit and walked out. The dark of the library blotted him up; soon he was a tan coat floating in space. Then the dark of the library blotted up the tan coat too.

～

After I'd been in Los Angeles a month it seemed like a long time. Not forever: forever would preclude the days in a metal truck, and I hadn't been anywhere so long as to forget those. Forever in Los Angeles would have precluded the experience of my conscience, the life of which stayed with me like the flashes of previous incarnations. Jon Wade did not come up to the tower again. It was the nature of the way and time I had been here that every such incident became a landmark. I left the library more and more. I don't think the police appreciated it, but nobody said anything. Their understanding of my case was such as to lead them to conclude I was beyond the persuasion of threat; and they were right. Large black birds covered the town streets in malevolent flocks. The canal waters were always filled with artifacts—chairs and framed pictures, masks of gold leaf and music boxes in which cartoon characters danced behind small windows. The sound of the buildings had indeed changed since the night my tower shook. Blasted abandoned eateries and black doorless taverns gurgled and hissed in a new key. To most of the town's population, which was largely old men and frightened indigents, it made life all the more disorienting. For myself it was one of the things that made a long time seem less like forever.

Another little landmark in my routine came about four or five days after Wade's appearance. A couple of guys from the town hall came to open up some of those locked rooms in the library. I was up in the tower when it happened. They poked around a while and then came up and brought me down to outline some of the new duties of my parole. Someone had decided it was a good idea for me to go through all the old manuscripts on the shelves, read them and file them and offer some estimations as to their value. Value to whom, I asked. Value to civic interests, value to territorial interests, they said. Value to the annexes or the government. Of course it was clear to me at once that none of this could have any value at all. I was supposedly a political subversive; if this were work of value, why would they have me sorting it out for them? I was right in thinking these people would not be giving me

any important keys to important rooms; this was work to keep
me occupied. I took the keys and thanked them for their profound trust in me. One of them laughed and said, That's all
right, Cale, you're on our side now, right? Then the keys felt
like the proverbial silver in my fingers, one piece for each day
of a month that fell short—by virtue of what silver buys—of
a redemptive foreverness, forevermoreness.

I am thirty-eight, thirty-nine. I look in a mirror and it tells
me I'm fifty, fifty-five. My hair is the same color it has been
since I was seventeen but my beard is white and my eyes are
red. How did I get so damned tired. When I was young I despised those who gave up so easily, I couldn't imagine anyone
could ever feel that old and that tired. In a musicless tower
above an empty waterworld I grieve for what I felt and how
much I felt it. Once I supposed I recognized my own voice
when I spoke to strangers; it was something to know your own
voice, to know it as well when you finished speaking as when
you began. How is it I'm so old now I don't know my voice
anymore. How is it I'm so exhausted by what I once believed
that the things I love affront me with the effort to love them.
Prison was a good place to be tired. There I taught my conscience the art of fatigue, as a consequence of which passion
and integrity died immediately, without protest.

I went walking that night, the day they gave me possibly
important keys to possibly important rooms. I took the radio
with me as well as the keys, zigzagging the streets eastward
past Broadway. The city became deader and deader until I
reached the quarter before the canal, where I found the rare
sights and sounds of a half dozen bars going and guys laughing; I realized I'd been in L.A. a month and not heard anyone
laugh. I didn't go in any of the bars but instead to the boat
landing where I caught a boat going down canal. All this way
no cops followed me, there was none of the usual company. A
big mistake on their part, I thought. Let down your guard
once and those like myself who are genuinely depraved will

rush to betray a trust: they can't betray it fast enough. The canal would come out on the coast near San Bernardino and then the boat would drift down to Riverside. If I were still alive the day after tomorrow I might then get another boat and slip into port somewhere near the Yuma-Sonora annex. On the deck of the boat this night I felt the last of me fading away. I was barely aware of the land gliding by or the cold of the wind, or of voices around me talking about the pirates hiding in the Downey coves waiting to take cargo of value. I had possibly important keys in a coat pocket, I had contraband radio in the other. I might cast one or both overboard. I might or might not remove them from my pockets before doing so.

The water beneath me in the dark, it was gray and windowless too as we continued sailing out of the city. I just stood with my back to the broken bitter skyline fumbling with this stuff in my pocket, keys in one hand and the radio in the other, wondering which it was going to be. Clouds soared by overhead like the evil black birds in the streets at noon, and then there was nothing but the moon, mammoth and skullwhite, laughing light all over the boat and the riverbanks. The voices around me stopped; I felt stricken by the stillness. No one else was in sight. I can go now, I thought. The banks were bare and distant for about fifty yards up canal until the bend ahead, where a small beach jutted outward. I stood watching the approaching bend and pulled the small radio from my pocket; I turned it on for a moment and then off. I looked to the right and left and behind me on deck, and the boat reached the bend and began to steer southward, out into larger water, leaving Los Angeles behind once and for all. On the jutting beach were two people.

One was sitting or kneeling in the sand. He was motionless and silent, facing away from me, and he held his hands behind his back. The other was standing before him as silent and motionless as he; with one hand she touched his head, as though she was running her fingers through his hair. Her face was as clearly visible to me as his was not. She looked very young; I doubted she was all of twenty. She wore a plain dress, and in the bright moonlight it had no color but pale. As the boat turned southward it came closer to shore, and at one point I could see her eyes though she wasn't looking directly at me. She didn't seem aware of the boat at all. Against the embankment behind her, white in the light of the moon, her black hair was like a cloud of gunpowder, which framed her brown face; she looked Latin or Mediterranean. I kept expecting her to acknowledge the boat but the boat had cut its engines. I kept expecting her to look my way, but she touched the head of the other man. In the moment I saw her I stopped grieving for my losses. It seemed impossible to see her eyes from the boat or to know her face that well. I despised the guy at her feet; I would have told at that moment any lethal joke that would have hanged him too.

He turned to look at me.

As his face shifted into the light of the moon there was another light, a flash that went off between his face and my own. It was soundless and instantaneous, and as it dimmed I expected I would get a good look at him. Except that his face wasn't there to be seen. I looked again, and again, and nothing else had changed; there were still the two of them on shore; but his face was gone: and then I saw it in her hand, the source of the flash, a two-foot-long blade that had flown from beneath her plain pale dress and caught the light of the moon and very efficiently separated the head she held in her hand from the rest of the man's body. It was all in an instant, and with her blow I turned to follow the orbit of a small human sphere launched out into the dark above the water.

NEXT THING I knew I was sitting in a car overlooking the quays drinking some coffee, and all over the beach below me were local cops and feds. The feds drove the large brown coats they wore as if they were army tanks. The car I was sitting in was the first I'd seen since getting on the boat in Seattle; it was unadorned and functional. I didn't drink much of the coffee they gave me. I didn't need it. After a while I saw him coming over and my throat tightened. My head and heart were already pounding. I kept seeing over and over that other guy's head flying off into space, and how long it took for his body to drop in the sand, how long it took for his body to understand what had happened. I kept seeing her in that dress that had no color, and the whites of her eyes like fireflies beneath her swarm of hair, and the way the clean knife changed in an instant to something wet and red.

Wade made a motion to me to get out of the car. Unlike our first meeting we were both standing now, and I was even more aware of how he loomed over me. In the dark it looked as if he had no hands. "First of all," he said in the same whisper as when I'd met him before, "you want to tell me what you were doing on that boat?"

I took the radio out of my pocket. "This dangerous instrument came into my possession," I said. "I wanted to get it as far from centers of population as possible before it went off. I was ready to throw my body across it if need be." It was supposed to sound clever but my voice cracked and when I held out the radio my hand was shaking. Wade didn't take the radio; I put it back in my pocket. "I saw a woman decapitate a man tonight," I said after a moment.

He didn't miss a beat. "Yes?"

" 'Yes?' It's not enough?"

"It's not enough," he said. He took my coffee cup from my

other hand and threw it on the ground. "Not without a body, with or without a head."

"Meaning you don't believe me."

"Meaning maybe I believe you saw something, since the captain of the boat says you were stone quiet all the way down canal and then went off like a string of firecrackers. You remember that?"

"No."

"So I believe something made you lose it, and someone getting his top lopped off might be as good as anything else."

"But maybe I imagined it," I said, "maybe it's in my mind." There was still a funny sound in my voice, I could hear it.

"Who are you arguing with?" Wade said, with something that finally approached irritation. "Were you heading for Yuma-Sonora, or contemplating the bottom of the canal?" He motioned back to the car and I got in, and then he walked away, heading back for the beach. Another cop came along, a thin wiry little man with red hair, and drove me back into town. I went to the station and gave a statement, but I had blank spots all night. Only later did I remember the sun coming up sometime before I got to bed, but when I went to sleep I could have sworn it was in the dark.

❧

I did not dream. Later, thinking about it, I expected that I would have dreamed, since the next day and the day after I kept seeing it in my head. But when I slept there was nothing but a pitch-dark sweep of water before me, and then I'd wake to see her at the foot of my bed with her long bloody knife and him on the floor not yet bleeding. The head always rolled off somewhere in the shadows, and sometimes I got within inches of its face before the whole thing faded.

They came and asked me one or two more questions but

that was it. That first month I presumed a rhyme or reason to the way they'd let my leash out and then pull it in, but now I saw there was no rhyme or reason. Now I saw they didn't know what to do with me. They kept saying I was on their side now but they didn't know that, because I didn't know it. Sometimes you can know someone better than he knows himself but I wasn't necessarily that guy, or at least no one could be sure. If you can't be sure then everything's a gamble, and I was their gamble. They were trying to decide whether I was of any advantage to them or whether the best they could do was neutralize whatever disadvantage I might be. After that night they must have thought long and hard about taking away possibly important keys—if they were possibly important at all.

I spent some time in possibly important rooms, arranging the manuscripts and writing files on each. Their significance escaped me. Letters between people never heard of, brochures and programs and articles, sometimes an extended piece of writing either factual or not; some of it was handwritten and some of it was in typescript and some of it was published. It was difficult to imagine that any of it was of any value to anyone. It all looked old but in this town that didn't mean anything.

Sitting back in the recesses of these back rooms I'd play the radio as loud as I wanted. Maybe Wade figured he was doing me a favor letting me keep it but I wasn't going to let him get away with thinking that. I wasn't going to let him or any of them think I was on their side just because they let me keep a fucking little radio. So I played it and every once in a while a cop would wander through and peer in the doorway in the direction of the sound. Then one night I woke abruptly to another thud in the distance and the tower shaking like the time I thought it was a quake. Then there was another thud and then another. Three, including the one that woke me. Outside the symphony of the buildings went berserk; I didn't sleep that night for all the shrieking. The next day and night were the same. After that a cop came by one afternoon and peered in the doorway as usual; this particular time I wasn't playing the radio but he came in anyway. He was the thin wiry little man with red hair who had driven me to the police station. "I got to take the radio this time," he said.

"That ungodly wail outside and you're worrying about my radio?"

"Got to take it, jack." I gave it to him and that was the last I saw of it. One could ignore the constant din of the days, but the nights were impossible. L.A. turned into a town of somnambulists. I went walking the fifth night of it. I got up from bed and came down from the tower and out into the streets. In fact the sound was a lot worse in the streets, but I still decided I'd rather be walking around in it than lying in bed listening to it. I headed back in the same direction as several evenings before because I remembered the part of town where there were bars and people's voices.

The sound wasn't as bad once I got past Spring Street. Going into one of the small dives next to the East L.A. Canal, I could lose the sound altogether. The clientele wasn't exactly the cream of society. Most of the men were smugglers from down coast, along with some out-and-out pirates, bringing into town under the cover of night dope or cheap Sonoran liquor or bits of outlawed technology, whatever it was this month the feds had decided was dangerous. There were few women, maybe half a dozen, all of them in their late forties. The younger prettier ones did their business out in the mansions across the water where traveling merchants with some money could afford to sail.

There was one woman, however, who looked no older than her late twenties. You couldn't help but see her and none of the other men could help it either. She wore a dress that was either blue spotted with white or white spotted with blue, and she had long amber hair. She sat in the corner of the bar smoking a hand-rolled cigarette and fooling with a camera. The men, by and large, left her alone. They'd talk to her and buy her a drink, but in the half hour I was there no one put the make on her. She was so rare to this place and these men, and her presence was so valued, that it was worth it to everyone to have her in the corner in the dark and not scare her away. She kept getting free drinks and she'd smile at the guys who brought them, but her smile invited nothing except drinks and no one overstepped the terms of her invitations. She kept fooling with the camera and I decided cameras weren't on the blacklist with radios; unlike sound, the images of the earth were not in conflict with the images of men.

The bar was an underground grotto, descending some twenty feet in the earth and entered by one long winding stairway a little like the stairway I took every night up to my room. The grotto was cut in stone and dirt, and one of the underground rivers of the city came roaring through in a ravine. Most of the booths and tables were constructed on an overlooking platform. Sometimes the water would lap over the shoulder of earth where the bar stood, splashing against a customer's feet. The air was thick with the smoke of cigarettes and hemp and wet with the heat of the river, the flat roar of which was a lull after days of screaming cities. I sat watching the woman with the camera awhile. The shadows around her seemed to stretch to the grotto's ceiling, and my own shadow shot in her direction. Only it wasn't my shadow at all. I had a drink of something vile and waited for him to make his move; he sat down across the table from me. He had discharged the tan coat somewhere and looked hot.

He ordered a drink of something vile too. "Cale," he said, "can a man hate himself so much he's not even alive anymore?" He wiped his face with a handkerchief and pulled at a white shirt that actually looked baggy on him.

"You *sail* into town in that shirt, or parachute?"

Wade pushed the sleeves up his arms and opened the collar some more. He put the handkerchief away and drank half his drink. "It's sweltering in here," he muttered, gazing around at the water. It was the first time I'd seen him ruffled; it was hot all right, but it really got to him. "What are *you* doing here tonight," he said.

"To tell the truth, I was getting away from the racket up above."

"So something gets to you after all."

"I was just thinking the same about you and the heat."

"I think," he nodded, "I prefer the noise to the heat." He finished the drink and ordered another; he was sweating the alcohol as fast as he could consume it. His parachute shirt was turning into a white blotch.

"Any new developments on the other night?" I asked, and regretted it immediately. Initiating a conversation with him seemed a fundamental concession.

"What other night?"

I licked my lips. "The woman on the beach," I said slowly, "with the knife."

"What's to develop?" he said. "No body, no head, no knife, no woman."

"You think I'm crazy."

"You keep saying that," he said, getting his second drink. "Nobody else has said it, just you. I wouldn't presume to suppose what your mind is or isn't capable of inventing. My understanding of your state of mind is such as to lead me to conclude it's capable of anything, except an outright lie."

"You don't think I'm capable of an outright lie?"

He thought a moment as though to be sure, but he was already sure. "No," he said, "no, if you could live with a lie you would have begun with lying to yourself. You have a lot to lie about. Where were you born, Cale?"

"America."

"As I thought. America One or America Two?"

"I never could get straight on that. I think it must have been somewhere in between."

"You're what, forty-five? Fifty?"

"Thirty-eight or thirty-nine."

"You look rather poorly for a man your age. I guess that's to be expected."

I took his second drink and threw it in the river. In retrospect it was rather comic; we both calmly watched the glass float out of sight into the tunnel. The guy behind the bar gave me a look, as did a couple of others. "Why don't you get off my back, Inspector?" I said. "You already said something once about taking my own prison with me, don't you think I take this sort of shit with me too? There's nothing I can confess to you I haven't confessed a thousand times to myself."

"I'm not interested in your confessions," said Wade in his cool whisper, though he was still sweating a lot, "I'm interested in either infuriating or humiliating you into staying alive and in a condition that would pass with most people as sane. You dead or crazy would be bad form from a government point of view, and my superiors don't want it. I'm not a political man—"

"Horseshit."

"—but I have my orders. You're on our side now, Cale—"

"Horseshit I said. I'm not on your side. I was never on anybody's side—"

"That was your problem."

"Maybe and maybe not. I have to live forever with the fact that one moment of stupidity and indiscretion on my part hung a guy. But I don't have to live with the idea that it was a political act or that because of it I've assumed a political role I never chose. That the powers-that-be can't understand the difference between a personally stupid act and a politically willful one is their problem. All I have at this point is what I did and the real nature of it, and not you or anyone else is

going to take that and make it something else. So leave me
alone. There's nothing to stop me from how I choose to live
or die with my own particular sort of treason. If you haven't
noticed, I've been living in a very high building these days.
Your people put me there."

"I've noticed."

"If you haven't noticed, the window of the room at the top
of my high building isn't so small."

"I've noticed."

"For people who are so worried about my life and sanity, it
was careless of you to put me in such a high tower with such
an adequate window, wouldn't you say? For people who are
so worried, I mean. The honor guards that follow me around
have grown casual in the extreme—maybe they're here tonight but I haven't seen them, and I didn't see them a few
days ago when I caught that boat leaving town. That tether
gets longer and longer after all. There've been a hundred opportunities for me to do almost anything drastic, starting with
when they sailed me in the first evening."

"You're correct there."

"So what it comes down to is I don't think you people can
make up your minds whether you want me alive or dead,
murdered or suicided, sane or nuts or whatever, and I think
that's because for all this talk about me being on your side,
you're not so sure I'm on your side or that I was ever on your
side, which makes me the most uncertain kind of individual
for you to have to deal with. By your own actions or inactions,
by your own contradictions, you've acknowledged *my* contradictions, and by your own insistence on my political role—a
role your actions and inactions contradict—you've acknowledged *your* political role."

"I'm lost."

"Well don't bother finding your way out. It doesn't matter
to me and I'm not sure you're so lost anyway. I just don't

want to hear about how you're not a political man. Where were *you* born, Wade?"

I stood up. I thought he might stand up too but he didn't. He sat in his wet parachute looking at me and sweating but for the first time not aware of the sweat. The bartender still had nasty looks for me and the woman in the corner with the camera was gone. I put some money on the table. Wade had nothing to say, and I left the grotto and went back up into the caterwaul.

≈

I was born in America. It was somewhere inland. At the junction of two dirt roads about three hundred yards from my house there was a black telephone in a yellow booth; sometimes walking by you could hear it ringing. Sometimes walking by you'd answer, but no one ever spoke; there'd either be the buzz of disconnection or no sound at all. By the time I was eighteen I thought I had outgrown the sound of telephone calls that weren't for me.

I never understood the borders; they seemed to change all the time. They were borders of land and borders of years, but wherever and whenever they were, clearly, in that time and place I was born, it was America. Whether it still is I can't be sure. I'm not sure I want to know. About the time I was eighteen and had learned to let the telephones ring, I saw my first body of water. It was a wide river that ran to my right. I heard later it was an American river, but I knew that was a lie. I knew there was no such thing as American rivers or foreign rivers; there were only waterrivers with waterborders of waterland and wateryears. Believing such a thing was my first step in the direction of danger. I never believed in American skies either. But it never meant I did not believe in America.

When I sailed from Seattle to Los Angeles, it was a nice

idea to think I was in a waterplace and watertime. But there was no fooling myself, I knew I was in the place and time I'd brought with me from Bell Pen and that America was another distance; and I'd heard the legends of L.A. clocks and how the hour hands race across their faces while the minute hands never move.

I dreamed about Ben Jarry the night after I drank with Wade in the underground grotto. It was my first dream in a while, I'd assumed that when I dreamed again it would be of a woman. In my dream Ben Jarry, with his hands bound behind him, was led down a long hall by two guards and I was led up the hall to begin my parole. I saw him from far away and we kept getting nearer and nearer, and everything in me went dead. I realized when he was only a few feet from me that he was being led to his execution. He said nothing to me, he only looked. I was fortunate that nothing in his eyes forgave me. If his eyes had forgiven me I am genuinely certain I would have killed myself; so maybe that's fortune for you. Or maybe it's misfortune, since forgiveness would have provoked in me the courage to exchange my time and place for that of the water around me on a trip from Seattle to Los Angeles. And yet I never actually saw Ben Jarry walking down a long hall. Ben Jarry was dead before they ever released me. He was also born in America.

I began to notice that the archives of the library's back rooms were filled with the recorded legends of murdered men, who may or may not have actually lived. The most striking was of a man murdered in Los Angeles in a kitchen. It was late one spring night and many people saw it; he bled on the floor and did not die immediately. They caught the guy who did it. The murdered man had been born in America One. Whether he'd died in America One or America Two wasn't clear to me from the documentation. I wasn't sure if this was something I was supposed to keep on file or not. I wasn't sure if this was of value to civic interests or territorial

interests. I would have somehow supposed the feds preferred
not leaving such information around. So I kept the manuscript myself and after a while I found myself sequestering
more and more such manuscripts, usually for reasons I could
never have explained. I took them up to my room in the
tower in the dead of night and kept them in a box under the
bed. This particular legend stated that this particular murdered man came from a family of murdered men. I would
have liked to have found the legends of these other murdered
men; I was studying the distinction between murders that are
acts of martyrdom and those that are acts of redemption.

The word was out I let the squatters sleep in the library
halls, and as the nights went by there were more of them.
Live squatters in the library halls seemed to multiply with the
documents of murdered men beneath my tower bed. A cop
came by one afternoon and said, You're supposed to keep
these people out of here. I said, I understand perfectly, officer. There were more squatters and more cops that followed,
but the cops knew they couldn't threaten me with prison,
they knew they couldn't hurt me more than my dreams.
When I taught myself to love the cacophony of the city,
when I taught myself to sing along with the noise of the
buildings, I began to dream less and less of meeting Ben in a
long hall. Instead he became a squatter in the corner, a cut-
off rope around his neck, and when he opened his mouth, out
came the noise of the buildings.

Among the recorded legends of murdered men you can
dream of almost anything. But it was no dream, what happened the night I woke still slumped in the chair where I'd
been working in the back room, manuscripts piled around me
in the dark. I didn't know the hour but I couldn't have slept
long; I figured it was just past nightfall. None of the library
lights was on; I had to do my work in the days because there
was no power in this wing of the building. Only a glow from
the street outside the windows made anything visible. I had

that usual anxiety you feel when you fall asleep where you haven't expected to, waking alone to a change of light. But I also had a feeling that clashed with the anxiety of being alone in spent light. I stumbled up from the chair. It's not true that one wakes knowing someone else is in the room. No one ever wakes knowing that. People who believe that give too much credit to human instinct. They forget that as children they woke knowing something was beneath the bed or behind the door when in fact nothing was there at all. At Bell there were many nights I woke knowing someone was in my cell; in fact no one was ever in my cell. Now I woke feeling both alone in spent light and that there was someone else in the room, even as I knew too much to believe it. I kicked the manuscripts away and moved toward the back of the dark archives, and the glow from outside the window never changed. I passed one aisle of files and then another and then found the two of them in front of me as though they'd just appeared.

I jumped where I stood and felt the percussive slam of my heart in my ears. She turned to look at me, as she had the first time; he turned to look at me as he had the first time, from his place on his knees. I waited for the image to come apart, like a fetus smeared into an ephemeral jelly, and then not be there at all. But this wasn't an image of my aftersleep, like the other images of other sleeps; it didn't go away. I'd lived in a cell too long not to know the real thing. Then I saw the knife.

Her blow was faster than I could speak. His head sat so still on his neck for a moment it was as though she had missed altogether, and then it seemed to come floating toward me. If I had wanted I could have caught it, cradling it in my arms and pressing its face against my chest. It landed behind me with an awful soft smack, not unlike the thuds of the nights when the city shook and its sound changed. Like the first time, the body took a long while crumpling at her feet, and she stood and raised her head and watched me. She parted her lips and then said something in another language. I stepped toward her and she raised the knife to me, and the color seemed to go out of her face and her mouth was wet. Her eyes were wet.

I looked to the body. She bolted from where she stood, darting for the aisle behind one of the shelves. I just stood looking at the body and turning to its head sitting some distance away on the floor. It was leaking slowly while the body erupted at the neck, deflating like a bag.

I had this momentary burst of composure. I had this momentary burst of composure in which I thought I would just walk over to the head and pick it up and look at its face; I was certain I'd see Ben Jarry looking back at me. But I never got that far. Suddenly I was sitting in a chair in the corner of the archives and Jon Wade was standing over me and the glow of the street was still coming through the windows and another familiar light was flashing in my eyes like the electricity of a storm. All around me were other guys in coats and a lot of activity. It wasn't as though everything had just changed at the snap of someone's fingers; rather I was vaguely aware of a passing period of time during which I traveled through the things that happened around me without paying any attention to them whatsoever. I put my hands in front of my face and looked up. "Don't tell me," I said, not especially to Wade. I knew it was a little too convenient. He didn't say anything, he was waiting with his hands in his coat. He didn't look happy. "Like last time," I said.

"Last time?"

"What are you doing here?" I said to him.

He still didn't look happy. "What happened?" he finally said.

I shook my head. There was this damn flashing light. "Nothing. I had a dream. It was nothing."

Wade reached down and put five huge fingers around my collar. "What are you trying to hand me," he said, and now I realized for the first time how angry he was. He took hold of my arm and pulled me across the room. The cops stopped and stood watching us, and I stood watching them, and then I saw it. There was no body and there was no head, but there was more blood than I'd seen in my life, as though it came from ten men instead of one. Blood where the body had been and a streak of blood across the pages that filled the shelves and on the floor near where I'd been working. A trajectory of splattered blood from where the man's head had been ejected to where it had landed beyond me. I looked at it and looked at Wade and then at the cops and then at the raggedy crowd in the doorway, squatters from the halls risking eviction to peer in on the scene. I don't know if any of them understood the relief I felt seeing all that blood. "Then it wasn't a dream," I said to Wade.

He took me by the same arm and brought me back to the chair. "This is progress," he said, "we've now established that all this blood is not a dream. Sit down." I sat down. "Let's see," Wade said, "what other information you and I can glean from this. We'll begin with your most immediate recollection. Whatever it was that preceded this timely catatonia you seem to lapse into whenever something interesting happens."

I knew it was too convenient. "Like last time, I told you."

"The headless man and the woman of the dunes," he said. He pissed me off and he knew it and didn't care. "Same woman?"

"Same woman," I said. "Same guy."

"Same guy?"

There was another flash of light and it was getting to me. "Yes."

"Same guy who lost his head last time lost it this time too?"

"Yes."

"Is this man a snake?"

"Even a snake doesn't grow a new head," I said.

"I know that. Do you know that?"

"Then it was a dream," I said.

"It was a dream that bleeds," he said. "Did you *see* this guy?"

"I know it was the same guy."

"Did you see him?"

"Of course I saw him."

"You saw him clearly? I didn't think last time you saw things so clearly."

"I haven't seen his face. I don't have to. I know who it is. I didn't last time, but I do now."

"Does he have a name?"

"Everyone has a name."

"You're a fuck, Cale," he said, angrier and angrier.

"His name is Ben Jarry," I said.

"Shit."

I looked at the raggedy crowd in the doorway. "What about them?"

"This is my investigation," Wade said. But he looked back at them.

"She ran out," I said. He looked back at me and I thought of something else. "She also said something this time, she said something to me."

"What?"

"It was Spanish I think."

"Are you sure?"

"If I knew for sure what she said I would know for sure if it was Spanish."

"Like you know this was Ben Jarry," he said, "the man with the world's unluckiest neck."

"I told you it was a dream," was all I could say, and then there was the light again, and that did it. It was no electrical storm. I jumped up from the chair. "What's that damned light," I said. I looked in the direction it came from and so did Wade.

"Sit down," he said and pushed me back into my chair.

"Mallory," he called, turning to the wiry little man with red
hair who had taken my radio. I could see a form moving for
the door and it set me off and I jumped up from the chair
again. Wade saw her too. He called to his man again.
"What's she doing here," he said furiously.

It was the woman from the grotto in the blue-and-white
dress, with the camera. "She's a cop," I said out loud to everyone who could hear it. I turned to Wade and said, "She's a
cop and you've got her following me taking pictures. That's
why she was in the bar that night."

She was out the door with that, pushing aside the squatters
who were still watching. The red-haired guy named Mallory
started after her and so did a couple of others. Wade was
looking at me in absolute amazement and then back at his
men and then back at me, all within seconds. "Wait a minute!" he bellowed, and Mallory and the others stopped. In
the distance in the lighted hall I could see her disappearing
around a corner.

"She's a cop," I started in on him again.

"Shut up," he said. He turned back to his men and then
back to me. He was genuinely confused and he wasn't pushing me into the chair anymore. His eyes narrowed. "You
really don't know who that woman is, Cale?"

"She's a cop," I said.

For a long minute he said nothing, and then he shook his
head slowly. "No," he said, and looked back down the hall,
"she's no cop," and he got tired all at once and sat in the
chair I'd been in, sagging into it almost the way the headless
body had sagged onto the floor twenty feet away. You want us
to go get her, Inspector? Mallory asked. "No," Wade answered quickly. The cops looked at each other and didn't
move. "Cale," Wade exhaled to me softly, "I had high hopes
that you and I would have a low-key relationship. It hasn't
been turning out that way. It's disappointing to me. Now I'm
in a situation where I have several imponderable circum-

stances and no way to resolve them." He said, "Tonight something happened. Somebody bled enough for an army. But I still don't have a body, I still don't have a weapon, I still don't have a perpetrator, and as a witness you're a bit on the unreliable side. But I guess you know that. There's nothing I can do except take blood samples and a statement. In the case of your statement, I'd rather not have it. It's the kind of thing where I'd like to pretend something never happened but I can't. You know what that's like."

"Yes," I said quietly, "I know what that's like."

"Yes," he said, "I suspect you do." He got up. "You were easier to deal with," he said, "when you were paralyzed with guilt. What's gotten into you?"

"I don't know," I said. I wasn't sure that I wasn't still paralyzed with guilt. But not so long before, before I saw a woman with a knife and hair as black as a gash in the day, I didn't care who was my spy, or who thought I was on whose side of things, or how many times Ben Jarry died. I didn't care if I was crazy or sane, or dreaming or awake, or alive or dead. Now I just wanted to see her again, and take her next time, Spanish or no Spanish, knife or no knife, and seize the chance to save Ben Jarry's life once, for the once in which his neck had snapped on my account. That redemption was worth any measure of sanity or, for that matter, my life itself. Wade had to have seen some of that.

"Tell me when you figure it out," he said.

"What about the woman with the camera?" I said.

"Stay away from her."

Like hell, I thought.

THERE IS a tree by a river, it is out west. A man comes to the tree and looks up and sees among its branches a nation of men; they're living their whole lives in the tree. The man calls to them and says, What are you doing living in that tree? And after some silence, from the deepest foliage of the tree's highest limbs, someone answers . . .

I forget. I forget the answer. It's a good punch line and now I've forgotten it. I heard it in New York, I'd been living in a tenement where I had met a woman with whom I fell in love. She loved me for a month in return, until it interfered with her work. She was involved with a cadre of political outlaws. They met in secret among the tenements of New York and left their meetings carrying in their heads little bits of America One, to which they gave voice in the streets. I wasn't one of them, I had never been one of anything. I distrusted being one of something; I knew it wasn't real, I knew the only oneness that was real was my own, being one of me. I met Jarry relatively soon; the woman whom I loved said to me, You're lucky, you met him relatively soon. She said, I was involved in the cadre eighteen months before I met him. He traveled from cadre to cadre; as the leader he was the only one who knew all the cadres and who knew all the people who carried bits of America One. He was the only person who could put all the bits together if he wanted. Of course he didn't seem particularly commanding at all. My height, with light hair and skin like alabaster, translucent and white-blue; the expression of his eyes was elfin and amused. He was the sort of person who shook your hand and smiled and judged you all at the same time. Are you interested, he said to me then, in becoming one of us? I'm not good at becoming one of things, I explained. How long, he said, you think you can be neither one nor the other. Then he said, There's a tree by a river, it's out west. A man comes to the tree and looks up and sees among the branches a nation of men; they're living their whole lives in the tree. The man calls to them and says, What are you doing living in that tree? And after some silence, from the deepest foliage of the tree's highest limbs, someone answers . . .

Damned if I can remember. It was a good line, but later, when I thought about it, I wasn't sure it really proved his point. I sort of thought it proved my point.

I was arrested with the cadre one night. I was there because she was there. The others in the cadre never really trusted me, but I had resolved that if I was not one of the cadre, neither was I one of those who arrested us. In the questioning I did not identify Ben Jarry. They tried many tricks, little things to slip me up. They knew Jarry was their man but they couldn't pin him down, they couldn't connect him with us. They sent me to jail with the others. They split up the cadre so everyone was in a different place. They sent me to Montana-Saskatchewan I think, they charged me with having a bit of America One in my head. I'd been there over two years, alone, without much contact with any of the other prisoners, who seemed to be there for similar reasons. The men who ran Bell Pen kept such contact to a minimum. I managed to make friends with a man named Judd who had an ingenuous expression in his eyes and the laugh of a little kid. He said he didn't even know what he was in for, and if he was anything like me, I could believe it. His fatalism about his imprisonment struck the rest of us as something almost angelic; he did not seem to know malice. One day he was a little sadder, and at dinner I put my elbows on the table and said, to cheer him up, Well Judd, I heard a good one not so long ago. There's a tree by a river, it's out west. A man comes to the tree and looks up and sees among its branches a nation of men; they're living their whole lives in the tree. The man calls to them and says, What are you doing living in that tree? And after some silence, from the deepest foliage of the tree's highest limbs, someone answers . . .

Nobody laughed. Nobody said anything. I looked around, and then I knew they had all heard it before, and they had all heard it from the same place. And I looked at Judd and he had this awful smile on his face, and I knew he had heard it too. And I looked in his eyes and he didn't look so ingenuous anymore, he looked like a man who knew malice. And I knew he wasn't a prisoner at all. He got up from the table and smiled the whole time and walked away. I never saw him again. What Ben Jarry and I had in common after all was that we were both stupid enough to repeat the same joke to the same wrong person.

The other prisoners just sat looking at me. Later I would be astonished to learn how many of them thought I told the joke on purpose, how many of them believed I had just been waiting all along to finger Ben Jarry.

I waited in my cell all night, eyes open, for them to come get me. After two days passed I had almost convinced myself that a joke could mean nothing, as it had meant nothing when I told it. I heard it years ago, I said, when they finally brought me in for questioning. I heard it from my grandfather, who told it all the time when I was a kid. Everybody's heard that one, it's a common joke.

It's not a common joke, they said.

The man calls to them and says, What are you doing living in that tree? And after some silence, from the deepest foliage of the tree's highest limbs . . .

I don't remember. Since that day I haven't been able to remember; the bit of America One in my head was the punch line to that joke.

But then was then and now is now, and after the night in the back room of the library there was nothing in my head, no punch lines at all but Spanish words and a trace of the voice that carried them. And after I heard those words and the voice that carried them there was nothing but more such words; I found pages of them. I found them the next day and it didn't seem like an extraordinary coincidence; instead it seemed like perfect. The fog that morning hung like snow on the tall empty skyscrapers of Los Angeles and the gnarled little bridges that joined them a hundred feet above the streets. Men were there bright and early to clean up the archives, slopping wet mops on the dry carnage of the previous night and smearing the floor into a rusty red, packing up the manuscripts that were streaked with blood. The idea, I suppose, was to eliminate everything but the trace of a voice speaking Spanish words in my head. I came in as someone in a gray worksuit was pulling down the offending volumes from the shelf and loading them into a box. I took the box from him and took the manuscripts from the box and put them back on the shelf. He blinked at me in stupefaction. What do you think you're doing, I said. We have instructions to confiscate this material, he answered. I don't give a fuck what your instructions are, I said. You can clean up the floors but you're leaving these manuscripts. He shrugged and signaled his crew, and they picked up their mops and pails and left.

Then I began going through the manuscripts strewn at my feet where I'd fallen asleep the night before, and there it was; and as I say, it wasn't much of a surprise. It was natural it should have been there for me just as it was natural she should have been there in the archives or on a passing beach as seen from the deck of a boat. Of course it hadn't been there before, and it wasn't even a manuscript so much as a sheaf of papers; but it was ageless like all the rest of it and splattered with blood like the rest of it. In fact it was more splattered than the rest of it and that made sense too. The paper was dry and brown and the writing was faded. It was a thin collection of maybe fifty or sixty verses and poems. I sat in the chair and read them the rest of the day. Some of it was hard to make out because of the blood and the faded words. All the pieces were concerned with one subject, and anybody could recognize her immediately, the hair the color of night and the rage to match, and her mouth the color of Ben Jarry's blood. He wrote of her eyes as having the opaque rushing depthlessness of the blind, like the color of white skies and seas meeting at some point in the distance. The author said nothing of her body, just as her body when I had seen her had said nothing of itself: it was all about a face that was ignorant of its own image. When I finished the poems I realized I hadn't been breathing; I was high-tuned and frozen like a thief in a room with a single way out, and through the doorway of escape come the footsteps of capture. It didn't even occur to me—well, maybe it occurred to me but not seriously—that there could ever been another woman in another place or time with raging gunpowder hair and such eyes. That these poems hadn't been here before this dawn was insignificant, except in the ways it was perfect. Finally the poet described the rorschach of her tongue and the accent of her past, the language of topsy-turvy question marks and its languid lustful music. He never understood Spanish either but he knew it when he heard it, and he preferred it to the broken English with which she sometimes violated the prison he made for her from his dreams. If he loved her, he never said. If he made love to her, he never told of it. If he lied about her, I would have known it. But someone knew her and said so, and somewhere left me his poems of it, written of her in a place where or when the woman I had seen could never have been.

I kept the poems in the tower with my hoarded documents of murders. I was constructing my own house of conscience with the transgressions of conscience on exhibit. I found myself poring over the verses for days and nights trying to break their code. There was another week or ten days of this snowy fog; the tide was up and the city became a cluster of dark lighthouses amid moats and rivers. About five in the evening a red mist came pouring out of the sun beneath the clouds. It got so you could set your clock by the moment the sun dipped beneath the clouds and the red mist poured out of it. I talked to a boatman one evening about navigating the lagoon; I'd been watching the Hancock Park mansions out there, their doors caught in the bare black trees and the ocean snarling around them. If there was a beautiful woman with black hair to be found in Los Angeles, she was out in the mansions with the other beautiful women. Can't take you out in this fog, mister, the boatman said carefully. But he shot me a look while coiling a rope in his hands, and the look said not everything in this town was run by Wade and the feds, including guys who sold you boxes of music and guys who took you out in boats. The mansions in the distance turned to stars as the sun went down. I slipped the boatman some money and a look of my own that meant This conversation has been strictly between us.

I left him. I made my way through the high reeds that blew back and forth between the remains of two stone pyramids, rumored to have been built by Chinese barons back before the marshes shifted. They gleamed a tarnished gold in the sun, and in all the gaping holes pocked by the sea burned the fires of nomads. I headed for this bar I knew over on Main Street. By the time I got there it was dark and a few of the streetlights were on. Old boxes blew up and down the sidewalks, and scurrying across my path were what I took to be huge rats until I saw the eyes of men looking out at me from under their black coats. I had come to this bar a couple of times before; it had a red door with no knob and a window smeared with silt. The counter inside had a total of four different brown unlabeled bottles. There was no point being very particular about what was served to you in this bar. I wouldn't have come back after the first time except for an old man who sat at the end of the bar talking to himself. The bar-

tender called him Raymond. Though Raymond may or may
not have cared that anyone listened to him, there were always
three or four who did, and it was never the same three or four.
The bartender explained Raymond sailed in from the desert
every day to sit in this bar and talk to himself. More interesting was the bartender's claim that Raymond actually used to
work in the Downtown library. I have no idea whether or not
this was true. I have no idea whether the bartender knew who
I was when he told me this. But I tried to imagine Raymond
living and sleeping in the tower where I now lived and slept.
Raymond looked to me about seventy or eighty years old but
I knew from firsthand experience this meant nothing; like the
buildings in this city there was no telling how ancient he
really was. Raymond talked of the early days. He was a walking history of the town with the chapters out of order; but it
wasn't Raymond who had the chapters out of order, it was
the town itself. I sat in the bar and listened to him tell of
when the Asians first settled the blank little islands of Los
Angeles: Chinese warlords with palaces in the Hollywood
moors who rode the plains all the way to Nevada and clashed
with the huns and samurai who lived in the caves along the
coast where wild children now banded in tribes. A barbaric
context, Raymond rumbled to himself at the bar, but at least
it was a context, until the Portuguese gamblers brought in
their South American slave girls. And now there's no context
at all.

I left the bar and wandered a while, waiting for someone
with some sort of official responsibility to pick me up. After
half an hour I realized I'd walked to the underground grotto
where I had talked to Wade and seen the woman with the
camera. There I overheard sailors murmuring about a score
that night in Downey. I didn't expect to see Wade. I didn't
expect to see the woman with the camera either, but she was
at the same table as before. The bartender watched me casually. I looked around and sat at another table with my eye on

the other side of the room. A few people straggled in and out, and after about five minutes I got up and went over to her. Like the first time I'd seen her here, she was fooling very intently with the camera. Sitting in the ashtray on the table next to her was a cigarette and two or three burned butts. The smoke smelled like Sonoran hemp, but when she looked up at me she didn't appear narcotized; the distracted look in her eyes was something else. She also had three glasses sitting in front of her, all of them empty; she seemed just as impervious to the liquor. There was a pause in the way she looked at me. It seemed a long time—five or ten seconds—after I said hello that she reacted, and then she gave me the same smile she gave the others; it was goofy, which was interesting because she didn't have a goofy face. It was a sculpted face, high cheeks and eyes far apart except thinking about it now maybe her mouth was just a little off-center and that was what made it odd. At any rate the effect of the smile was calculated to be both pleasant and unpromising, and she used it with success. It got her many drinks and no trouble.

I didn't offer to buy her a drink. I'd given the boatman out by the lagoon too much money and now I was short. I told her my name and she smiled again in a way that said she already knew it or that it didn't matter. Her own name was Janet Dart or Dash or Dot; Wade would tell me later. Come here often? I asked. She laughed; it looked like I was putting the make on her. I decided I should say something that would change that. "Are you a cop?"

She looked down at the camera and then back up, sort of surprised. "No," she said.

"But you were over at the library, the night of the murder."

"Was it murder," she said, "I didn't hear anything about a murder." She looked at me cautiously. I hoped she wouldn't say something like What did you say your name was again?

"But you were there at the library."

"I was taking some pictures." She picked up the hemp and took a drag.

"Been in Los Angeles long?" I said.

"No." She looked at me evenly; she was remarkably composed for all the dope and liquor and questions. "I got here not long after you did," she said. That was when I knew she knew who I was, and she knew I knew it.

"Where you from?" She still looked at me evenly and didn't answer. "Did you come to take pictures?"

She thought about it. She wanted to be precise in her answer. "I don't go anywhere," she explained slowly, "with the primary purpose of taking pictures. The primary purpose is always different. But everywhere I go, taking pictures is the secondary purpose. Which makes it the thing all places have in common for me." She smoked some more hemp. She picked up the most recent glass and stared into the bottom of it as though something might be there that wasn't easily visible to the naked eye. She put the glass down and glanced at me wondering if I was going to buy her a drink. I bought her a drink with the rest of my money. "Aren't you going to have one?" she said.

"No."

"I don't like that."

"We'll share this one."

"I don't like that either," she said, but we did share it when it came, at least for a while; then it became her drink. "I'm looking for someone," she finally said after it had been her drink for a while.

"Yes?"

"Yes," she said. The camera sat in her lap and for the first time she seemed completely unaware of it.

"Are we getting to the primary purpose now?"

"Yes," she said, "we're getting to the primary purpose now. Do you know where he is?"

"Who?" I said, surprised.

"Who I'm looking for."

"Who are you looking for?"

She didn't believe me in the least. "You don't know?"

"No."

"He hasn't made contact with you?" And then she thought a moment and answered her own question, in a mumble, "No, perhaps he wouldn't have," and finished the drink.

"Who is it?" I said.

"Why don't you tell me who you're looking for?"

"Did I say I was looking for someone?"

She shrugged. "My mistake."

I shook my head. I said, "Actually, I *am* looking for some-one."

"I know," she said. "I saw her."

"What?"

"I said I saw her."

I adjusted myself in the chair and put both my hands flat, palms down, on the table. I must have sat there with my mouth open for half a minute. "You saw her?"

"That night," Janet Dart or Dash said calmly. "I was by the library and she was in the door, or it was more on the steps I guess. Right there outside the library. I remember the light of the library behind her, so the door must have been open."

"I don't think," I slowly shook my head, "we can be talk-ing about the same—"

"Oh hell," she said suddenly in exasperation. "I'm talking about the dark girl, she looked like she was from one of the southern annexes. Maybe South America. Brown skin and black hair and she had a light-brown dress and no shoes. There was something all over her and I thought it was mud, but later of course I realized it was the blood. She had something in her hand that was hard and bloody too. You know we mean the same person."

"You got it from the police report," I said, but I knew there was something wrong with that: the light-brown dress and no shoes, I hadn't told the police that because I'd seen her in a dress that had no color and, incredibly, I hadn't noticed the shoes or no shoes. Except now in my mind I saw her on the beach and then I saw her in the back room of the archives and I still wasn't sure about the color of the dress, but there was no doubt about the shoes. In my mind she was plainly barefooted now. How could I have not noticed that before? So the police couldn't have known about it unless they knew about her all along; this might, I suddenly thought, be part of a plan to keep me unhinged. "You're in with the feds on this," I said to the woman across the table. "It's part of a plan to keep me unhinged." She looked at me as if I were already unhinged. "There is no such woman," I said, but I didn't believe that either. It didn't go with the look on Wade's face that night in the archives. It didn't go with all the blood.

"All right," she just said.

"What happened when you saw her on the steps of the library?" I said.

"She went back in."

"Back in the library?"

"I think I frightened her. I think the camera frightened her."

"The camera?"

"When I took her picture."

I stood up from the table. "You took her picture?" I said.

"Perhaps it's Indian superstition, about cameras. Are Indians superstitious about cameras?"

I came around the table and stood in front of her chair. "You took her picture?" It must have appeared a little threatening; she looked around the room and I looked too, and there were guys watching us as though they thought I was about to get out of hand. She smiled and said to me, with her eyes still on the other men, "I think you should sit down." After a moment I said, "Do you have this picture?"

"Yes." She put out the hemp in the ashtray.

"With you now?"

"It's with my other pictures. You know I wish you hadn't pointed me out to the cops like that, the way you did that night. I'd just as soon stay clear of them."

"Why?"

"Because I have somebody to find too and I don't think I can with cops everywhere."

"What were you doing there if you didn't want to be around cops?"

She paused a moment and said, "To be honest with you, I thought something had happened. When I saw the girl come out of the library and she was all a mess like that. I thought something had happened to you."

"So you knew who I was and that I was working in the library."

"Yes I knew that."

"You knew who I was the last time I was here in the grotto."

"I wasn't sure."

"You want to tell me what's going on?"

"What do you mean?"

"I mean how you know me and why you know me and why what I do and what happens to me is important to you."

"What did you say your name was again?"

"It's too late for that line."

"I should have used it before," she agreed.

"Or not at all."

"Would you like to see the picture?"

"Would you like to tell me what's going on?"

"No. Would you like to see the picture?"

We left the grotto together. The other guys in the bar hadn't stopped looking at me. Up above ground she was transfixed by the sound of the buildings; it stopped her in her tracks a moment as if it reminded her of something. Is it the same, she said to me, it's the same isn't it. What's that, I said. The sound, it hasn't changed has it? she said. No it hasn't changed, I said, and I hope it doesn't either. It takes me a long time to get used to it every time it changes, and every time it changes the sound gets worse. I don't agree, she said. She said, I wish it would change every single day. I wish it would change every single minute.

We went to where she lived. It wasn't far from the canals but in the direction of the library and the center of town. This was the former industrial section of Los Angeles; the buildings were lined up like bunkers, gray and windowless except for skylights near the roof some thirty feet off the ground. Janet Dart or Dash was living in an old warehouse where the merchants of Little Tokyo used to keep rice and fish that came into the harbors. The bulb in the warehouse doorway was the only light on the street; we could see it from three blocks away. Janet Dart or Dash had a possibly important key that, at the very least, opened up the warehouse; when we stepped inside and the door slammed locked behind us, I was for a moment back in Bell. The feeling didn't change as we went up the stairs, and it didn't change when she unlocked another door and it slammed behind us too. Then there was a long hall with no windows she led me down, and it turned left and went about ten or fifteen yards to another door, and through that we turned left again and zigzagged right. By this time I had no idea which direction was which, and that felt like Bell too. She unlocked another door and it could as easily have led us into another hall; but here was where she lived.

At first I couldn't see if the space was big or small; standing there I was just aware of this void in front of us. It was pitch-black and cold. Over to my right I could see one of those little narrow skylights next to the ceiling, so I knew we were at the top of the building. The window was open. The sky was black beyond it. There was the sound. It's cold, I said, and immediately stumbled in the dark to close the skylight. What are you doing? I heard her say in the dark. Don't do that, leave it open. I turned to where her voice came from. This felt like Bell too, exactly like Bell, more like Bell than anything, in this dark room with one narrow high opening and everything cold. To hear her voice like that in the dark of a cold high cell brought back a thousand things I'd imagined when I lived in a dark cold high cell in Bell, imagining what it would be like to hear a woman's voice, any woman's voice, at that moment in that place. When I lived in Bell I'd found that if I could just imagine a voice, if I could just conjure that much, the rest was easy: I could make her look like anything, I could make her touch me in any way—once I had the voice in mind. Now I was standing here in the dark and I heard her voice and something ran up my back, everything felt poised and alert and tense; and when she spoke to me she sounded Spanish in my head even though she wasn't really Spanish at all. I knew what I was doing to myself. I knew what I was doing to her. This isn't Bell, I said to myself. It's cold, I said to her again. Leave it open, she said in the dark. I have to be able to hear it if it changes, that music that comes from the ground.

She turned on a light. Why are you looking at me like that, she said.

There was a rumpled bed in the corner and a small table by it. There was a box of clothes and another part of the room, shaped like an L, that was unrevealed by the light. If there were bars instead of a wall and a toilet in the corner, it would have been exactly like a cell. Show me the picture, I said.

She shrugged and lit another roll of hemp. It's over here

with the rest of my pictures, she said, I have kind of a gallery. Some of them aren't as good as the others, she explained. She walked across the room and brushed past me on her way to the dark part of the L, where she turned on another light.

I stood there staring at the "gallery."

They were photographs, all right; the wall was covered with them. From top to bottom and side to side nothing but glossy prints, every one of them with a large black spot in the middle as if she'd taken them in the dark of night or the very dark of this room, or in the dark of her own camera, never uncovering the lens. The alcove of the L was filled with glossy black spots, all lined up in rows, each one looking exactly the same as the other.

I turned to her. I expected she'd be standing there in her blue-and-white dress laughing with a smile that wasn't nearly goofy enough to make it funny. But she wasn't laughing at all, she wasn't even looking at me. She was studying her pictures, stepping up to one or another to check it out closely, looking from one black spot to another in comparison. She shook her head. Some aren't as good as the others, she said again.

She took, from the third row from the bottom, the fourth black spot from the right. She handed it to me. I told you it was her, she said, looking at it as I held it in my hand, while I looked at her. That same strange feeling ran up my back again.

Is this a joke, I whispered.

She barely betrayed consternation at the question. But something jumped in her eyes when she said to me, You mean it's not her? She looked at me suspiciously. Are you sure?

I stared at the black spot in my hand and swallowed. I kept trying to think what to say. There's nothing in these pictures, I told her quietly.

She flinched a little. She took the picture from my hand and dropped it on the floor like an abandoned bride dropping a dead bouquet.

It was dark when I took them, she said coolly. It was hard to see. But I can see these pictures and it's not my fault if you can't. She went over to the wall and ran her hands along all the pictures. What is it? I said as she gazed at the black blurs. She stopped and stood back from the wall. What are you looking for, I said. After a moment she answered, What I'm looking for isn't here. The picture I'm looking for isn't here.

She said, There was a tree on a hill, it was back east. In the no-man's-land between Manhattan and the Maritime annex. There was a tree on the hill, and a fence behind it where he lived with the others. The branches of the tree curved into the sky like roads, and the leaves were intricate and patterned like subdivisions of houses and buildings. The bark was white. His hair mixed with the leaves perfectly in the wind. The hills in back were very white and the edge of their tops was only a line. It ran into the profile of his brow as though his face was the horizon.

I took his picture, she said, one day when he didn't know I was there or who I was. Actually I had seen him many times before, from the other side of the fence of course, when I went to shoot the tree. He just blended the way some people blend. But I lost the picture. I don't know how, it was just gone one morning. I went to see him the next day during visiting hours to tell him I had taken his picture and now it was gone. He came into the visitors' room and sat behind this glass that divided us. Everything was dark and his face was like the white shadows of men's faces you see in limousines with black windows. He kept saying Who are you, over and over, even when I'd told him. I don't know you, he kept saying. You do now, I said. He jumped up behind the glass and ran through the door in back, and the guard looked at me.

When I tried to see him again they told me he'd been transferred to another place, but that was a lie. I waited for him to get out.

He's coming soon, she said to me, turning from the black pictures. When I hear the sound from the ground, I know he's already here.

The thing about him, she said, raising a finger intently, was that when I took his picture that afternoon on the hill by the prison, it was without a flash in the very late afternoon. I knew I didn't need a flash, the light was in his face. And I've been looking ever since for the picture that doesn't need a flash and that has its own light. I know if I keep taking pictures in the night, his face will show up like a fire.

I crossed the three feet between us and I took her by her wrist: she jerked in my grasp. You're lying, I said. She looked up at me frightened, and when I pressed her against the wall she seemed to sink into it. Her face was inches from mine and she was watching the hollow of my neck, not my eyes. You're lying, I said again. Are you trying to tell me you took all these pictures without a flash? What about the pictures in that back room of the library, what about that night with all the cops and all the blood? Are you trying to tell me you took all those pictures in the dark? She shook her head a little, then nodded a little. I shook her by her wrist and behind her on the wall some pictures loosened and fell; she stepped on them, trying to move with me when I turned her by the wrist. If, standing this close to her, I should close my eyes, I wondered if she could speak Spanish, I wondered if her hair would turn black; now she wasn't looking at the hollow of my neck but at my eyes. With her free hand she fingered the top button of her dress. Is that what you're trying to tell me, I said, that you took all those pictures in the dark? But I saw you that night, remember. I saw you because the flash of your camera kept going off in my face and it was driving me crazy. I kept thinking it was a storm, I kept thinking there was lightning in the room. It was that kind of light, like the sort you see only in the night, and I know that sort of light, I've had many nights without any light, and when you've had those nights you don't forget when you've seen such a light—

And then I stopped. Not because I was babbling but because of the nights and the lights forgotten. And I saw it again, right then, that light, not in that room but in my head.

In my head, I was standing on the boat. In my head, the girl with the black hair was standing on the beach. The man was kneeling at her feet. In the light of the moon was another light, a flash of something soundless and instant, that went off between his face and mine. Then I saw the blade in her hand. Then in my head I was standing in the back room of the library archives and there was a glow through the library windows from the street. There were cops all around and Jon Wade standing in front of me. Looking just over Wade's shoulder I saw Janet Dart or Dash with her camera. And just beyond the cops and Wade and Janet Dart, I saw her in the corner, hidden as deep in the dark as she could bury herself. I saw all this in my head as though I were looking at the enlargement of one of Janet Dart's photographs, sharpening its background definition; and Janet Dart was right, some faces have their own light. Her hair was blacker than the corner itself so that only her face was a pale haze, and only her eyes shone with the glint of the weapon that caught the glow through the windows and cut me across my eyes.

She was there, I whispered. I let go of Janet Dart or Dash, who dropped her hands and rubbed her wrists. She was there all along, right in front of us, I said.

Of course, said Janet Dart.

I turned from the gallery of black spots and walked to the wall that would have been bars had this been Bell Pen. I waited in the middle of the room for a long time.

I thought, How could we have not seen her? Cops all over the room and she was right there in the corner; how could we have not seen her? But in fact I had seen her. I knew I had seen her because I could see her now, back there in the corner, flashing the knife in my face. And if she had not wanted me to see her, why didn't she put the knife beneath her dress, why was she there at all? Why was she watching me and what was she waiting for me to do? How was it I never noticed anything of her but her knife and her face, not her dress or her feet or her very presence in a room filled with many people?

I turned to Janet. Of course? I asked.

Of course, she said again. I told you she went back in the library after I found her on the steps in front.

So you saw her there too, I said.

I have her picture, said Janet. She pointed at the black photos. But it's not the picture I'm looking for, she said. For Janet Dart's camera it was not the face with its own light.

Did you think you would find it that night, I said, the picture you were looking for?

Yes, said Janet.

Because she was there? I said.

Because you were there, said Janet.

But I'm not the one you're looking for, I told her.

You're the one everyone's looking for, she told me.

I left her. As I walked out the door I thought I heard her say, from a far place, She has such a hold on you. Whoever she is, it's such a hold. I spent half an hour trying to find my way down to the street through all the zigzagging halls of the warehouse. Doors locked behind me. At some point all the doors lock behind you instead of before you. Every place has its point of no return. All the way back to the library I was followed by cops.

I WAS BORN in America. Thirty-some years later a storm blew in from Sonora to lash the far outpost of L.A. where I lived in a tower that held the legends of America's murdered men. The rain beat against my home. My tower rose like a secret passage into the maelstrom. At night I read the white maps of a woman as charted by a phantom poet, and in my head I carried the black spot of her photograph. The storm lasted five days and the water that ran through the streets carried doors torn from their hinges. The peaks of the waves took the form of birds, white foam extending into wings until wild white gulls were everywhere, flying into each other and falling into mauled heaps on the water. When the storm had passed, it took with it the fog that clotted the bay, and when I rose from five days and nights of rain and poems and black portraits and looked from the top of my tower into the blue city below, the sea itself was black. Thick white rain had fallen leaving a black smoking sea. The trees were bare and leafless, cold bald amputees after the white rain, and from the top of my tower Los Angeles was a seashell curling to its middle. The roof of the shell was beveled gray, the ridges pink where the clouds edged the sky, and as with all shells there was this dull roar, you know the roar, the sound of the sea they told you when you were a child.

I was born in America: and I have to finish this soon. I have this feeling of urgency, that penultimate flush before the end, the last rush of blood to the face and light to the eyes. I once supposed I was bleeding in order to bleed myself dry; now I wonder if it was the flow itself I loved. Now I wonder if it was the spilling itself that held me speechless. It isn't that my voice is failing; rather, it almost sounds familiar, the voice of a dead relative from the bedroom closet, from back behind his clothes and shoes I've been wearing since he left. I won't delude myself that integrity can be reborn or that passion can grow young. But the maps I've stolen from the archives navigate more than just the face of a woman. And if she was there in the corner of the archives that night as I believe, then she knows it too, and she's waiting for me with the light of her face and her knife.

The evening the storm cleared I went out to the lagoon. In the twilight and the smoke from the sea the mansions sat in a green and silver cloud threaded by a tangle of empty trees. I found the boatman I'd talked to the week before. I'll put you out there buddy, he said, but I won't hang around to bring you back. We run into any feds I turn right around, I don't need trouble with them. Feds go out there much? I said. Every once in a while, he said. It's not the girls they care about, the girls have got their system. It's the others, the ones they don't know. Guys like you, said the boatman, guys with their own reasons. The feds hate people with their own reasons.

As we got closer to the mansions he told me of the pimps who used to live in town and bring the men out there. The pimps had operated under the assumption that they kept the girls out there in the lagoon like animals in a wildlife sanctuary. As usual, such a mistaken assumption, said the boatman, leads to other mistaken assumptions. The girls put up with it for a while. Then one day someone noticed there weren't any more pimps around. They were found by the cops on the banks of the Rossmore Canal, one of the three main waterways of Hancock Park. An entire beach of pimps, every last one with his throat slit, lined up along the canal, said the boatman, gulls perched on their foreheads shitting. The girls dawdling under the trees twirling their hair and smoking cigarettes, watching bored as the pimps were hauled away by their feet. Not a witness in the bunch of course.

Now we roared up one of the smaller canals and the boatman cut his engine. The girls had already been at work. On the sand I could see the imprint of couples. The tide came in and went out and the imprints were filled with white foam, so the sand was spotted with the wet white pictures of lovers. The sun was down when he dropped me off; his farewell wasn't exactly profuse. Ten feet from me there was nothing left but the noise of him. I was standing in front of a huge earthen house that was dark except for one gaslight coming from a front corridor. The house was arabic and like all Los Angeles houses it could have been built anytime in the last five thousand years. As I walked up to the gaslight the sound of the boat disappeared completely and there was nothing but the faint din of the coast in the distance, the sound of the city buildings slivering through the stripped webbed trees. I got to the corridor which led to a door but off to my left were some steps upward and I took them. They led to a veranda. From there I could see the rest of the canal and some of the other houses; for a moment the water ignited from the sun as if someone had set a match to it and then went dark, a new fog drifting in and hanging on the fences like foliage. Creaking wooden bridges swung in the wind over the water between the houses. Three or four small boats were tied to shambling makeshift docks and someone was moving from dock to dock lighting the lanterns on the posts. After a while I could make out lights all over the lagoon, lanterns and gas lamps and a few fires.

I came down from the veranda and walked back out where the boat had left me off. The woman who'd been lighting the dock lanterns was coming my way in one of the boats, a torch burning in her hand. She sailed past me and then beached about fifteen yards away, where I could now see another dock in front of another house. We were separated by a small slough. She lit the lantern and got back in the boat, and I waited for her to see me. I called to her and she looked at me across the water. Who's that? she said in a voice that didn't carry very well. I'm from the city, I called. She said nothing but the boat came in my direction. The boat had no motor or oars; I couldn't figure how she got it going where she wanted. About five feet from me I could make her out: she was blond with a small face and slight body, and she wore loose casual clothes, jeans and a blowzy top. She could have been any age between twelve and twenty-five. What are you doing here? she said when the tip of the boat touched the shore. I started to pull the boat up but she said, Leave it. She sat in the boat with the fire of the torch burning by her face, looking at me. There's nothing over here, she said. "I'm looking for someone in particular," I said. "About your height. Black hair, she might be Latin. She may not speak English."

"Listen," the girl said laughing, "I can manage the black hair and some words so nice you'd never know they meant nothing at all." She said, "But I have the torch shift tonight and I don't guess improvisation's what you had in mind. Get in and we'll see who we can find. Like I said, there's nothing here anyway." I got in the boat. I pushed off from shore and she watched me as we seemed to drift in exactly the direction she wanted to go. "You must be very undercover," she said. "Whoever dropped you off out here didn't want to be seen by nobody."

"I'm not a cop," I said.

She shrugged. "Doesn't matter to anyone here if you are. Actually I assumed the opposite."

"What?"

"Forget it. Your business with cops is your business." The mansions of the park were gliding past us now, becoming more and more colossal. I could see into the houses where the tide flooded the lobbies and lights shone on the water lapping against the inner marble stairs. The first steps were covered with sea debris and the original drapes on the upper landings were rotted by the salt air, hanging in tatters and bleached in color. Every once in a while we could hear low laughter in the dark and sometimes arguing. In the distance on the southern shore of the main canal was a huge structure sitting alone on a knoll. "That's the old hotel isn't it?" I said.

"Yes."

I watched for a while, then I said to her, "Do you know the person I'm talking about?"

"There's a woman named Lucia, up near the next river."

"You think it's her?"

"It might be her."

"Are we going that way?"

"Eventually. I have another five or six lights."

I looked around me. "Can I ask you something?"

She became impatient. "Not why am I doing this for a living."

"Two questions, actually."

We pulled into another dock and she leaned across the boat, bringing the torch within inches of me. With one sweeping motion she lit the lantern. "Well?" she said.

"How do you direct the boat?"

"I know the water," she said.

"Were you born in America?" I said.

"No." She waited. "Were you?"

"I'm sure of it." We sailed beneath a row of overhanging trees and then into the lobby of the mansion where the woman named Lucia lived. The mansion was built in an antebellum style. Inside the lobby were several very small fires burning in different wall alcoves; the light from them was dim. We sailed through some doors in the back of the lobby, and at the end of this second room I could make out the stairs. We bobbed around a little from wall to wall. For the first time she had to physically push the boat where she wanted it to go. Back here, she explained, the water's unknowable. She got us to the stairs and I got out; it was impossible to be sure but my guess was the water came about a quarter of the way up the steps. She also got out and we pulled the small boat up the stairs to the top. We were standing in the dark and the girl called Lucia's name, and when she didn't get an answer we started down the hall. After a minute we saw some faint light coming from a room; she called Lucia again. I was thinking of her peering out at me from the dark corner here; I was looking for the flash of the knife but there was no moon, and the fires were too dim to catch the glint of it. Walking down the dark hall it occurred to me I didn't really want to find her here. If she lived here then I would know the man at her knees was just another pimp for whom a little throat-slashing was not enough; I didn't want to believe that. I didn't want to believe the man at her knees was any common stranger other than Ben Jarry, because I needed him to be there, I needed to save his life. When I'd done that I knew I would free all of us, Jarry and myself and this Lucia; then he and I would be through with each other. Then she and I would be just beginning.

Lucia! the girl said, and we heard something from the room with the light at the end of the hall. A woman's voice and a Spanish word.

We got to the doorway of the room. There was a large tousled bed and the threads of a canopy hanging from the posts. A white matted rug was on the floor and wallpaper ran down the sides of the room like brown water. A small dresser was directly opposite us, with a mirror.

In the mirror I caught the momentary dark reflection of someone's black hair. There was a movement to my side, I saw it out of the corner of my eye. I turned and lurched for it, my hands in front of me to catch the blow of a knife.

Lucia, said the girl.

Lucia said something in Spanish.

The woman called Lucia indeed had black hair. She wore a black robe. But she was ten years too old and her hands were one weapon and one victim too empty. She looked at me like I was crazy.

I stopped and stared back at her. Then I looked at the other girl. She looked at both of us, and Lucia said something else, or maybe it was the same thing she'd said before.

Not your Lucia? the girl said.

She said something to Lucia and while they talked a moment I went back into the hall. I waited for the girl to come out. When she did she said, Sorry. That's it for Spanish women with black hair, at least around here.

I knew it wasn't her, I said. I'm glad it wasn't her.

The girl shrugged and we headed back for the stairs. She sighed and said, I'm going to have to take you up to the Rossmore. That's the best place for you to catch a ride back to town. If I put you back where I found you, you'll never get anywhere.

I have one more favor to ask, I said to her.

"What's that?"

"Take me out to the old hotel. You can drop me off there."

She shook her head. "I can't do that, mister. I'd help you out if I could, I've tried to help you. But that hotel is *out there*, and I don't just mean the distance. There are people who have been in that hotel for *years*."

She wasn't going to change her mind. We got to the stairs and dragged the boat down the steps; I was in front pulling the boat behind me, and she followed. I felt bad that she didn't catch on. She had tried to help and she trusted me. I got the boat in the water and she was three steps behind me. I got in the boat and looked over at her, and she reached out her hand.

I pushed off alone. She stood on the steps watching me drift away. In the dim light of the room she seemed even younger, childlike, which she had not seemed before. It took her several full seconds to figure out I was leaving her there.

I'm sorry, I said. I heard my echo in the dark and on the water.

You bastard, I heard her say.

I said, I'm sorry. But I have to get out to that hotel.

You don't know the water, she said.

I'll bring the boat back, I called to her.

Don't fucking bother. You come back and I'll fucking slit your throat.

So I've heard, I said. I pushed my way out into the lobby and then glided toward the doorway. She stood in the distance on the stairs as though at the back of a cave, the water black and wounded with occasional light. You don't know the water! she shouted. I nodded and turned a corner, and she disappeared from view.

I emerged from the house and floated out into the canal. She was right of course; I didn't know the water, and all I did was meander aimlessly between currents. Finally I got myself to the nearest of the docks where I tore off one of the posts that was lit at the top. I doused it in the canal and pulled it back into the boat with me. It wasn't flat enough to use as an oar but it was ten or twelve feet long and, kneeling in the boat, I could push myself along the shallow part of the river. I kept as quiet as I could, heading back up canal until I reached the main waterway from where we had originally come. I imagined a tribal horde of women suddenly emerging from the houses with weapons, to get back their boat and take care of me good.

I got to the southern edge of the lagoon and could see the old hotel plainly in the distance. But I could also see the girl was right: the hotel was far, farther than I'd thought, and now I was in some trouble. The water was too deep for the pole to do any good. I was somewhere between lagoon water and ocean water; the sea itself wasn't a quarter of a mile behind me, and while the tide was washing me in rather than out, the island where the hotel stood was still far away. I was sitting in the dark staring into the distance and trying to gauge whether I had the remotest chance of making a swim for it when I heard a voice that sounded as though it were directly behind me. I turned and a large schooner was some twenty feet away, sailing silently by; someone on deck shone a light. Need a tow? came his voice, and out here on the flat water beneath the flat black sky his words carried as though he were sitting in my boat.

I'm trying to get to the hotel, I said.

He answered in an even lower voice than before, I can't take you there, that's off limits you know. I can tow you in to the southern harbor, though.

The southern harbor was not the one in Downtown but rather where the East Canal emptied out onto the coast, near the beach where I'd seen the Latin girl and Ben Jarry the first night. All right, I said. Toss me a line and I'll follow you in.

The schooner edged up to me and this guy in a jacket and T-shirt tossed me a line. In the dark he looked as if he was probably friendly. Then we started on our way.

Everybody trusted me tonight.

Because the point was, of course, that since we were heading to the southern harbor rather than Downtown, we were going to pass the island with the hotel—if not right by it, then a hell of a lot closer to it than I was now. It's possible the guy on the schooner suspected something. He insisted that I ride in his boat instead of remaining in my own, which dragged along behind us at the end of a rope. So the blonde in the mansion wouldn't be getting her boat back after all.

I kept watching the island, waiting. When we had almost passed by, skirting its eastern tip on our way to port, I knew this was as near as I was going to get, about half the distance from where I had been before, out in the middle of the water.

In another three minutes the island would be irrevocably behind me. I never even thought of not going.

In midair, when my hands were inches from touching the water, I could already feel the cold of it. Then there was the shocking black rush, and when I came up the first time I almost thought I might have heard shouting in the distance. But I went back under, and for a moment I saw her in the sea, where blood knows no stain but only rivers. That was only for a moment. I've been acting funny, I said to myself. I've been doing strange things.

I began swimming hard. The most difficult thing was maintaining my orientation, keeping my head clear as to where I was and where I was trying to get. After it seemed I had swum half an hour I began to panic; I felt my effort collapsing. In fact I probably hadn't swum half an hour at all. Probably it was more like ten minutes. I was treading and thinking to myself, I'm thirty-eight or thirty-nine; my body does not believe it. My body believes my face, which believes my heart, and it makes me an old man in the water, who believes his panic and exhaustion. For the moment I cared nothing about her, I cared nothing about Ben Jarry. This, I said to myself, maybe aloud though I don't remember, this is as my damned traitor heart would have it. It would have me in my tower living in the gloom of moral death. I began to swim again. I swam against my face and my heart, I swam as though I had my face in one hand and my heart in the other, and I pummeled the sea with them in order that they would take me, against their will, where I chose to go.

On the island I slept. I dreamed I buried my face and my heart in the sand, the first wrapped around the second.

I didn't lie there very long. The cold woke me; I was wet through and through, and there on the edge of the sea was a hard wind, though an hour before the night had been still. The hotel hovered before me, a monstrous dark yawn, and I got up and headed for it. I was walking around it ten minutes before I found the entrance. There were no doors, just a gouge where glass had been. There was no light. I was cold and inside the building it wasn't much warmer. A corridor turned south and shot off in the distance, each side of it lined with little cubicles: empty ticket agencies and barbershops and clothes boutiques and post offices and rental centers filled with busted mirrors and dilapidated shelves and counters, maps across walls and racks with old postcards and magazine stands and ledges filled with small cracked bottles and things I couldn't make out. At the end of the corridor were some stairs. I stumbled up in the dark and could see the main lobby of the hotel open up before me, a black expanse, rows of motionless elevators and a dining hall and beyond that a lounge. I thought I heard some sort of music overhead and caught a glittering of something framed within the gash of the ceiling. I found myself staring up into a huge tunnel that ran through five or six floors of rooms to the sky; the glitter was stars in the distance.

A light was coming from the lounge. I held myself, shuddering. I'm damn cold, I said out loud. I got to the doorway of the lounge and it was immediately warmer. A bulb was burning at one end of the room dirty orange electricity. I said to myself, What, they have someone come around and change the bulbs? The lounge was gritty and lined with webs; a bar was at the back shadowed and still, with liquor bottles on the shelves behind it and glasses sitting upside down on what was once a white cotton towel. All of it was dimly visible to me in the light of the hearth at the other end of the room, where a fire was burning. The hearth was set in large flat stones and surrounded by large worn chairs. I went over to the fire and was standing there several moments before I realized someone was sitting in one of the chairs. "Lee?" he said, blinking at me in the dark.

I looked at him in stupefaction. He stood up and came over to me. He was tall, probably as tall as Jon Wade but

nowhere near the mountainous build; he moved like an
aristocrat. As far as I could tell from the flames of the fire he
was in his mid-fifties. He was stylishly dressed and groomed
but his face had a certain thickness to it, as though he drank
a lot. At this moment, in fact, he was holding an amber
glass with ice clinking in it and seemed just the slightest bit
tipsy.

"My God, Lee," he said, touching my shirt, "you're
drenched. What the hell happened to you?" He pulled me by
the elbow to one of the other chairs and I sat down in it.
"Look here," he said, "can I get you something from the
bar?" He was watching me with utter concern. I stared at him
and then over at the bar in the dark with all the dusty glasses
upside down on the dirty white towel. I looked at the glass in
his hand and back up at him, and water ran from my hair into
my eyes.

"No thanks," I said.

"Here," he said, "pull the chair closer to the fire." He
started to pull me out of the chair so he could move it closer
to the fire.

"It's all right," I said, resistant. "I'm fine here." I looked
around me.

"What happened to you anyway?" he said. "I've been
waiting damn near forever. The damn phone doesn't work or
I would have called." He squinted at me in the dark.

I shook my head. "I'm not Lee."

He kept squinting at me. He sighed heavily. "No, I can see
that now." He took a gulp from his amber glass and turned to
the fire, anxious. He turned back to me. "Well I hope you're
all right," he said a little absently. He sat in his chair and held
the drink on one of its arms, thinking. Presently his attention
came back to me. "Someone turn a hose on you or something?" he said, regarding me from head to foot.

"I took a swim," I explained.

"A swim?"

"Out in the water." He stared at me. "The lagoon," I said. "It was the only way I could get here."

"The lagoon?" he said in complete bafflement. But he waved it away. He sighed heavily again and looked toward the door, muttering. "Where is he anyway?" I heard him say under his breath.

I turned toward the door too. "Waiting for someone?" I asked.

"If we don't come up with this script, it's over for both of us," he said. He was clearly agitated. "I can't afford to lose this opportunity. I'm . . . I'm forty-five years old and I need a vehicle." He was older than forty-five. I knew that not by the way he looked but by the way he said it. "I've been patient with Lee a long time, and I've been waiting a long time for the right vehicle."

I nodded. "Who's Lee?" I said after a while.

"Lee's not fucking here, that's who Lee is," he said, his voice rising. He finished his drink. He was still a moment. "Name's Richard," he said, extending his hand.

I took it. "Cale."

"Are you an actor?" he said.

"No."

"Do you work in pictures at all?"

I kept looking around me, at the bulb burning at the opposite end of the room. I was finally becoming warm from the fire. I didn't know what he was talking about. "No," I said.

"Good for you. Bloody good for you. I mean it. It's a fucked business and a fucked place. I admire anyone who can avoid it altogether. What is it you do?"

"Can you tell me," I said slowly, "where the kitchen is?"

"What kitchen?"

"The kitchen of the hotel."

"I think it's downstairs behind the ballroom," he said. "Or maybe that's the dining room." He added, "The dining room's closed."

"I have to find the kitchen," I said.

"Are you a chef?" he asked, distracted. He was getting agitated again. He stood up from the chair. "The hell with this. I've been patient with Lee a long time. I've been waiting a long time for the right vehicle." He looked around. "Maybe I should catch a cab into Beverly Hills, phone from there."

I stared at him. This man thought he was going to take a cab somewhere.

"Lee?" he called. He was calling into the dark beyond the doorway behind me. I turned and then he said, "There's someone there. Is that you, Lee?" he called. "I've been waiting."

I saw a form move in the dark; there *was* someone there. I stepped toward the door and the form backed away, and when I got there I could hear the light steps of someone running across the lobby. The guy behind me called again but now I took off after the footsteps and reached the stairs that went back down the way I had come.

There was music above me and the shine of stars, and I looked up into the sky six floors away. The tall silhouette of the actor was small in the far door.

I turned back to gaze into the mouth of the stairs, and I saw her. It was absolutely black but I saw her anyway; she held the knife in her hand. It already had blood on it. "It . . . is you?" I heard her say, in awkward English.

It's me, I said. I stepped toward her, down the stairs. She ran.

At the bottom of the stairs I heard her steps fade away down a long corridor. At the end of the corridor was another light and in the light I could see a small glowing object on the floor. As I came closer I could see it was the knife, glistening red. I half expected that, when I reached it, it would vanish. I half expected that, as I bent to pick it up, it would dissolve in my hand. It did not. When I held it, it felt ordinary, nothing epiphanic at all. It took me ten minutes to find the kitchen. It had a burning bulb too, like the lounge and the corridor from where I'd just come. The kitchen was strewn with utensils and appliances and pots, and the large white doors of the freezer were wide open. It looked as if it had been abandoned only a moment before, and there was the barely lingering smell of rotted food. Next to one of the freezer doors lay the headless body of a man, still bleeding. I reeled for a moment, not looking at him; I wasn't used to that yet. I didn't see the rest of him and I wasn't inclined to search for it. I went over to a place some ten or twelve feet from him and took off my clothes and lay on the ground with the knife in my hand.

Maybe I slept, maybe I passed out. I say maybe because later, when I learned how much time had gone by, sleeping or passing out seemed the only explanation; I felt as though I'd been lying there only a few minutes. Occasionally I would raise my head to see if the body was still there. But then I must have fallen asleep, because a voice woke me. Cale, the voice said, what are you doing?

I opened my eyes. A very big shadow was standing over me. "Wade?"

"What are you doing?" he said again.

I held my hand up in front of my face. I still had the knife. "I'm guarding the body of Ben Jarry," I said. When Wade didn't answer, I said, "Don't tell me. Don't tell me there's no body over there." When he still didn't answer, I raised my head from the floor and looked over in the direction of the body. There were a bunch of cops and there was something on the ground with a sheet over it. I nodded. "Finally. Finally got a body. There's no eluding you forever."

"No," came Wade's voice out of the big shadow, "there's no eluding me forever."

"I knew you'd get him sooner or later," I explained, "I always had confidence in you. No matter how tough the assignment, you were bound to snare him. Millions of murdered men, true, but not having a head is a distinguishing characteristic. No way you can escape notice very long if you don't have a head. You guys are aces. You guys are cracker-jacks."

"What are you doing, Cale?"

"In the archives of the library are the legends of murdered men, Inspector. Maybe some are real and maybe some aren't. I'm familiar with most of them at this point. I've been smuggling their legends into my tower, I've been poring over them in my sleep. My favorite is the one of the man murdered in this kitchen. This very one. Like Ben over there, except this murdered man would be a little harder for you to track down, since he had a head. He was shot with a gun. Do you know about this man?"

"No."

"In this very kitchen. Shot with a gun. By an Arab of some sort. Late one spring night and many people saw it. He bled on the floor and did not die immediately. He aspired to lead his people and at the moment he was shot he was in the throes of triumph, his people had acclaimed him on this very night just outside this very kitchen. Before him, his own brother had led the people, and his brother was another murdered man, and the brother that came before them was a murdered man as well. A whole family of murdered men. They were born in America."

"America One," came Wade's voice from the big shadow, "or America Two?"

I got up off the floor. I stood toe to toe with him and held the knife hard. I held the knife as hard as his eyes held me. "Not America One or America Two," I said, seething. "Just America. They were born in America."

Wade licked his lips. "I have to arrest you."

"Why?"

"Because we have a body here and we have you holding what by all appearances seems to be a murder weapon."

"You don't understand," I said. "That's Ben Jarry over

there. You can't arrest me for murdering Ben Jarry. You've already set me free for helping *you* murder Ben Jarry, remember?"

. Wade slowly blinked. "Put your clothes on." He looked down at my side where I held the knife hard, and he put his hand out, palm open and draped with a white handkerchief. We stared at each other a good half minute before I put the handle of the knife on the white handkerchief. He wrapped the knife and called over Mallory and gave it to him. I put my clothes on. We walked from the hotel kitchen up the stairs into the lobby. I could still see the light of the lounge where the bar was. "There was somebody else here earlier tonight," I said to Wade, nodding at the light. "Some sort of actor, your height, fiftyish. I talked to him." Wade lumbered over to the lounge, looked in and came back. "No one I can see but check it out," he said to Mallory. Check it out, Mallory said to the cop next to him. Wade walked on ahead, and Mallory and another cop led me out into the night, where we followed Wade to a boat down by the beach, where there were still more cops.

They had spotted me taking off with the boatman that evening. They hadn't picked me up at the time because they wanted to see where I was going and why. They'd lost us in the fog and only when they got the boatman coming back could they make him show them exactly where in Hancock Park he'd dropped me off. You must have made great friends with the little blond hooker, Wade said to my surprise, she wouldn't tell us shit. They'd been stymied again until they got a report from a schooner that docked in the south harbor with a small boat tied to its tail.

Back in town they took me to the station. It was now nearly dawn. A few cops were standing outside smoking and in the front room a couple of women who did not look as though they worked the lagoon but over by the East Canal were sitting on a bench that ran along the wall. Next to them

on the bench a guy was slumped over. Wade talked to the
cop behind the desk and then after a few minutes we went
through the door down a green hall to a small windowless
room. Everyone was exhausted. I should have been exhausted
too. Instead everything in me was fired, I couldn't remember
when I had felt this fired. Perhaps I had never felt like this,
even before prison. I had this ridiculous sense of being in
control of everything, I had this feeling of calling all the
shots. It was ridiculous because I wasn't calling any shots at
all, it was ridiculous because everyone thought I was out of
control. We sat in the small windowless room at a single table
with two chairs. I was in one of them and Wade was in the
other. Mallory stood by the door and another cop stood in
the corner. I sat looking wild and fired; Wade looked exhausted. "Have you settled down now?" he said to me.

"What do you mean?" I looked at the other cops.

"Are you clear in your own head?" he said.

"Everything in me is fired," I explained. With perfect tim-
ing someone knocked on the door, and Mallory opened it. It
was the police doctor. He said he wanted to take some blood
and a urine sample. Wade said, Fuck that, this man isn't
drugged. "Everything in me is fired," I explained to the doctor. The doctor had me open my shirt; he took my pulse and
put his hand on my head. He turned to Wade and said I was
burning up, and I said, What did I tell you.

"I don't care about that," Wade said slowly, "this man and
I are going to have a talk now."

"This man should be hospitalized," said the doctor. He
and Wade argued, and that ended with Wade still sitting in
his chair and the doctor outside the room and the door locked
between them. "Tonight," Wade said to me, "you're going
to tell all about it." He was still speaking very slowly but bit-
ing the words so hard I could hear the pain in them. "You're
going to tell me who you went to meet in the lagoon tonight
and why."

"A woman," I said.

"We found a woman," he said, meaning the blonde, "and nothing happened between you as far as we can tell from what she told us."

"A different woman."

"A woman named Janet Dart?"

That confused me. "Who?"

"Janet Dart," he said. "We know you met her a week ago and we know you went to her place. I told you to stay clear of that woman."

"She was showing me her pictures. Have you seen them?" I said, "I thought she was a cop."

"My understanding of your case," he whispered, smoldering, "is such as to lead me to conclude you never thought she was a cop. My understanding of your case is such as to lead me to conclude you know why she came here." He was hot and his face was wet as it was in the grotto that night, but now he didn't notice it at all. "We know about her connection," he said. "We know she came here to Los Angeles to see a man who was a member of your political cadre in New York City two and a half years ago. We know he escaped from an upper-annex New York prison seven weeks ago. We know your former political cronies have sent him for you and we're reasonably certain he's the one who's been setting off the undergound detonations. My understanding of your case is such as to lead me to conclude you went to the lagoon tonight to meet Janet Dart and perhaps this man, though we're not sure why. I guess you're right about one thing, we still can't quite figure whose side you're on."

"Listen," I said, "that woman's crazy. She doesn't care about politics. She's in love with a guy who doesn't even know who she is. She's in love with a face that doesn't need a light. Check the places with no lights."

"Did you murder her too?"

"I haven't murdered anybody." I looked at him. "You

think I murdered the man in the kitchen? What about those other times? On the beach and in the library. What about that." Wade looked at me incredulously, and suddenly I saw it too. Suddenly I stopped seeing everything my way and saw it his. "Shit," I said, still looking at him, "I keep forgetting. I keep forgetting you never saw those other times. I keep forgetting I'm the only one who ever saw those other times."

He leaned back in the chair and waited. "Was it your contact, Cale?"

"It's Ben Jarry," I said. "And I did kill Ben Jarry once, as sure as if I had done it with a knife in my hand. But I didn't kill him tonight."

Wade didn't even hear it. "They've sent someone for you, very possibly to kill you. Do you understand? I told you to leave that woman alone." He sat up in the chair. "Stop jerking us around and we can make a case here for self-defense."

"That would put me on your side for sure, wouldn't it," I said.

"But you have to level with us," Wade said, nodding.

"Check out that body," I said to him. "Check out the fingerprints and the blood type. Maybe it doesn't make sense but I *know* it's Jarry. I have a feeling you know it is too."

Wade looked at the other two cops. "Get him out of here," he said.

"Take him to the doc?" said Mallory.

"Take him to fucking jail," said Wade. He got up so furiously the chair flew out behind him, hitting the wall. He slammed the door open and left.

They took me to the cells, toward the back of the building and down half a level. They opened one and threw me in. Up until this point they'd been relatively civil, but I guess now their general frustration with me bubbled over. They weren't particularly gentle about introducing me to the prison floor. They also gave the cell door an extra rattle when they slammed it shut. In the dark I could distinguish several other cells, and though I couldn't make out any other prisoners I could hear them sleeping. I lay on the ground against the wall thinking about being in jail again. A month ago, a week ago, there would have been something comfortable about it. It had been very uncomfortable to feel imprisoned, as I had felt, and not have the bars and floor and the physical evidence of a jail to confirm the feeling. If one is a prisoner by nature, it is best to have a prison as home; it's a hard thing to be a prisoner trapped in the body of a free man. But then I escaped. I escaped the prison of my free body, and became a free man—at which point the free body was no longer a prison but a natural habitat. I would probably never understand how I had made this escape, I would probably never understand how she did it; but I knew she had done it, that she had cut me loose with her knife. I knew I was a step away from becoming another legend in the archives, I knew I was writing the documentation of it this very night. The poetry of the lines someone had once written about her from some other place came to me easily; I felt around in my pockets to see if I had the pages. It didn't matter. I knew all the verses anyway; my brain was exploding. Sitting there in the cell I started doing something odd: I began composing in my head the next poem, the one that was to be written next. Not the last poem of those I had read but the poem after the last poem. Not a new poem, not my poem, but the poem written in the head of someone who may never have existed but who had certainly written another poem nonetheless, and just never had the chance to commit it to ink and page. So there I sat with the poem that came after the last poem, knowing I didn't belong here in this jail, that I didn't want any more jails. Knowing that now I was a free man trapped in the body of an imprisoned one.

There is a tree by a river, it is out west. A man comes to the tree and looks up and sees among its branches a nation of men; they're living their whole lives in the tree. The man calls to them and says, What are you doing living in that tree? And after some silence, from the deepest foliage of the tree's highest limbs, someone answers . . .

Suddenly I was exhausted. Suddenly I wasn't fired anymore. I went to sleep and slept through the dawn and through the afternoon. Once I woke up to the daylight and another time I woke up to someone walking outside my cell. Both times I went back to sleep. When I woke again the sun was already beginning to go down again.

I looked up and she was standing right in front of me.

She was across the cell, and she knelt down and looked at me. She looked tired, and brown splotches of dry blood were on her arms; she looked at my hands warily, a little frightened. She was watching to see if I had the knife. I opened my hands before me and turned them to show her they were empty. I put them on my legs. She would start to say something and then stop; she would look at me and then down at the ground between us. I knew she was trying to explain it but she couldn't. She turned her head to take in the dark jail around us.

"How did you get in here?" I said to her. "I know you weren't here before."

But I thought about it and now I wasn't so sure. She could have been here, back in the shadows of the cell, when they brought me in, just as she'd been in the shadows of the archives that night. She could have been brought in by the cops while I was sleeping; once I would have jumped to such a conclusion. She cocked her head and watched my lips the way people do when they don't understand the language. "You can't stay here," I said. "You understand? They found the body. They have the knife. They'll check it out and they'll see I couldn't have done it." I thought about that too and now I wasn't so sure that made any sense to me anymore either.

The door at the end of the hall opened and closed, and she stood up. Mallory had come in to check things out, and now he stood there outside the cell looking in at me, and then looking at her. His mouth dropped a little and he got this queer look in his eyes. He looked at me and then back at the girl and said, Who the hell are you. I thought, We're making progress. First the blood, then the knife, then the body, now the girl. Who is this, Mallory said to me. I didn't answer. He was going to open the cell and then he thought better of it; he said, I'm getting the Inspector, and took off. He'll be back, I said to her, with a man you don't want to meet.

She didn't move. I began inching to her across the floor and she watched me still wary and suspicious. I could make out small puddles in my cell now; the jail smelled like the canals outside. The windows were at street level and sometimes when the canals rose around the city, water came over the ground and poured into the jail. Steam was rising from the floor. She didn't seem to notice it. She blinked at me and her mouth was fuller and redder in the dark; she sighed heavily. A great sense of pain seemed to go through her. Her eyes were dazed and precise ovals in the small pool at our feet, and I could actually hear the sound of her lips parting. She shook her head a bit, as though to wake herself. In the deepening blue twilight of the windows in the opposite cells I saw a candle go by; I wondered if the people of Los Angeles had come to wear fires on their shoes. The flame reared like the trunk of an animal and the puddles of the jail caught the reflection of the candle and still held it after the candle had passed. Every small wave on the surface of the puddles of water multiplied the color of the flame; a red and fiery sheen seemed to lie across the cell in the dark. She was a shadow framed by a ring of candlelight. At that moment I'd come too far down the white hourless hole of Los Angeles to give in to her so easily. Her face had smoke around it and she reached out to the bars of the cell when I caught her. I kept thinking that any minute someone would come to put out the flame of this candle, wherever in the city it was, so as to extinguish the reflections of the water's surface. Old trash from the city lay by the doors. The shadows of the bars burned themselves into the water. A large dark cloud settled in the hall; for a moment I thought it was Wade. It's Wade, I said to her. Her hair ran in black curls down her face, and I pressed myself to her. She was right against me. She shuddered at the sight of me. What is it, I said, I haven't done anything.

We watched each other, pressed to each other, and I looked down at my hand holding her arm. I let go. For a moment she didn't move, and then her eyes became sad and she stopped shuddering. I dropped my hands to my sides, and she turned and pushed open the door of the cell.

I know they locked that door. They gave it an extra rattle when they slammed it shut. But she pushed it open and walked through and stood in the hall looking back at me. I took a step; the door of the cell was still open. I swung it back and forth. Where are you going, I said. She walked into the dark end of the hall and I waited, looking at my fingers which had on them the blood from her arms that was not quite dry. For a moment I wasn't sure if I was in a cell in Los Angeles or in a cell in Bell Pen somewhere in the ice of the north continent. At that moment it didn't matter to me whether Ben Jarry had been hanged or whether my indiscretion had hanged him. I would have traded Ben Jarry a hundred times to have her pressed against me again. I looked at the shadow where she had vanished; I knew she wasn't a ghost. I'd held her and she had opened the door and it was still open, and she had been too tired and afraid and suffering to be a ghost. The door at the other end of the hall opened and I looked, and there were Wade and Mallory. Wade was looking at me calmly. Mallory saw me standing in the open door of the cell and his face went white. Through the window was coming the last light of dusk, and the fire in the puddles all over the floor was gone.

I stared at my bloody fingers. "Inspector," Mallory said to Wade, swallowing hard, "I swear to you we locked that cell."

Wade was still calm. He looked as though half of him were receding into the night, as though he were disappearing by the moment. His clothes hung on him and his face was sunken. He blinked at me. "How did you open the cell, Cale," he said. I could barely hear him.

"She opened it," I told him.

Mallory was still swallowing. He exhaled and said, "There *was* a girl, Inspector." He worked up the nerve to look at the side of Wade's face and said, "She was in there a few minutes ago, I swear it. She had black hair and looked Mex maybe, or—" Wade turned to him. Shut up Mallory, he said quietly. He turned back to me.

I showed him my hands. "Well this isn't *my* blood," I said, "and I think you know it wasn't on me when we came in last night." Wade had his back to me before I finished talking. He was walking to the door at the end of the hall, and when he got there he pivoted imperceptibly and said to Mallory, Bring him along. He drifted out the door as though the ground were moving him. Nothing he did seemed of his own volition, not what he saw or what he said or did. Mallory gave me an utterly baffled look and motioned me on ahead of him. We followed Wade toward the front of the building and into his office. There were a few guys sitting around at their desks drinking coffee.

In his office Wade walked behind the desk and, not even looking at me, said, "I'm putting you under house arrest. You won't be leaving the library except under exceptional circumstances. We'll have your food prepared for you and bring you those supplies you need." He said all this so softly I could barely hear him. He looked five or ten years older than the night before; he looked like someone who had seen something amazing and inexplicable. I noticed something else. I had to listen for it and then I had to figure out what it was. I realized it was the sound of the buildings: the sound had changed again. I tried to remember if I had felt the rumble of the ground; I thought of the pools of fire on the floor of the jail.

"Am I still under arrest for murder?" I said to him.

"No," he answered. "If you were under arrest for murder you would be in jail. You're under arrest for violating conditions of your parole."

I smiled. "It was Jarry wasn't it," I said.

Wade let out a deep breath.

"It was Jarry," I said, "and you can't arrest me for the murder of a man who's already dead. That's it, isn't it?" I was angry. "You know what I think?"

Mallory was pulling me by the arm, toward the door. "Come on, jack."

I was sure I had it all figured out. My mind was racing, inventing and discarding one theory after another, all in the course of seconds. For a moment I was sure Jarry had never been executed at all. For a moment I was sure it was all a setup to make me a scapegoat, to make me bait for whoever was coming here to get me. Whoever this Janet what's-her-name was looking to meet up with. My mind was racing, trying to get it all straight, but it was going faster than I could follow, I was blathering to myself. "You know who she is," I said to Wade, my eyes narrowing at him.

"Your Spanish girl? No."

"But you know there is such a girl."

"I have no reason at this point to disbelieve it." I could still barely hear him. "But listen to me," and as he leaned across his desk his voice did not so much rise as solidify, "if there is a Spanish girl, you stay away from her. I'm telling you for your sake. You can believe that body was Ben Jarry if you want, it doesn't matter. But for your sake, you stay away from her."

"You can't admit it was him, can you?" I said, shaking my head. "It's that hard for you, isn't it."

He came around from the desk and took Mallory by the shoulders and nearly lifted him up and out of the room. He slammed the door and stood facing it with his back to me for several seconds before he turned. When he turned he had this exhilarated mirthless grin on his face. I went nauseated and weak; suddenly I knew I hadn't figured it out. Suddenly I knew something was very wrong. He stepped up to me and put his face an inch from mine. "It's *you*, Cale," he whispered. I looked at him and he looked at me, and his eyes had become eminently satisfied, but he was still too afraid to quite laugh in my face. "We checked it all out, just like you said," he nodded, with the same wild sickening grin. "The prints and the blood, we went over it and over it. Didn't that corpse look just a little familiar? All those times you got a look at it? You decided it was the object of your guilt, but you know it was a little more familiar than that. Because it's *your body*."

I was confused. "My body?" I said.

"There's the lab report." He pointed at a manila folder on his desk. "Fired back from Denver on the double, twenty minutes ago. Feel free to look it over. History of your death." He was enjoying this now. "So I'm sure that you, being a man of a rather interesting intelligence, see my dilemma. I'm holding you for your own murder. I have in my morgue the corpse of the man who's accused of killing him. Do you see the dilemma? Were that it was so simple as to be the body of Ben Jarry. Now I suggest you accept my offer of house arrest because the next time your mystery lady shows up with her knife, she may do all of us a favor and introduce the witness to the witnessed in a fashion more permanent and less complicated than she has done until now."

"I believe," I managed to say a few moments later, "you once said we live in silly times."

"I believe I once did." He opened the door. To Mallory waiting outside he said, "Take him home."

THEN TAKE me home. When I left at eighteen, night was imminent; I reserved dawns for retrenchment. I turned my back on the sun sliding downward. In the last dusk of my adolescence I came to the fork in the road with the black phone in the yellow booth and it was ringing. When I answered this time there was that same void of sound, I knew it was someone on the other end dying. I knew somewhere on the plains around me someone lay in a bed clutching the telephone in a wordless gasp of demise. I let the phone hang to the ground and followed the one line that stretched from the booth across the road to the pole, and continued until a mile later where I came upon the line lying severed in the dirt, its ends exposed and jagged. It had a hum. It had small fire dancing around it, singeing the weeds and frying armadillos. The rest of the line was nowhere to be seen, not a pole in sight. The exposed ends of disconnection burned themselves into the planet. There was nothing I could do but go to New York City.

Twenty years later I walked from a station in L.A. with a cop at my arm, informed of my own murder. It didn't take long to find her again. We were crossing the wharf for the patrol car when I saw the boat that had come sailing to me out of the sun the night I bought the radio down behind the

Weeping Storefronts. The boat had the same blind Asians and Latinos; as before, they were still standing on deck staring in the direction of the spray. I realized they hadn't docked yet. I realized they had sailed into the harbor and on into the East Canal, down the other side of town out near the southern gulf, and had turned north again just to repeat the course. I realized they didn't even know they were here, they didn't know they'd been here for weeks. Nobody called to them from the shore; in Los Angeles you have to figure out for yourself when you're there, nobody calls to you from the shore. There at the edge of the boat she was standing watching me. Nothing at this point surprised me. She could have been sitting in the front seat of the patrol car receiving dispatches, she could have been wearing one of those suits the feds wear. But she was there on the boat that kept circling the city, among all the blind people, her eyes directly on me; and she might have told them they were there too, but maybe she spoke a Spanish no one else did. Maybe it wasn't Spanish at all. Maybe she spoke their language fluently but didn't tell them anyway. Maybe this was her sanctuary where she was unreachable, out on a boat that never docked, among those dispossessed to whom no one called from shore. I grabbed Mallory's arm as he was opening the back door of the car. He was staring at the ground, he was staring into the backseat. Look, I said, grabbing his arm, pointing at the boat gliding by. Get in, he said. But Mallory, look, I said again. He would not look. He would not turn his head up; his eyes were glued to the ground or the backseat, straight in front of him. I shook him by the arm. Just get in, he said furiously, now turning to stare straight into my face. It's her, I explained, out there on the boat. Just get in the car, he said, shaking with terror. He knew she was out there. But he wasn't seeing anything tonight, he didn't want to see it. He had the same look Wade had when he told me about the lab report. The town was terrorized by her. America was terrorized by her, by the mere foot of her being. The only one not terrorized by her was I, the man she'd murdered three times.

The city was going crazy with sound. There was an explosion even as we stood there on the wharf; we could hear it and feel the timber rattle beneath us. There were two more explosions in the five-minute ride to the library, the car swerving both times. The sound was changing every time. Just when you thought it couldn't get louder or more harrowing, it did. What the hell, Mallory muttered, is going on?

That was nine days ago. I've been waiting in the tower, watching you.

I've been waiting for the time to move. I have been, indeed, under house arrest as Wade promised. Indeed, as he promised, someone has brought my meals twice a day and asked if I needed anything. I haven't seen Wade himself. I somehow don't think I will. Not after the last time. Every once in a while I ask one of the cops what's going on out there. They always pretend they don't know what I mean. But they do know what I mean. I heard from one of them about Janet Dart or Dash. I heard she was in the grotto over on the east side where I always saw her and one night she stepped off one of the overlooking platforms and dropped like a stone into the river that ran past the bar. Not a sound from her. As though it would carry her out beneath the city to whomever it was she'd been looking for. As though to pursue her passion to the edge of her world and then beyond. She was gone in an instant.

I don't read the legends of murdered men any more. Instead I finish your poem. I've seen you go by eight times in nine days—not actually you, of course, though I wondered why you didn't simply appear at the foot of my bed or in the back rooms below. But I've seen your boat, or the top of it, pass every day at a different time, only once a day; though I haven't seen you on the boat, I know you've been there. During this period the entire city has become a radio. It transmits songs from the deadest part of the center of the earth, and they're living dead songs, zombie songs. Some of these songs last a day, some last only hours. Some last a few minutes before someone changes the channel in a flurry of geological static that shakes and recharts the underground rivers. Until yesterday I've been biding my time. The cops become lazier and more complacent. At the exact pitch of night, when the radio is turned to the right channel, I know it is no problem for a dead man to elude them. I could exit through doors they don't even know exist. I've been biding my time: but yesterday something changed. Your boat stopped still in the harbor and rested all night; it was there this morning when the sun came up. But then I watched it turn in the harbor and I saw the smoke, and I knew a new voyage was in the making. And then I watched in horror as you sailed away, out toward the sea; and for several hours I believed I'd lost you. I should have known you'd jump ship. It should not have taken the flash of something signaling me from out across the bay in the moors to the north. But I see your knife now, and it calls me, and I don't have any more time.

It was you, wasn't it. It was you on the other end of that line when I picked up that telephone out in the middle of nowhere twenty years ago, out in America, probably at the very moment you were somewhere being born. At the very moment you were somewhere being born I answered the phone and heard the silence of your dying in a bed. Sometimes one must live half a lifetime before he understands the silences of half a lifetime before—sometimes, if it's someone like me. Sometimes, if it's someone like you, one understands from the first the silences of a lifetime to come, the silences that come at the end; and one emulates them early, so as to recognize them later. I hear the call of your knife over the songs of a zombie city. I cast myself in flight for the decapitation of my own guilt, to live where I once died, to resurrect my passion, my integrity, my courage from out of my own grave. Those things that I once thought dead. By the plain form of my delirium I will blast the obstruction of every form around me into something barely called shadow. I sail. I swim to you. I know the water.

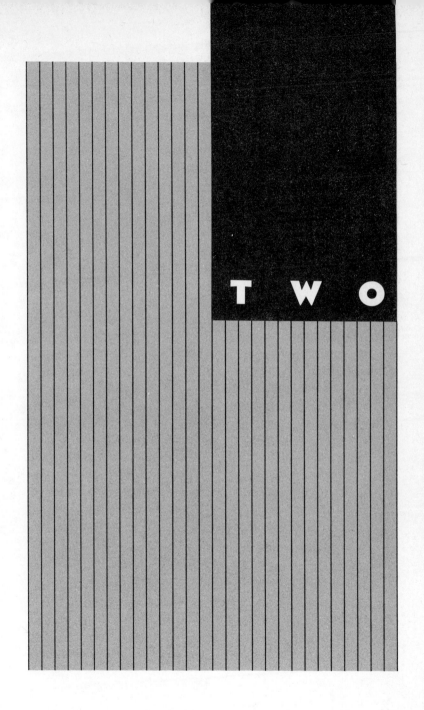

T W O

LATER, IN a Malibu hospital listening to a Malibu sea, she dreamed of the night of the shipwreck. She wasn't certain this was her earliest memory but it was the earliest memory of which she was certain. She had awakened as a small girl of three to the sounds of her brothers outside her window; sitting straight up in the dark, she was too self-possessed even as a child to open her mouth and cry. Rather, typically, she waited to correctly place her own consciousness, misplaced during the previous hours of the evening. She heard four of her brothers talking. The fifth, a year older than herself, slept three feet from her side. She listened for the sound of either her mother or father or sisters. She rose from the bedding of grass in the middle of the hut and went to the window and gazed out. The four brothers stood on the edge of the cliff that overlooked the bay jabbering among themselves with a quiet heat in their voices, their father watching the bay and speaking only to silence his sons. They were five dark forms before her. Catherine went into the other small room of the hut and found her mother in the door, the other two daughters watching from their beds. Calmly the three-year-old girl slipped beneath the skirts of her mother so that by the time the mother saw her it was too late, Catherine was off down the path toward the bay, where now there stretched out before her blotches of sand and dark water in the glare of men's torches, and unfamiliar people lying strangely on the beach, and also the scattering of toppled trunks and drowned lanterns, the splinters of the ship and the rags of its white sails washing in with the tide, and more motionless unfamiliar

people who didn't know enough to lift their faces from the
sand. At the bottom of the path Catherine stood watching
one such person gaze face down into the earth, in the way she
had seen her brothers gaze into the rivers looking for fish. To
the corpse at her feet the small child explained, Nothing
swims in the dust.

It was like Catherine that she did not exclaim joy at the
freedom of being on the beach any more than she exclaimed
terror at the night to which she woke, some moments before,
in puzzlement. On the path behind her she heard her mother
running and calling her name. The beach was covered with
men poring over the sand and its bodies and loot, and the
light of the torches was bright enough so that, as she wandered among and between them, she could distinguish only
vaguely the form of the ship out in the water. It looks like a
huge dead critter, she thought to herself. It's a tangle of
arms and extended things. She stepped out into the tip of the
bay and stood several minutes watching the dead ship. The
sights and sounds of everyone around her died away. It was
the earliest memory of which she would ever be certain again,
standing there in the middle of the night staring out into the
dark of a dead ship, lights and voices somewhere behind her.
Many years west of her, many thousands of miles to the north
of her, she thought of it; and lying in a hospital bed in Malibu, as she slipped from the oppressive care of her atten-
dants, she recalled last her father's laugh in her ear as he came
from behind and scooped her up from a white hooded wave.
It's time to sleep, she remembered him saying, for little girls
of crazy courage. When he carried her back up the path from
the tumult of the beach, her wet feet in his hair, they were
met by her exasperated mother and all her older siblings, jeal-
ous of her recklessness. For the first time that night, and
maybe in her life, she allowed her face to display delight.

ACTUALLY HER name was not Catherine. She would be given the name of Catherine later, in America, when the speechless beauty of her face so resisted naming that the relative banality of Catherine was the best anyone could give it. Her actual name was an impossible sound, a mutation of Spanish, Portuguese and an Indian dialect, just as her people were an impossible social configuration for which the name Village suggested too much communal fabric and the name Tribe too much common blood. The closest translation for what they were would be Crowd. When Catherine was five, a couple of years after the night of the shipwreck, the rains washed away their cliff and the Crowd moved into the South American forests. For miles it was difficult to separate the forests from the sea. The Crowd traveled north to a place where the edges of a monstrous river slipped in and out of the trees and the air was constant clouds of water lit by the green light of afternoon. The people of the Crowd lived in nests. Overhead they constructed canopies of black wood. They did not consider themselves wild people. They didn't live naked, and they did not love ritual. In the dim ambitions of Catherine's father Colombia might be a place of ultimate migration; he'd lived there a little as a younger man. He remembered the bars. What wildness was in him was of a man-made strain.

The boats didn't stop crashing into their lives. Rather than floundering on the beaches they caught themselves in the weird wicked roots of the forest. Sailors who survived spoke of spotting these roots slithering off the coast of England, licking the hulls of their ships with pink vulvalike mouths. If this seemed improbable even to a girl as small as Catherine, it nevertheless imparted to her a sense of the world's smallness, which she never got over. She would think to herself, If I were the forests of my home, my face would be a cloud of water lit by the light of green afternoons, and my legs would cross the sea to England; she hadn't the slightest idea what or where was England. The mornings of her childhood were of wreckage in the trees and the lies of sailors, and the dusks of her womanhood never forgot them.

WHEN CATHERINE'S father was a young man of twenty-five he fell in love with women who made his heart stop. When he was an older man of thirty-five he fell in love with women who made his heart melt. When he looked into the face of his small daughter she made him feel the older love that was characterized less by desire than the beauty of sorrow. In this way he might have been of the Orient. In the evening, after he'd hunted the family's food or chopped it from trees, he took Catherine in a small canoe on the river where she sat between his knees with her back to his belly and he pointed out to her the visions of the forest. They paddled among a hundred green clouds hanging from the branches that crossed the water; these clouds were like the snow walls of northern countries which formed long spiraling mazes. Corridors of the river, framed by the green wet walls, hurtled off in wrong directions. Her father knew no wrong directions. Her father knew the mazes of the river as he knew the mazes of the trees. At dusk he knew the mazes of the sky as he knew the mazes of the river. His breath in her hair was as calm and steady as the current and left a small bright trail in the twilight, so clear that when they turned back Catherine could navigate the way, following her father's breath faultlessly and certainly home.

One day out on the water, right before the sun fainted into dark, her father picked her up to gaze over the side of the boat. There, for the first time, she saw her own face. She thought that it was a strange and marvelous watercreature, like the roots of trees with pink mouths off the coast of England or the fish that dead men watched in the dirt. Had her father looked over the side of the boat with her, she might have understood it was her face. Rather she grew up believing that this creature accompanied her wherever she went, that she could call to it in her mind and see it by her side when she walked along beaches. She claimed it for her pet. She threw it food it never ate, and when she tried to catch it, it swam from her so fast it seemed to vanish at her touch.

THEIR PART of the forest, sitting as it did at the mouth of the sea, became a burial ground for ships, the Crowd waking each dawn to another skeleton caught among the trees. Usually no crew, or only the remnants of one, was to be found. The Crowd picked their way among each disaster with hard-headed consideration for what was of use. If there was food it was eaten and if there were clothes they were worn. The Crowd would not have objected to the honor of being deemed scavengers. They did, however, become impatient with the clutter of the boats themselves: only so much rubble of so many decks and cabins and cavernous husks could be absorbed into the thicket of the wilderness. They pushed the boats out to sea only to watch the water bring them back. Soon each tree in the village became a boat unto

itself, draped in the cloth of sails and terraced with the plains
of thirty bows. Sometimes on the high branch of a tall tree
Catherine thought she might sail the whole forest somewhere
east and north, where the mazes had walls that dwarfed the
trees, and separate rooms for day and night.

BY THE time Catherine was twelve her father had
come to believe she would never stop the hearts of men. She
would in time, he believed, melt the hearts of men as she
melted his, but by then he'd be gone. He laughed in relief at
this, since it meant he wouldn't lose her, and then he cried at
his own selfishness, because it meant she would never be
happy. That she was so composed and resolute as to survive
unhappiness would not make the unhappiness any less. At
any rate, as it happened her father was wrong, though he
would never know it. He reached his conclusion and confirmed it to himself over the next five years of her adolescence, because her body, while strong and self-sufficient, was
without the voluptuous gifts young men valued. So the boys
of the Crowd pursued other girls while Catherine with her
straight solid form watched alone. She was too proud, even at
sixteen, to rage at the betrayal of her breasts.

They did not see her face.

They took her eyes to be the large fiery insects that buzzed
among the reeds of the river. They took her mouth to be the
red wound left by hunted animals or perhaps their own
women each month. They took her chin to be the bend of a
bough and her hair to be the night when there was no moon.

Her father saw her face for the first time the winter she was eighteen; for eighteen years he'd loved her face because it belonged to *her*. But he'd never seen it as something separate from her.

A terrible rain came lashing the forest and he took refuge after a wild night with the Crowd of setting floating bonfires to sea. In the distance a huge black ship battled through the deluge. A huge black ship battles through the deluge, he told his wife under shelter, a ship huger and blacker than we can know. One overpowering wave and the ship will come overpowering us like our own shadow gone monstrous: one ship too many for a forest of ships. He turned to look out at the bonfires sent floating out to sea to ward off the ship and now saw only sizzling embers doused in the rain. The ship loomed larger. Do we move? his wife said. Not in this rain, he said; we wait: and then he turned to look at his children and saw his favorite sitting and watching, and saw her face. Her eyes were the brightest lights he'd ever seen. For a moment they were something separate from her; for a moment her mouth, her chin, her hair were all something separate from her. He made a horrible sound. He was beset by the disassembling of his life: the upheaval of home, the visions of a deathship crashing down on them in revenge for all the other ships that had caught themselves in his forest, and now his favorite child with a face that had a life of its own. Panicked, he began to sob. His head buried in one hand, he reached over, groping in the dark, to lay his fingers gently on Catherine's forehead and bring them down over her eyelids, in the manner of one who closes the eyes of the expired so as to keep the soul inside a little longer.

WHEN HE woke she was gone. He looked up and his eyes followed his own arm to the end of his own hand, to the tip of his own fingers that had touched her; and they were empty of her. He looked around him and she was nowhere to be seen. The rain was pounding the shelter furiously. He woke his wife and she too looked for Catherine. They checked the spaces between each of the seven other children. Catherine was nowhere in the nest. Frantically the father ran to the base of their hometree to look for his daughter. The sea was in utter turmoil; the sky was black and the ship in the distance opened the night like a hole. Leaping from tree to tree, he called her again and again. His neighbors watched as he seemed to dissolve from sanity. All he could remember was the night of the shipwreck fifteen years before and how instinctively Catherine had rushed from their home to the edge of the sea, watching a boat die in the distance. Yet now it was different. Now they lived beyond the edge of the sea. Only the efforts of the others kept him from launching his own small canoe out into doom; they pulled him back and held him pinned and listened to him shout himself into exhaustion.

Over the course of the next few hours they noticed something. They noticed the boat turn dramatically away from shore, even as it was pillaged by the rain and the wind. By morning, when the wind was broken and the rain was a drizzle, the boat was in the distance, small and diminishing. That was when they found her.

She was high in the tallest tree, where she had often gone in hopes of sailing her forest home to another place. She had taken her long ferocious hair and wrapped it around the tree where it held like a bond of wet rope. There she'd signaled all night to the ship with a light no rain could extinguish, the incandescence of her eyes. In any other circumstances she would have understood this to be futile; on any other night, after all, her eyes would only have been two more stars in the sky. But on this night, a storm-blotted night of no moon, there were no stars. The ship steered clear. Six hours she swayed in the tree, holding her eyes open against every force of nature that conspired to close them. She was battered, thrashed, mauled, pilloried by a night that hated her. Her flesh was beaten bloodless cold. But she had stopped, on an approaching ship, the hearts of men, and thus had freed their passion to survive. The men of the Crowd had to hack through her black hair to free her from the tree. Though her eyes were wide open, she did not hear when her father spoke to her. They knew she was alive by the way her mouth quivered with frozen shock. Her father grabbed her and pulled her to his chest, and he cried into her chopped thicket of hair. It's time to sleep now, he whispered, for young girls of crazy courage. They took her to the nest. He closed her eyes and she slept. The people of the Crowd watched her, while somewhere else sailors read the memory of her face, the compass of mazes.

ANOTHER DAY passed before the first signs of him drifted into the forest: splinters of the huge black ship whose luck had run out; a chest of scarves, coins, a deck of cards; the crescent fragment of a wheel by which the boat had steered. He washed up himself some hours later, at the moment Catherine, in the nest, woke from her recuperation. She sat up looking out to where several men pulled the sailor from the water. He was laughing. Flung twenty miles by the storm back to the site of his ship's averted disaster, half-drowned by the water and cooked by the sun, he was laughing. He had a shock of yellow hair. They hadn't gotten him from the water two minutes before he'd rattled off three obscene jokes, which the men of the Crowd might have found amusing had they understood Portuguese. By the time they laid him across the roof of a low breakwater he had sung several sea chanteys. He laughed himself out of consciousess. Gazing around him, he fixed momentarily, before blackness, on the eyes of the most extraordinary face he'd ever seen. These eyes watched him across the short distance of a small slough, from beneath hair so black that in his delirium he took it for a mass of feathers, fallen from malevolent black birds plunging somewhere to their doom.

WHEN HE looked at her she caught her breath. At that moment she understood he was the instrument of destruction. When he laughed it was the sound of destruction's motor, and his hair was the static of its revving. As he slept she looked in the river for her watercreature, pointed at the sailor lying in the sun and ordered the creature to eat him. The creature didn't move until she jabbed at it in the water and it disappeared.

BY EVENING the sailor was still there, uneaten by the watercreature. Catherine said to herself with grim dissatisfaction, It's my own fault. I climbed the tree and tied myself to it with my hair. I signaled the boat all night when the sea and the sky had other plans for it. It might now be at the bottom of the ocean had I kept out of it.

I must take command of things again, she told herself. As night fell and the sailor slept, she crept across the fallen tree that bridged the slough over to the other side. At one point on the bridge she looked into the water and saw her creature beside her, dim in the light of the moon. She angrily kicked it with her foot, almost toppling in. On the other side she walked calmly to the sailor and knelt beside him. She listened to him sleep, then she began to roll him from where he slept into the river. She would kneel on his back and hold him under the water with all her weight. When he was dead she would sail him out into the mouth of the sea. She would point him in the direction of the maze's worst and most confused dead-end passage. His disappearance in the morning would be accepted by the Crowd with the same fatalism as his appearance.

He hadn't touched the water, however, before she found him sitting up looking at her, one hand around her wrist. He had an amazed smile. With his other hand he reached out to hold her face, at which point with her other hand she hit him so hard his head would have made a complete pivot but for the stubborn intractability of his spinal cord. Given his madness, he thought this fairly hilarious. He laughed as he had when he was pulled from the sea, throwing back his chin. She calmly belted him again. He laughed some more and she did it again and again, each time without a flicker of fury anywhere but in the deep white lava of her eyes. She would have been content to beat him to death, but after she'd struck him hve times he stopped laughing. His jaw tightened; he raised his hand to her and someone grabbed it.

The sailor looked up to see her father. The other men of the Crowd stood with him. We rescue this man from the sea, they said in their language, and he tries to violate our young girls. This bitch, said the sailor in his language, tried to fucking drown me. What happened? Catherine's father asked her. I was trying, she explained, to drown him. I was trying to sail him into the maze's worst and most confused dead-end passage. The men looked at each other confused and slowly let the sailor go. Catherine's father looked at the sailor in rage, but it was compromised rage. He looked at his daughter in exasperation but it was compromised exasperation. But why? he said. That he is here, she said to him, is a consequence of what I have done: I bear a responsibility for that consequence. Her father nodded as though he understood her.

CATHERINE TOOK her face back across the fallen tree to the other side of the water. The men dispersed. The sailor watched and smiled his amazed smile. You touch my daughter, said Catherine's father in his language, and I'll make you yearn for the thighs of the sea. The sailor answered back in his language, Some night, huh, captain? Catherine, on the banks of her river, beat at the reflection of her face twenty minutes, splashing in the water until her flock of savage hair lay wet and listless on her back.

From then on, the Crowd regarded Catherine with guilt and dread. Their gratitude for the night she saved the village mixed with contempt for the madness of her sacrifice. When she attempted to drown the sailor, this perception of her madness was only affirmed. When she raged at herself in the water, the issue was placed beyond doubt. That her eyes held their own power inclined the Crowd to believe she was a sorceress. Her father felt uneasy; he sensed a prevalent wish among the Crowd that Catherine had perished at her post high in the tree, for which they would only have had to deal with her martyrdom.

THE SAILOR'S name was Coba. Fully revived some thirty-six hours after his rescue, he sauntered about the village jauntily mixing with the others. He continued telling jokes no one laughed at and conversing in a language no one fully understood, though the common Portuguese of their tongues served as an uncertain basis of communication. He also watched Catherine, and from her spot on the other side of the water she watched him. From his third spot on either side of the water Catherine's father watched them both. When Coba saw Catherine and her father watching him watching her, he laughed as though it was one of his jokes. He plotted his revenge. From the chest that had washed up with him he pulled a deck of cards.

FIRST HE told them stories from the cards. He told stories of sensitive kings and adulterous queens coupling with adulterous jacks. The jokers fulfilled eponymous roles in these small dramas, but the aces might be anyone: a spy in the court, a magician, a sailor washed into port. Then after he'd been with them a week Coba took to playing solitaire across the back of a huge black pod from the reeds of the river. Once the men of the Crowd got the game, they laughed at the sailor's defeats. He laughed too. Soon he was wagering fruit on the fate of his games. He lost a lot of fruit. Soon he wagered the scarves from his chest. He lost a lot of scarves. He'd mix up his act with more stories about adventurous jacks and chameleon aces; he'd finger the queen of clubs, flickering her image to the other men in the light of evening fires. This one, he said to them, has hair nearly as black as *that* one; at which he pointed across the slough to Catherine. The men watched the girl of no voluptuous value. Coba saw they didn't understand the value of her face. Catherine's father saw the way the men of the Crowd watched his daughter. Soon Coba wagered coins from his chest on the fate of his games. He lost the coins one by one. He laughed when he won but he laughed louder when he lost.

HER FATHER came to her one night and said, Go away. Why? she asked him. They don't understand you anymore, he said to her. They haven't understood you since the night you saved us. I haven't asked that they understand me, she said. She said, Do you understand me? Something sad came into his eyes. I don't ask to understand you, he said. She got up and went down to the riverside in the middle of the night. When she pulled the canoe up to the shore she looked at her father and said, Oh papa, and clutched at him angrily. He gently pushed her from him. She got in the boat and left.

She ENTERED the maze of the river; on a continent in which every other river ran east, this one ran west. She slid her boat into one of the river's green and blue boxes, expecting to trigger secret panels and swiveling walls; all that was constant was the sky above her, latticed by the coils of the trees. She pushed the boat along with the oar, letting it guide itself. She descended farther into the maze of the river as the dark turned to day and the day turned to dark. She followed what she supposed to be an unerring instinct, waiting to emerge from the other side, out beyond the edge of everything that had been her world.

After many hours, when the sun rose to its apex and glared down into the river's maze, Catherine saw her watercreature swimming right before her. Remembering how it had failed to devour the sailor at her command, she took the oar and smacked it on the head. A moment later it was there again, nagging her. I don't want you here, she said angrily, go back to the village. It insisted on trailing along at the front of the boat. She made the disastrous mistake of turning her boat away from the creature in order to lose it behind her. Soon she was sailing down passages that looked distressingly familiar. Every time she glanced behind her the damned watercreature was still there, and the faster she sailed from it, the more familiar the maze became around her. She realized soon she was crossing her own path. She got so turned around in the maze that by dusk she was completely lost. In fury she stood in the boat and slammed the oar down hard on the watercreature over and over until the sun had set and, on a dark night, the creature vanished. If nothing else, she whispered to the water, I've finally killed you. She sailed on a little farther and came out of the maze, only to desperately discover she had emerged at the point she'd entered. A few minutes later she drifted back into her village, with the Crowd standing by the banks watching her return, and none too pleased about it either. She saw her father at the end of the slough, his face in conflict between the part of him overjoyed to see her again— when he'd thought he never would—and the part of him that feared for her. He folded her in his arms. When they tied the boat in the torchlight of the harbor she saw the watercreature, unbloodied and very much alive. She cursed it and it cursed her back.

THE MEN of the Crowd became increasingly consumed with two things: what they considered Catherine's sorcerous inclinations, and gambling. They couldn't have too little of the former or too much of the latter. Moreover, the sailor linked the two in their minds: the queen of clubs became the very emblem of Catherine in his games, and the very appearance of the queen turned the men of the Crowd black with hate. As time went by Coba continued to lose his nest egg bit by bit, one coin after another going the way of the men in the Crowd. Both the men and Coba enjoyed the spectacle of it more and more, with the Crowd's passion becoming more frenzied. Soon Coba wouldn't have many coins left.

CATHERINE'S FATHER was beside himself with worry. He grew alarmed at the way the others looked at her; there wasn't much doubt they considered her a witch. He spoke to his wife from whose long deep stoicism he hoped to gather reassurance. But his wife's stoicism was founded on her own doubts. She's my daughter, the girl's mother said, but I don't know her. The other children were estranged from their sister as well. It's nature's fault, said Catherine's father, for giving her no voluptuous gifts, rendering her without value. It's nature's fault, said Catherine's mother, for giving her the face of a spot in space or a place in the middle of the earth. When she was young I should never have let her hair grow, I should have sewn a mask to her skull. But we never noticed it before, the father said. No one ever noticed it before, said the mother, it took them a long time.

It didn't, said the father, take the sailor a long time.

THE SAILOR had one coin left. He folded up his pack of cards in the squalid soggy little box from which it had come.

The men in the Crowd were in a tizzy. The games had come to an end. No more gambling. No more laughter from the man with the faggy yellow hair. But listen, said Coba sadly, I have only one coin left. He held it up between his fingers, moving it slowly in the air around the borders of the night fire so everyone in the circle could see it. My luck's been bad. Coba shook his head miserably. You understand now the premise of a gamble? It's not just the number of what one has but its relation to the whole of what one has. Another man may have five hundred coins. I have only one. Yet my one is worth more than four hundred ninety-nine of his because should he lose his four hundred ninety-nine, he still has one coin left. Should I lose my one, I have nothing left.

One more match, the men of the Crowd shouted. We'll each put up ten of our coins against that one of yours.

It's nothing, shrugged the sailor. He sighed deeply. It's nothing, ten from each of you, because you don't risk what I risk. You don't risk everything.

All right, the men said. Twenty coins from each of us. Let's play.

You haven't understood the game, Coba said. He kept sighing more and more deeply. Of course I'd like to give you a match but it's a violation of the code of what one risks. You have to match not coin for coin but risk for risk.

Meaning what? said the men.

Meaning I risk everything, Coba said, when I risk this single coin. He held it up again between his fingers. Each man sitting around the fire with a stack of coins before him gazed at Coba's single coin and smacked his lips. All right then, they shouted. You risk everything, we risk everything, but get those cards out and let's play. They pushed their coins into a pile and started jumping around as if their feet were on fire, excited about the big game.

But it's nothing, Coba said, gesturing at the pile of coins. The men of the Crowd stopped dancing around and blinked at him, dumbfounded. How can you insult me this way? Coba said. You offer me my own money, which was never yours to begin with, and argue that you're risking everything. He allowed himself a small smile. You see how it isn't so, he said. What do you want, the men said, the whole fucking village? The sailor saw he couldn't push things much further. Not necessary, he answered, waving his hands. Not necessary at all. The money, of course, is a good start, he said, pointing at the pile, but something of value of yours . . .

Such as, the men said.

Such as your best boat. Not a fleet, mind you. One very good boat.

Anything else? the men asked dryly.

Coba locked the fingers of his two hands behind his head and moved his shoulders up and down. He considered the cool pleasant air of the evening. Not too obviously he let his eyes drift as though he were thinking. As though it had never occurred to him. He grimaced a little as though with the difficulty of the decision before him. The men tapped their feet impatiently. Then he nodded. I think so, yes, he agreed. And he watched her across the water as he had done every day since he'd come. They don't know what she has anyway, he thought. They don't understand the irrational, nonfunctional, unprogenitive beauty of a woman's face.

The queen of clubs, he said.

The men looked at him and at each other and back at him. There was silence and then one of them chortled. Another man laughed and then another, and soon they were all laughing, slapping the sides of trees and kicking red embers with hilarity. The witch, they said, you want the witch? Sailor, if you *lose* you can have the witch as far as we're concerned. The sailor laughed along with them as if to say, Yes, it's foolish, isn't it? What an idea, gambling the witch. Then they stopped laughing and there was a nervous moment and it started up again for a while. They were all struck by the oddest notion that the sailor wasn't joking, this wasn't another of his wild stories. The men looked around for Catherine's father and then back at Coba. He wouldn't think this was so funny, they said, your gambling for his daughter.

He wouldn't think it so funny, Coba said, your putting her up for stakes. But then, you know, my luck's been bad.

They looked around once more and then back at him with dull leaden eyes. They crouched in the light of the fire.

They whispered, Deal.

TEN MINUTES later Coba explained, One's luck changes. He had before him a very large pile of money and a crowd of decidedly nonplussed former gamblers. The fire seemed to burn low very quickly. Coba put the cards away in his pocket. That's the way of luck, he said smiling. The men glowered and he scooped up the winnings into his chest, which just happened to be a few feet away, out of view of the others. It had all the appearances of someone planning to leave soon.

The boat, he said. The boat and the girl.

Later it would strike him that he had saved the day by insisting on the girl. Later it would strike him that the men of the Crowd had very well determined it was worth giving the sailor a boat and returning his nest egg to have him transport the witch from their village. But there was the matter of Catherine's family, so the men were careful about it. We gambled the witch, they said to him, because your luck has been so bad.

One's luck changes, Coba said.

Yes, you've explained that to us, said the men. But the girl, there's her father and family to deal with, they said.

But I won the wager, Coba said.

You have fairly won her in *our* eyes, answered the men, and we'll do nothing to stop you from taking her. But the taking is up to you.

Coba glanced across the slough with some anxiety; Catherine was nowhere to be seen. He quickly pulled together his chest and his few belongings and went down to the banks where a boat was now waiting for him. It wasn't the best boat in the village, as had been agreed upon, but it was a solid enough boat, and Coba decided he'd get while the getting was good. But the getting wasn't finished. He looked back over to the other side of the water and pushed the boat to the other bank. He stepped up on shore and turned to see the men watching him. He pointed in the direction of the trees and they pointed in the same direction, and he inhaled and nodded.

He went into the trees, where the mouth of the sea flooded the roots and the low thick branches formed a mass of walkways. He came to the shelter where Catherine lived with her family. Catherine was lying on her bed in the back of the hut, where she'd been the night of the storm when her father wept in his hand. Coba walked right up to her, took one wrist in one hand and another in the other hand, and pulled the girl to her feet before she was aware of what was happening. He drew Catherine out among the trees and pulled her along the branches to the land; they were halfway to the boat before she'd figured out enough to wrap his hair around her hand and give it a very earnest yank. He responded by bringing his fist not across her face, ever aware as he was of his investment, but into her belly. She went stone-white. At this moment her father could be heard yelling from the thicket and nearing the slough. Coba threw Catherine into the bottom of the boat as her father came running out of the trees.

He shouted to the men that the sailor had his daughter, as though the men of the Crowd, standing there on the banks of the river, didn't know this. He shouted to them to stop the boat. The men didn't move. Coba in the boat pushed away with the oar. The father kept screaming to no avail. Behind him ran Catherine's mother, also crying, and the brothers. Their tumult was utterly isolated, a smudge of action and noise in the midst of the silent still jungle, before the silent still witness of the Crowd.

Catherine's father ran into the water, reaching the edge of the boat.

Catherine, enveloped in nausea and a hush in her ears, caught her breath enough to raise her head and her eyes to the shore. She saw her father in the river, and her mother and brothers emerging from the trees.

She had to blink twice, then again, then many times when Coba, in a way that reminded her remorsefully of her attempts to kill the watercreature, took the huge wooden oar and brought it whistling down from the sky squarely into her father's skull.

She kept blinking many times at it, a funny befuddled expression on her face. If she could not convince herself of what she saw, she could not mistake, she knew there was no mistaking the sound of the crack, the sound of her mother, and then her own sound, a wail that was reeled from the pit of her, as though it was on the end of a string.

THEY ENTERED the maze of the river. They slid their boat into one of the river's green and blue boxes, expecting to trigger secret panels and swiveling walls. She wouldn't have expected anyone could find his way, when she had been so unable to find her own way. The sailor inched along carefully, his eyes watching everything and his ears hearing everything, feeling his way. It grew dark and they continued. He's a good sailor, she thought, this bastard who's murdered my father.

OF COURSE I'll kill you, she explained to him in her language which he'd come to understand better. He laughed back at her but bound her hands. He put her in the cargo hold. Night came and he lit a candle and peered into the hold at her. He touched his fingers to her face and she snarled at him, Don't even think of it. It's not even a possibility. When he was not dissuaded by this advice she carefully aimed and delivered her foot straight between his legs. He howled in agony, and when the pain subsided and the water had cleared from his eyes, he saw she was no longer in the cargo hold but at the front of the boat on the edge. I will sleep on the bed of this stinking river, she told him in her language, which he now understood with startling clarity, before you'll touch me again. He rubbed his chin and his pants alternately. It's better this way, he said, nodding. Nothing gets complicated this way. He wanted her less than the fortune her face would bring him.

BY THE end of the following day she saw the end of the maze before them, opening up in a white glare. It was then she noticed the watercreature guiding them out. Traitor, she whispered to her face, don't think you do this for me. If you were a friend to me you would have guided us back to the village the way you did the night I tried to escape. If you'd been a friend to me I would have gone and my father would be alive. Your treachery is no less terrible simply because you might have thought it was all a joke. Someday I'll kill you too, she said to herself, as I will kill him.

WHEN THEY emerged from the maze of the river, there hovered above them a mining town built into the side of a hill, small windows blinking out of the black earth. Those who lived in the town had spent ten years searching for gold.

At every point that they decided the venture was futile and considered deserting the town for good, someone would strike it rich and the promise of a new lode made the town come alive again. Coba and Catherine happened into port in the aftermath of one of these discoveries, so that the air of the town was charged with frenzy. In the evenings the miners came trudging back to town exhausted in body but not hope. A small saloon and brothel operated, the liquor of the one and the favors of the other flourishing only in a dearth of competitive attractions.

Catherine anticipated the sailor's schemes. Don't think you'll sell me to these men, she said to him. I'll sleep on the bed of this stinking river before— Yes, yes, Coba cut her off wearily. He took Catherine to the saloon where he kept her outside, bound in rope and rags under a cloth. As he had with the men of the Crowd, he lured the miners into a game. He told his stories of kings and queens and jacks. He gave special emphasis to the ace of spades, which would unearth, he explained, the treasure of the hills. He proceeded with efficiency to lose his money. In the early hours of the morning, among the pale crusty yellow of the lantern fires, beneath the sagging roof of the saloon and the constant drizzle of the jungle, he looked at the mangy faces around him aglow with new windfalls; he noted how they were primed for the eventuality of fortune by their belief in the lodes of the mines. Convinced after weeks or months or years that good luck was just beyond their grasp, they couldn't help but believe Coba was an omen of that luck and that, beginning this very night, none of them except Coba could lose. Coba did not refute this conviction. Rather he sat back, opened his arms good-naturedly, and said, What is it about me? Why is it fate hates me so? Is it that I tempt it so often? All right I'm a fool. But I'm a sailor and I love navigating the winds of fate even as they dash me on the rocks time and again. So I have nothing more with which to gamble now, virtually nothing I should say, nothing that

would interest serious men, my final possession would only
amuse you, gild the lily as it were, and what do you need with
more gold than that already at your fingertips though I suppose (he said, rubbing his chin) if there were no answer to
that you wouldn't be here on this mountain far from the
pleasures of civilization, stuck with the bad whisky of this es-
tablishment and the company next door, of whom you must
be presently tired assuming (allowing a moment for each man
in the room to contemplate the familiar whores of the
brothel) assuming you were ever much diverted in the first
place.

None of them knew what he was talking about.

It's nothing, said Coba, forget it. It's been an interesting
evening, he said, standing up from the small table of three
and a half legs and picking up the cards. I'll leave with what I
still have, my prized possession, get while the getting's good.
Whimsically he turned over the top card of the deck to reveal
the ace of spades, and then the next to reveal the queen of
clubs; he chuckled to himself knowingly and snorted with relief.

Wait a minute, the miners said, what do you mean, prized
possession? What does this mean, ace of spades, queen of
clubs?

It means I get while the getting's good, Coba said again.
Ace of spades is the card of your fortune, and the queen of
clubs is the card of a woman with hair black as this earth (he
stomped on the ground for effect).

Where is this woman? the miners asked with some excitement.

Coba squirmed as though placed in an uncomfortable position. You place me, he said, in an uncomfortable position.
My wares would only appear sentimental before worldly rev-
elers who know the cognac of empires rather than the trivial
aperitifs of women.

The miners still didn't know precisely what he was talking about, but by now they had gotten the drift, namely that the sailor didn't want to tell them about something important. You're trying to get out of telling us about something important, the miners accused.

All right, it's so, said Coba. But calling her a woman overstates the matter, she's only a girl, really. . . . He cast them a sly look and then, resigned, threw up his hands. He gestured for them to wait. He went out the back of the saloon while the miners crowded after him, fearing he would try to get away. He led in Catherine who was still under the cloth, and unveiled her like a statue.

For the next few moments they all stood in silence, the miners thunderstruck, Catherine seething in their midst, and Coba with his wide amazed smile. He'd never seen men so awed by a face. Men who'd spent years searching for nothing but gold forgot years and gold altogether. This, Coba said to them rather heavily, is all I have left. She's a wild girl, I found her living among the animals of the jungle. She's a river girl, you can tell by the way the water of the river lies on her naked body, what I mean of course is you could tell if you had ever *seen* the water of the river lying on her naked body. The miners still didn't say anything; they appeared dazed. So I found her, the sailor went on, and clothed her (he picked at her dress) and fed her and cared for her, and as you can see I'm still in the process of taming her (he pointed at the rope around her hands), though no man has yet done that, if you get my meaning. So I'd feel, well, irresponsible turning over such a girl to a man, in the way I'd feel irresponsible turning over a lynx. God knows what she's capable of. I think we all shudder to consider it.

The miners looked at each other.

Now that you understand the situation, Coba said, we'll call it a night.

Not so fast, said the miners.

If any one of you touches me, said Catherine, I'll bite his thing off and spit it down his throat.

She said something! the miners shouted, though they didn't understand the dialect. A river plea, Coba translated; she says she tires of her wild ways and longs for the hand firm enough to break her of them.

What do you want for her, sailor? said the miners, getting control of themselves. For several minutes the air was filled with offers: gold found, gold yet to be found, younger sisters in Bogotá, sisters yet unborn, cocaine and marijuana and exotic strains of peyote, anything the miners could think of that a stupid white European might want—offers including guest privileges, leasing arrangements, escape clauses. To all this the sailor became heated and indignant. I don't sell her—his voice rose as theirs fell—I'm not a bloody slaver. The miners said nothing and Coba peered around furiously. He wiped his chin and straightened the front of his shirt. He said, I'm a gambler. I scratch out a living making respectable wagers. I may not be good at it, my luck may be bad an inordinate amount of the time, but don't insult me with bullshit about buying a girl. This is the damned twentieth century.

The miners grumbled among themselves and apologized.

Coba said, If you want to propose a wager, then propose it. She's worth more than twice what you have. But I'll settle for twice what you have. Match every coin you've won from me with a coin of your own, there's a wager for you. If that's unacceptable, then good night.

The miners watched him and watched her. Something went tight in their bellies and dry in their mouths. They watched his resolve, they watched her hair black as the earth they plundered for gold (they looked at it beneath their feet). They each knew that no other woman any of them ever saw again would have a face of her own after they had seen this face, and the idea of spending their lives with women they had to hide from the light appalled them; it was as though learning they had only moments to live.

They whispered, Deal.

ONCE COBA had won back his fortune as well as that of the miners, he excused himself from their company with haste, took Catherine and made his exit. They were still a hundred yards from the boat when they heard the miners coming after them. We're lucky these men are so stupid, Catherine thought to herself as she ran with the sailor down the side of the mountain for the river. But sooner or later he's going to get his throat slit, which he deserves, and something worse for me, which I don't. Near the base of the mountain her feet went out beneath her and she tumbled the rest of the way, lying face down in the riverbank trying to get up, her bound wrists making the effort impossible in the slick of the mud. Coba took one look at her, chewed his lip, considered the horde of swindled men coming down on him, thought of the money to be made at mining towns all the way up the river. He ran to Catherine and yanked her to her feet by her black hair and out into the river, where they climbed aboard their boat to the music of guns.

BY THE third such town their escapes were becoming more hairbreadth. Catherine understood more and more each time that one night she would fall in the mud and he would look at her and leave. It's a race, she told herself, between his stupidity and the stupidity of the men he cheats: one day he will be stupider than they are. My only hope, she said almost out loud, is that the day he becomes that stupid, I will get him before they do.

THE FOURTH town was far down the river, after which this river that ran west among all others that ran east would curl even more westward into a denser, more foreboding jungle than either Coba or Catherine had known. In the time between the third and fourth towns their supplies dwindled; they'd gotten out of Town Three so quickly they'd taken nothing with them but loads of gold. Loads of gold, she said to him, and nothing to eat or drink. There's enough food and water until the next town, he said, I'm taking care of things. Sooner or later, she thought, word of mouth will catch up with us. She didn't say this out loud because if the sailor were to intelligently appraise the risks, he might intelligently conclude his scam days had run out on the river, which meant Catherine was no longer of value to him. In a floating context of finite supplies, one eats better than two. My survival, she thought, now rests on the arrogant indifference to danger this sailor has for brains. For the moment he must continue believing he's smarter than he is.

THE DAY Coba discovered he wasn't as smart as he thought he was, Town Four was in the distance, a rim of dirty white lying on the green of the river. He watched the town with satisfaction and brought out from the cargo hold the last couple of pieces of fruit, saved for the moment when it was certain more food was on the horizon. Catherine sat at the other end of the boat watching in the other direction. You're looking the wrong way, he called to her, and pointed to the town; she glanced at it briefly and silently turned back. He shook his head, relishing the day he wouldn't have to put up with this crap anymore. He took out a sharp knife and cut the fruit, and tossed her a piece which fell on the deck at her feet. Someday this business will be over, he said to her, and you can have the long siesta on the fucking riverbed you want so bad. He felt satisfied saying this because by now he was sure she understood him.

About this time he heard another voice.

He spun around to face in the direction of the town, which had now grown nearer. There, just a few feet from him, was another boat, somewhat smaller. Three men were in it. Two of them sat watching Coba idly while the third stood at the front of the boat, smiling broadly underneath a comic bushy mustache. Coba was confused; he looked at them and looked at Catherine and then back at them, wondering if he should rush to the girl and throw the cloth over her. Hi ho, said the man with the mustache to Coba; he tipped his hat to Catherine and called her señorita. Been on the river long? he asked cheerfully. Since the last town, Coba said; he laughed his laugh. Is this a welcoming party? he said, a bit more uneasily than he had planned.

Yes, that's it, said the man with the mustache. A welcoming party. I'm sort of the town's diplomatic service, let's say. Trying to fix things before they get broken.

Uh huh, said Coba, still confused.

That's it, said the man emphatically. Trying to fix things before they get broken, save everyone a lot of trouble. You, for instance. I'd like to fix you before you get broken, save you a lot of trouble. Give yourself a chance to take yourself out of the hand before it's too late.

Coba did not like the gambling metaphor.

Now you can do one of three things, the man with the mustache explained with great joviality. You can sail into town, where a more formidable welcoming party is waiting for you and where you'll find yourself put in a small jail and kept an undetermined period of time until it's decided what's to be done with you. Or you can sail back to the town from where you just came, at which place you might be given similar treatment if you're very lucky. Or you can continue to sail downriver where it narrows, and where the jungle thickens so as to blot out the day, and long living vines throttle men slowly, and there are fast rapids, fanged serpents, fierce wild cats, mosquitoes the size of oranges with malaria that runs like juice, and natives the size of children that eat men the size of you. How's that sound?

Coba said nothing.

The man with the mustache said, That's about how I figured it sounded.

We have no food, Coba said in a dry mumble. We're getting low on water.

Well now, that has to be your problem there, said the man with the mustache jauntily. During this discussion the other two men continued sitting idly in the boat, not saying a word but staring at Coba and Catherine with heavy lidded eyes. Now they picked up the oars and turned the boat in its place, starting back for town. We'll be waiting for your decision, the man with the mustache said with a wave. Adios.

Coba sat a long time staring at the other boat as it grew smaller and the approaching town grew bigger. When he was close enough he could see that, as the man with the mustache had advised, a throng was waiting on the makeshift dock. They carried hatchets, machetes, guns and ropes. Coba decided he didn't want to go there. He also knew he didn't want to go back to Town Three. So, aimlessly, without any real command on his part, the boat slid past the town and approached the beginning of a more astounding lethal maze than any he had sailed. The entrance to the new jungle seemed to ooze darkness. He noticed there was a funny roar that seemed to come not from the ooze but from all around him, or behind him; and then he realized that it came from the town itself, and the roar was the laughter of the populace, ushering him off to oblivion. As Coba closed in on the jungle the merriment seemed to grow instead of fade.

Or perhaps it was mirth at another turn of events. For he turned to find that Catherine, who was still at her place on the other end of the boat, now instead of bonds was wearing two ragged rope bracelets, the two wrists having been separated from their captivity to each other. In her hands she held the knife with which the sailor had been cutting fruit.

LATER IN Los Angeles, when the dreams began, she would remember, but only vaguely, the way the knife felt in her hands on that boat on the river while she was watching him. No vengeance coursed through her, and she was nearly beyond hatred, she was beyond the color of it, into something white. Rather she was caught by the necessity of it, as though by slashing the knife across the pale of his throat she would sever herself from a cord, through which she had once been nourished with food and air but by which now, at the moment of a kind of birth, she could only be strangled. He was not this cord of course, but her memory of him was a cord attaching her to what and where she had been before; and she wondered if every fetus regards the cord with the same sense of betrayal, as an attachment to something black, before memory, nourishing one's journey to something white, beyond hate, until the journey only stalls in another station, where the wait between departures is a thousand colors that never end.

For himself, one of the last of life's revelations would be a smell in the jungle, a smell he'd never known, after a life in which the vocabulary of sensations seemed to have exhausted itself early. By the second day of the New Jungle it was all around him, this odor. It wasn't fruit, it wasn't a plant, it wasn't the water, it wasn't the fine blue mist of the air; it was human. Not human in that the jungle was filled with humanity, though it might have been, but rather in that the boat was always entering a small black round cavity where the leaves had the purple texture of flesh pulled over a mass of broken capillaries and the branches clotting the river passageway were webbed with veins. The boat drifted farther into the dark epidermal tissue of the jungle, the smell getting stronger and stronger until he was mortified to even consider hacking through it, he was convinced it would splatter blood across his eyes. Huge drops hung from the trees. At the other end of the boat Catherine said to him, The jungle mourns that it has to foul itself with your death. Shut up, he whispered to her, peering around him.

The jungle got blacker. Have I been swallowed by a monster? he cried. She answered, You've been swallowed by yourself.

The river was moving faster, the momentary beams of sunlight that filtered through flashing by more and more quickly. Where does it go? he said, not really to her. There's a hole at the end, she explained, where the water runs in. You lunatic bitch, he snarled, rivers don't have holes. He watched the river carefully and tried to make out what was ahead. Of course he constantly had to keep his eye on Catherine too, who still had the knife.

Since she'd gotten the knife they'd been at a standoff. Coba had the oar of the boat, the reach of which was obviously a good deal longer than a knife's, the same oar that had cracked the head of Catherine's father. On the other hand, he wasn't sure but that she couldn't throw the knife; it seemed a more complicated skill than a young girl would have mastered, but cutting loose with her hands the very ropes that bound them was a complicated skill as well, and she hadn't had much trouble figuring that out. It was to Coba's credit that he didn't underestimate her. So he stayed at his end of the boat and she at hers, each of them waiting. By their second day in the jungle neither had slept. You think you can outlast me at this? he said laughing, his bravado becoming increasingly transparent since the welcoming party had met them at Town Four. Do you remember, she asked calmly, how you came to my village? You came to my village because one night I climbed a tree and tied myself to it with my hair and signaled your ship till dawn. I slept with my eyes open that night. You never know whether I'm awake or sleeping, I can sit as still as sleep (she demonstrated this by becoming absolutely still) or I can sleep while I appear awake. How will you know? It's fitting that having saved your life this way, I'll end it this way too.

You're a witch, he said to her, his voice breaking. I did your people a favor when I took you from them.

By the end of the second day he began to feel the mosquitoes; by the third day there were citadels of them, hovering over the river ahead. He might have taken refuge in the cargo hold, a blanket covering the open side; but to have confined himself to this space, without the advantage of the long reach

of the oar, would have compromised his position of defense
against Catherine, who wasn't touched by the swarms at all.
On the third day the vines of the trees seemed to be wrapping
themselves around his limbs; he overcame his fear of splatter-
ing blood and hacked his way loose, no sooner loosening one
than becoming caught by another. Of Catherine the vines
took no notice. By the end of the third day Coba heard the
sounds of the thicket, the crunching of grass and a distant
haze of drums.

On the fourth day the river was moving faster than ever.
The hole in the bottom must be close, said Catherine.
There's no fucking hole in the bottom of the fucking river,
Coba screamed. The boat was spinning wildly and he had to
use the oar to maintain whatever control was possible. Frantically he was trying to direct the boat and steer it clear of the
hungry trees while watching Catherine at all times; any moment she might hurl the knife at him. You know you can't
survive the river without me, he said to her, we're in this together.

We've never been in anything together, she answered.

By now he hadn't slept in three and a half days. He hadn't
eaten since the last of the fruit just outside Town Four. The
drinking water was virtually gone. Catherine was also hungry
and tired, but he could tell by looking at her that she was nowhere near his point of exhaustion; compared to him, she appeared refreshed. He knew she had dozed here and there,
fooling him with that sleeping trick of hers. Also, he didn't
understand how she could have been so unscathed by the
mosquitoes and the vines of the trees.

At the end of the fourth day the river came to a sudden
stop. It was in the middle of a clearing, framed by the jungle
but with a distinct circle of sky above them, as though they
were in a crater. The sun was shining through, not in flutter-
ing rays of light but in a big soft ball. Coba began to laugh.
He couldn't quite tell where the river went from here, unless

this was a lake; he didn't care if it went nowhere. He was delighted with the clearing and the big soft ball of sunlight. Hole in the river, he said, laughing at Catherine.

She just blinked at him and held the knife.

We're through it, he said with satisfaction, though to where they'd come he didn't know. He looked at her and had half a mind to risk the knife and get rid of her, just so he could get some sleep. Maybe later go into the jungle and see if he could find something to eat.

Then he felt the slow swirl of the boat beneath him and noticed the landscape beginning to inch past. Then he noticed the river was beginning to move again after all. At about the same time he noticed these things, a rapierlike flight of pain launched itself from his thigh. He was horrified to think he might look down and find himself bitten by a snake that had, unnoticed, slithered on board. Instead his leg had a small pink mushy puncture, out of which an arrow still quivered before his eyes.

Another arrow sliced past his cheek, and he had barely distinguished the sound of a third when a new flight of pain took off from the side of his belly. Again he looked down; he had now been shot twice.

He flung himself into the cargo hold out of a rain of arrows. The river was picking up speed with frightening velocity; the new blur outside reminded him, rather foolishly, of subways in Europe and the way underground walls flew by. The sound of the arrows was like that of countless orifices of the jungle each taking in a quick breath. The river was flying and yet the arrows kept coming, which meant the banks were filled with barbarians; there must be miles of them, he thought to himself. The pain of his thigh had grown cold while the pain of his belly leaked a flood of red. Between the cold below his waist and the fire above it, he expected he would divide in two.

The next thing he knew, everything was still again. The

sound of the arrows had stopped. For a moment he thought he had dreamed, but he still had an arrow in his side and an arrow in his leg; now all of him was cold. Nothing was on fire. He wanted the feeling of being on fire. He didn't like feeling this cold. He felt as though he were lying at the bottom of fear, waiting for someone to lower a rope. Then he realized something seemed sequentially missing from the last few moments; he realized he had passed out. For a moment he felt great alarm at having slept, then great relief. He knew she was lying at her end of the boat in a torrent of red arrows; if nothing else he had outsurvived her. At least that, he said. He was wrongly cold. He wanted to go to sleep.

He looked up to see her walk around the corner of the cargo hold, stand over him and look at him.

There wasn't a mark on her. Like the mosquitoes, like the vines. Fever inflamed him. She wasn't smiling or superior. She was waiting. He looked again and she wasn't there for a moment, and then she was. Damn witch, he cursed her; but it wasn't that she disappeared and then reappeared, though that was the effect of it. He looked again, and then he saw it.

It was like the puzzles he remembered doing as a child, in which one tries to find a hidden picture in a larger picture: you look and look and suddenly you see a cat in the wall, clear as can be, though a moment before you hadn't seen it at all.

They never saw her face. Not the Crowd, for a moment not the sailor, and not the jungle. They took her eyes to be the large fiery insects that buzzed among the reeds of the river. They took her mouth to be the red wound left by hunted animals or perhaps their own women each month. They took her chin to be the bend of a bough and her hair to be the night when there was no moon. She lived in a place where she did not know her own face; and where she did not know it, the jungle never saw it: identity was something known in a way utterly removed from the vessel that carried it. Here, far from the men who gave her face its beauty, she was impervious to the view of the jungle and everything in it.

Even the fever, he whispered. Even the fever doesn't see you.

So she waited for him to die. The boat drifted along peacefully now. He bled and he bled. When he tired of lying in his blood he pulled himself out onto the deck; wrongly cold in the cargo hold, he thought he might snatch some warmth from a big soft ball of sunlight. But there was no big soft ball anymore. She did not slit his throat. She would let the cord wither on its own, so that the memory might wither too. It would leave less of a scar that way. As he shed his life on the deck of the boat she went through his things in a casual, practical way, sorting out odds and ends. She thought of casting his coins overboard, but that seemed spiteful and overwrought. She came upon his cards and his scarves. Layering the sturdiest and plainest scarf twice, she wrapped a seemly number of coins in it. Then she watched him some more.

The night passed. Before dawn of the fifth day something erupted from down inside him and filled his mouth and nostrils. He was astonished to notice that it was the smell he had first noticed four days before, the smell he had thought was of the jungle but which in fact was the smell of his own recesses.

His head shot up from the deck. He gasped for a huge gulp of air, his eyes wide. She walked up to him and, putting her foot under the biceps closest to his heart, rolled him off the edge of the boat. His eyes were still wide as he sank, staring up at her through the water. There was a bubble from him.

In after him went the cards, queen of clubs and all. Deal, she said.

THE WESTWARD river spat her out somewhere in northern Peru. Since she was deposited on the right bank rather than on the left, she went in the direction of Colombia rather than Chile; by such accidents whole lives are determined. Bogotá was the first city she had ever seen, though all she saw were its lights in the night. She didn't stay long, entering at sunset and crossing through the middle of town; by dawn she had already come out the other end, and it was behind her.

SHE CONTINUED in the same direction, to the coast west of Barranquilla, where she decided, at the edge of the sea, to turn in the direction of the sun. Since it was late afternoon and the sun was on her left, she followed the coast to Panama rather than to Brazil, where she would eventually have stumbled on where she had started. Continually walking along the edge of the sea, she approached, after two weeks and another three hundred miles, a river she easily identified as made by men. She was shrewd enough to understand the value of her gold. With it she bought food and passage on a barge, which exited the canal on the side of the Pacific Ocean and sailed to a small merchants' port in the Gulf of Tehuantepec.

SHE LIVED on the beaches of the gulf for two months, sleeping in a hole she dug with her hands and covering herself with the sand that baked so hot in the day it kept her warm in the night. Each morning she got up as soon as the sun rose above the trees to get wood for a fire. She went down to the ships to buy food from the boatmen. She began to notice the way they looked at her; it was the way Coba had looked at her when he'd first come to the Crowd. One day she got up to get wood and kept on walking. She walked ten days until she finally came to the pyramids of southern Mexico. They gleamed a tarnished gold in the sun, and in the gaping holes pocked by the heat burned the fires of Indians. It may be that the pyramids of Mexico were the first thing to fire Catherine's sense of wonder since the night she stood on the beach when she was three years old watching the husk of a dead ship. For a while she lived with an old Indian woman in one of the pyramids where she would pass the time strolling among the catacombs. There were ancient pictures on the walls that told stories, none of which she understood since she had never seen pictures before. Some of the pictures looked alarmingly like the treacherous watercreature. She refused to believe that there might be a whole species of watercreatures, rather she preferred to think the one she knew was an aberration of nature. Sometimes she recognized the pictures of suns and stars, of mountains and waters. One day she came to the strangest picture of all, which didn't resemble anything she had ever seen. She couldn't make head or tail of it; perhaps, she decided, it was the likeness of a peculiar kind of forest or maybe the huge city she had seen in Colombia. The picture looked like this: AMERICA.

SOMETIMES PEOPLE with faces the color of Coba's came to the pyramids. They came in automobiles. By now Catherine had seen an automobile, moving isolated across empty terrain. But what she had not seen were the cameras the tourists brought; to her they looked like mysterious little boxes raised in ritual. One day Catherine met a couple. The man was a university professor in his late twenties and the woman with him was a postgraduate student. They spoke to Catherine in a language she didn't understand, unlike any she had heard. They were fairer than even Coba had been. By now Catherine was tired of living in the pyramids, and she pointed up the road from where the couple had come in their automobile and asked, in her own language, which they could never have comprehended, if she could go back up the road with them. She kept pointing up the road and pointing at herself, back and forth. The man was absolutely amenable to this proposal; the woman didn't say anything. They got in the car and drove the rest of the day, Catherine in the backseat with her scarf of gold coins. They came to a hacienda where the couple was staying. Catherine assumed she would find a patch of dirt somewhere out by the house and dig a hole where she would sleep; the young professor, however, would have none of this. He kept pointing at Catherine and pointing at the house where he intended to have her sleep. The other woman looked off in the distance during this "conversation." Catherine and the couple were together two days, continually driving up the same road and always staying at another hacienda or, as was the case on the third night, a small hotel. By the beginning of the third day Catherine understood that the woman hated her. She understood that the man looked at her the same way the other men had. In the hotel in the middle of the night, as Catherine lay in a blanket in the entryway of the couple's suite, she heard them have a terrific argument. She got up, took her scarf of gold coins and left. She walked up the road during the night and in the morning was still walking when a familiar automobile screamed past as though she weren't there.

SHE CONTINUED through Mexico, living for a while in the back room of an estate outside Guadalajara, working in the kitchens of a territorial governor. She was surrounded by Indian servants and didn't go beyond the large wooden doors that divided the kitchens from the dining room. Once, when she heard the sounds of many people in the dining room, she peered through the crack of the door at a large table covered with food, surrounded by elegant women and men. Sometimes the governor came into the kitchen to speak to the chef; Catherine had been there three weeks when the governor saw her for the first time. He pulled aside the Mexican woman who was in charge of the servants and spoke to her as his eyes watched Catherine the whole time. When the conversation was over and the governor was gone, the Mexican woman kept looking at Catherine with concern. The next day the governor came back into the kitchen and smiled at Catherine; he spoke again to the Mexican woman. After that the Mexican woman avoided the governor whenever possible, and the governor began coming back into the kitchens more often. The governor's wife, a tall thin but not unattractive woman with light hair and a long neck, noticed this pattern as well. She also kept looking at Catherine and had her own conferences with the Mexican woman in charge of the servants. Catherine found herself assigned to chores farther back in the

house, until she was confined to the laundry area and then
the grounds. The governor developed an intense interest in
laundry. He toured his grounds with new enthusiasm. His
wife regarded Catherine with frosty resolve. There were more
conferences with the Mexican woman, and the other servants
watched this spectacle with amusement. Finally the Mexican
woman came to Catherine. Go away, she said kindly. It's not
your fault, but for your own sake you should leave. Catherine
didn't fully understand all the words but nevertheless grasped
the point. The Mexican woman drew Catherine a map of
where to go; Catherine had seen it before. The map looked
like this: AMERICA. "America," the Mexican woman said
when she handed the map to Catherine. She repeated it until
Catherine repeated it back.

SHE FELL in with a caravan of wagons and mules led
by a gypsy couple with four small children. The caravan made
its way up through Durango and Chihuahua, across the flat-
test emptiest lands Catherine had ever seen, beneath skies
that chattered with starlight, so bright as to pale the lumi-
nance of her own eyes. In the lives of the gypsy couple the
magic of Catherine's face was prosaic. The caravans moved
five hours in the morning, stopped four hours in the afternoon so the couple and the children could sleep through the
heat, and then moved another three hours in the early evening. In the second week rains came, stranding the caravan
where it stood for four days. For two months Catherine lived
with the gypsies and crossed fourteen hundred miles of Mexico to the northeastern part of Sonora, where they finally

came to Mexican Nogales, which stared across the border at Yanqui Nogales. "America," the gypsy man said to Catherine. "America?" she said. She parted as she had joined them, a stranger after two months. Outside the border crossing she walked up to a man leaning on his truck drinking a beer and said, "America?" pointing at the ground. The man smiled. "America," he repeated and pointed across the border. "America," he said again, and opened his empty hand. When she gave him half the gold coins she had left, he looked at them curiously, squinted at her suspiciously, smiled again and shrugged.

THAT NIGHT, in the back of the truck with two men, a boy and an old woman, Catherine rode across the border. She heard a discussion between the driver and the border guard; the talk was good-natured and friendly and there was laughter between them. There was a protracted moment of silence, during which Catherine understood the surreptitiousness of her journey. The old woman was watching her, and one of the two men raised his finger to his lips. They waited in the dark. One man made a signal to the other that reminded Catherine of Coba when he used to deal cards, except that in this case it was not cards being dealt. When the driver and the guard had finished their business there was more laughter, discreet and conspiratorial, and the truck began to move again. After three hours the truck stopped, the driver got out and came around to open the back. The six of them were in the middle of Arizona in a desert not unlike the Mexican desert Catherine had crossed for two months. They looked around them in the dark. "America?" Catherine said to the driver, pointing at the ground. "America," he said and pointed to the western black. "America," he said again and rubbed his fingers together. Catherine gave him another coin, and when he continued to hold out his hand, gave him another. He looked at the coins still askance but smiled slightly and shrugged again, and after the others had paid him they all got back in the truck, driving west.

THEY DROVE all night. What woke Catherine the next day was not the glimmer of light through the edges of the back flap but the din, unlike any din she'd heard since the river sent her and the sailor roaring through the jungle. When she woke to this din it was ten and a half months since Catherine had left the Crowd, ten and a half months since the day she had watched Coba murder her father. It was nearly beyond memory altogether. Some hours later, in the early afternoon, the truck came to a stop. Catherine and the other four passengers heard the door of the truck open and close and the footsteps of the driver coming around to the back. He threw the flap open.

The five got out. Catherine got out last.

They were on a hill. Trees were behind them, across the road; they stood on a dirt patch overlooking a basin.

The basin was filled with a city bigger and stranger and more ridiculous than the city she had seen on her one night walking through Bogotá. She'd never imagined there could be such a big and strange and silly city. It appeared to her a monstrous seashell curling to its middle, the roof beveled gray

anything, the driver gestured. "Hey," he said, "any way you want it." He walked back to the truck and said, "Tomorrow we go to America. Be ready." He said it with Coba's easy cheer. The truck left and Catherine had a feeling it wouldn't be back. The five of them went to sleep. Well we'll just have to see what comes with morning, Catherine said to the white kitten. After the girl dozed off the kitten ventured on her own into the trash again, until she heard the howl of another dog. She hurried back to Catherine and stayed there.

BUT THE truck did come back in the morning. By that time the illegals had been up and waiting four hours. Nothing was said; the driver simply got out and opened up the back flap and the five paraded in. The driver held out his hand; the old woman at the front of the line held out her money. Catherine, standing behind her, snatched it from her fingers. "America, money," she said to the driver, and gave the currency back to the woman who watched with frightened eyes. The driver exploded with a furious epithet.

They drove through Chinatown into Downtown. At Wilshire Boulevard the truck turned west, winding past Mac-Arthur Park where Catherine saw the lake glittering in the sun and people sitting on the grass. The roads and buildings were bigger than anything she'd seen since the jungle except the pyramids, but the people looked the same as they had in Mexico. Beyond MacArthur Park and Lafayette Park, the truck rolled to the corner of Wilshire and Vermont, where there was a great deal of traffic and a policeman stood in the middle of the intersection, giving directions in lieu of a broken blinking traffic light. On the corners stood pedestrians waiting to cross. The driver pulled to the side of the street and put the truck in park. He turned to his passengers in the back and pointed across Vermont Avenue.

"America," he said.

"America?" they said.

They all sat gazing across Vermont Avenue as a stream of traffic lurched by. The driver sat patiently, letting them take it all in. Catherine looked across the street, looked at the other four passengers and then at the driver. Holding the white kitten to her chest, she started to laugh. The others turned to her as she laughed for several moments; when she stopped she said to the driver, "You think we're imbeciles."

"What did she say?" the driver asked the Mexican who spoke English.

"I said," Catherine retorted without waiting for the translation, "you must think we're imbeciles. This is no border," and now she was becoming angry, "look at all the people just walking across. Don't you think I've crossed enough borders by now to know one when I see one?"

"What's she talking about," the driver said with some agitation to the Mexican, who was also becoming agitated.

Catherine turned in the back of the truck and threw open the back flap. "Hey!" said the driver; and with her kitten and her scarf of one gold coin, she stepped out of the truck. She looked once to see if the others would follow; they were frozen in their places. She snorted with disgust. The driver was now out of the truck and coming at her, and as she stepped onto the sidewalk, she dodged his reach and ran for the intersection, clutching the cat to her.

She got to the corner and started for the other side. By now the driver was some yards behind her, torn between pursuit and the risk that the others might also leave the truck. Catherine stepped into the middle of the street and heard someone call her; it was the cop in the intersection. He pointed at her and yelled something, and suddenly she believed she had made a terrible mistake, this was a frontier after all, and the border guard had immediately identified her as a trespasser. She jumped back onto the sidewalk and looked at the driver, who was also backing away from the cop. Catherine turned from both of them and ran down Vermont Avenue, where she hid behind an electronics shop, people on the sidewalk watching as she fled.

The cop whistled again and then looked at the driver of the truck. "You're in a no-park zone, mister," he said. "Move it if you don't want to get cited." The driver waved in acquiescence. He got back in the truck, took one more look in the direction the girl had run, and quickly drove his cargo across the street.

SHE HID in an alley until long past dark. Then she wrapped the kitten in her scarf with the coin and came out to the empty intersection, where the broken traffic light was still blinking. Once in a while a car would drive up Wilshire from either direction and cross Vermont at will. Catherine saw no sign of police. On the other side of Wilshire under a street-light sat a taxicab, the red glow of someone's cigarette floating in the dark behind the wheel. I can pay him my last gold coin to drive me over the border into America, she thought. She kept looking for guards and looking at the cab, from which the man behind the wheel was now watching her. Because of the way he looked at her, she changed her mind. I've had enough of navigators, she said to herself. They've gotten me nothing but trouble; she considered Coba, the professor at the pyramids, the truck driver. From now on, she said to her scarf, we transport ourselves. The kitten did not answer. She walked from the shadows of the street, turned suddenly and bolted across Vermont, greeting her first midnight in the new land.

BY MORNING she was famished. The kitten in her scarf was squeaking with hunger. The two of them started west on Wilshire, where they entered a coffee shop. Catherine held her one last coin in front of her. "Only dollars here," said a woman behind the counter, "can't come in with bare feet anyway." Catherine continued to hold the coin out, then gestured to her lips that she wanted to eat. The woman behind the counter was looking around at the other customers. "That money's not good here," she said; she pointed at the coin and shook her head. Catherine was crestfallen. She unwrapped the kitten from the scarf and held her up to the woman, now pointing at the kitten. The woman sighed heavily, gave Catherine two pieces of bread, a tin of jelly, and two tiny cartons of cream. Catherine took them in her hands and put them in the scarf as the kitten started to scoot under the tables. "Oh Lord," said the woman behind the counter. But Catherine got the kitten back and offered the coin again; the woman shook her head and frantically waved Catherine and the kitten out the door.

On the sidewalk in front of the restaurant Catherine opened the tiny cartons of cream and held them up to the kitten. Then she put the jelly on her bread and ate it. A few minutes later the woman from the restaurant came out and told Catherine she couldn't sit there on the sidewalk, moving her hands at the girl as though she were bailing water. Catherine wrapped up the kitten and left.

She walked several more blocks west on Wilshire Boulevard until she came to a huge building with a map that turned in the sky and looked like this: Ambassador Hotel. A parking lot was in front and a long circular drive ran from the street to the lobby. People were arriving at and departing from the lobby in buses and cabs, bellhops carrying luggage back and forth through the glass doors. A line of newspaper racks barricaded the entryway. America, Catherine thought to herself with certainty; these people looked altogether different from those she'd seen on the other side of Vermont Avenue. The truck driver had been right after all; Catherine hadn't understood this was a place of invisible borders, so formidable that only those who belonged would even dare to cross them. She immediately felt threatened: I've breached something so terrible that only fools risk breaching it, she thought.

But she'd come very far, over a long time, and she wanted to be sure. She told herself, I have to find my crazy courage once more.

A tall, well-dressed, middle-aged man was opening one of the paper racks. She walked up to him and touched him on the shoulder. He turned and looked down at her with curiosity. She pointed at the ground and said defiantly, "America. Yes?"

"America?" he said, laughing. "This isn't America. This is Los Angeles."

"AMERICA?" LAUGHED Richard. "This isn't America. This is Los Angeles." The girl looked at him oddly, and he shut the rack. "Just a joke," he said wearily. "Of course it's America." She still wasn't sure she understood him. "Yes," he said emphatically, "America, yes." He pointed at the ground and nodded.

She sighed with relief. She nodded to him and stepped back, gazing around her at the bustle of visitors in front of the hotel. Richard regarded her with more curiosity and then went back to looking at the racks. He put the *Times* under his arm and asked a bellhop what had happened to the racks for *Variety* and the *Hollywood Reporter*. The bellhop told Richard he could get them at the newsstand inside. "I know that," Richard said to him; he hated the newsstand inside because it was always mobbed with people. "But I've been in this hotel eight months now and until this morning there have always been racks for both papers."

"Cleared them out, sir," the bellhop told him. "Making more room around the lobby for the guests this June."

Remind me, Richard said to himself, to vacate the premises by June. What was happening in June? A Japanese computer convention? A conclave of world-renowned entomologists investigating whatever exotic pestilence was tormenting the local agriculture this year? Not the Academy Awards, that was next month; besides, he thought, nobody will be at *this* hotel for the Academy Awards, I'm the only actor so hopelessly behind the times as to be staying in *this* hotel. Momentarily Richard wondered if, as long as he was going to be moving anyway, he ought to do it in time for the Academy Awards. This line of thought reminded him of his general situation, which reminded him why he never followed this line of thought and why, as a consequence, his general situation never changed. And if I leave, he smiled grimly to himself, they'll want me to pay my bill.

He started back into the lobby to fight the crowd at the newsstand. He saw Catherine still standing by the drive; she was looking around, wondering what to do next. In a way it was the contemplation of his general situation that led him to spontaneously devise Catherine's future. She's a perfect sight, he said to himself. Her eyes caught his; she looked as if she hadn't eaten in a week. "Excuse me," he said to her, "do you have the faintest idea what you're doing?" She didn't respond. "Well something's occurred to me," he said to her, "why don't you come up to my room." She still said nothing and he explained, "Just to give you something to eat and so I can make a phone call. Nothing that will tarnish your image or mine, believe me." Leading her through the glass doors and into the lobby, he thought, My image should be so tarnished.

STILL, HE hadn't seen the kitten. They got to his suite, which struck Richard for the first time in the eight months he'd been there as tidy in a way that indicated inactivity. It had always been so tidy but it had taken this experience, leading this strange young girl through the door, to make him realize that it looked like the room of a man with nothing to do but keep it tidy. He wanted to rush ahead and dishevel it. Instead he sat her down at the small round table by the window that looked out toward the Hollywood Hills. There was a bowl of fruit and a basket of pastries left over from the morning. "Sit," he said, taking her by the shoulders and directing her to the chair. When he went to make the phone call in the bedroom she unwrapped the kitten. She took the coffee creamer and poured some cream into a clean glass ashtray and put it in front of the kitten.

In the other room Richard made his call. "Maddy?"

"Hello, Richard," she said on the other end, and added, without a moment's pause, "he's not home now, he's at the studio." She was decidedly cool.

"Maddy, I have an astounding surprise," said Richard, "I am not calling to talk to your husband. I am calling to talk to *you*." She was surprised at that. "Still without a housekeeper since the last one quit?"

"No housekeeper," answered Maddy, "the house is a shambles and Janey's home from school sick. Care to work for a living, Richard?"

Richard laughed theatrically. "That's extremely amusing, Maddy. In fact I have a solution to your troubles."

"Such as."

"Such as a housekeeper of course," he said, peering around the door. Catherine was sitting at the table staring out the window. "A girl I just found in front of the hotel, with no shoes and, far as I can tell, not a syllable of English in her—"

"How can I resist."

"And," he added emphatically, "nowhere to be and probably here very illegally. Which means, as hired help goes, rather in your price range." He had to twist the knife a little; there was silence on the other end. "Since you've had problems financing your housekeepers lately, I thought this might be just the ticket. How much sign language does it take to get a dish washed?"

"This is very thoughtful of you, Richard," Maddy replied acidly.

"I freely admit self-interest in the matter. Domestic bliss in the Edgar household means Mr. Edgar gets down to business a little sooner, which means *I* get down to business a little sooner."

Maddy said, "Do you ever think what happens if he doesn't get down to business soon? If he doesn't get down to business ever?" Said in a way that betrayed worry; said very quietly.

Richard answered, just as quietly, just as worried, "No, I don't think of that."

He heard her sigh deeply on the other end of the line. "I don't either."

"Bad news for me, Maddy, if he doesn't get down to business soon, let alone ever. I'm counting on it."

"So am I." She said, "Send the girl over, Richard. Has she a name?"

"I haven't the faintest."

Down IN front of the hotel, Richard had trouble getting Catherine into the cab. "I've had enough of navigators," she told him, standing away from its open rear door. "I transport myself from here on." Richard got in and out of the cab several times trying to show her it was all right. "See," he said to her, "I'm in the cab now. Nothing happens. It doesn't eat me." He thinks, Catherine told herself, that I'm afraid of the machine. "I'm not afraid of the machine," she said to him. "I've been in one before." All this conversation, of course, took place between them with complete incomprehension.

Richard wound up taking the cab with her, finally determining it was the only way he'd get her in it. He was nervous

anyway since his discussion with Maddy, and when he got
nervous he always went somewhere. He had gone to Beverly
Hills to see his agent when he felt like this, but lately his
agent had made him more nervous, not less. "Hancock
Park," he said to the driver. The cab cruised down the long
Ambassador drive onto Wilshire Boulevard and west on Wilshire to Rossmore, where it turned right. During this trip
Catherine didn't watch out the window but stared straight
ahead of her; she was keeping the city at bay. Since the river
had deposited her on the northern banks of Peru months earlier, she had switched off her capacity to be overwhelmed.
She had never been in a place like this before and she was
concentrating on retaining her faculties of self-possession. She
acknowledged what was around her while refusing to submit
her consciousness to it. I've been falling, she thought, and
until I land there's no use watching the scenery. She absorbed
each new shock as one absorbs the light of the sun without
staring at it.

In Hancock Park she was surrounded by homes so large she
assumed they housed whole tribes. I'm in a forest of Crowds,
she was thinking, at the center of this monstrous village
erected on borders no one sees but everyone knows are there.
The trees sheltered the street and the taxi sailed beneath
them as though on the rivers of her home. Richard gave the
driver the address. The house was red brick with a white door,
near a corner at the edge of the park; it was one of the smaller
houses in the neighborhood. The driver seemed a little disappointed when he saw it. "Right here," Richard said. They
parked on the street; Richard got out and ran up the lawn to
get Maddy, trying to think of a way to get her to pay the fare.

MADELINE EDGAR was an athletic-looking red-
head in her early thirties. On this day, beset by circumstances, she answered the door with even more impatience
than usual. Catherine was inside the house about twenty seconds when Maddy whisked her to the back. "Richard, are you
sure about this?" she said to him; actually he didn't look all
that sure. "What are you doing here anyway, does the girl
need an escort?" Richard explained he couldn't get her to
take the cab alone. Maddy gave him five dollars for the cab
and another twenty, which she called a "finder's fee." She
cracked, "If she doesn't work out you can give it back." Richard handled the twenty as though it were soiled.

A service area was behind the kitchen, and there was a
room behind the service area: very bare, with a single bed and
a chest of drawers, a sink and a tub. "This is where you'll
live," Maddy told Catherine, "I'd rather you ate your meals
here as well. Do you understand what I'm saying?" Catherine
gazed at the room around her; Maddy was already on her way
out to the kitchen, beckoning Catherine to follow. She explained everything to the girl and then found herself miming
as well; she knew little Spanish and was not used to dealing
with Latins. The last housegirl had been British. Her name
had been Catherine. Within five minutes Maddy was calling
the new girl Catherine. Catherine had no idea why she was
being called Catherine but didn't contest it.

That night the two women had their first breakthrough in
communication. Both understood the word "leche," on
which Maddy produced for the girl a glass of milk. When the
mistress was gone, Catherine gave the milk to the kitten, who
now lived in the bottom drawer of the chest.

THE WORK Catherine did in the Edgar house wasn't unlike the work she had done in the governor's hacienda at Guadalajara, except on a smaller scale. She cleaned the kitchen and handled the laundry, and on her second night she helped Maddy prepare a meal. She met the Edgar child the first morning, a six-year-old recovering from the chicken pox who came into the kitchen and gurgled, "Hello: orange juice," at the new housekeeper. Maddy came in and said, "You don't need Catherine to get your orange juice, Jane. It's where it always is." Jane said to her mother, "Catherine? Is everyone in the universe named Catherine?" When Jane was gone, Catherine noticed Maddy looking at her the way other people had looked at her; she was seized by dread.

Maddy realized with some annoyance that she'd passed some twenty-four hours with this girl under her roof and hadn't really *looked* at her. She could be anybody, Maddy thought; she's a complete stranger and I've brought her into my house where my six-year-old sleeps. The other thing that annoyed Maddy, as a thought that didn't coalesce until later when she was driving Jane to the doctor, was that for the first time ever, in the midst of a thousand girls in Hollywood with whom her husband came into contact all the time, Maddy was intimidated by a woman's beauty. She may be the most beautiful girl I've ever seen, Maddy realized: how could I not have noticed that yesterday? I must have been distracted. It was as though her face weren't there, as though it became part of the house as soon as she stepped into it. All Maddy had seen were her bare feet. Maybe it's an attitude I have about servants, she thought, maybe Lew is right: growing up in Pasadena made me a rich bitch whether we had money or not.

In fact she still hadn't told her husband about the new housekeeper. He had passed an entire night without knowing that someone else was in his house. That night she told him first thing. "I hired a new housekeeper yesterday."

"Oh," he answered. A moment later he said, "When's she start?"

"What?" said Maddy.

"The new housekeeper, when does she start?"

"She started. Yesterday."

"Oh," he said again. He looked in the direction of the kitchen door. "Is she here now?"

"Well, she's in the back room. Richard recommended her." She said this as though it would bolster her case, though considering Richard, she supposed it didn't.

"Richard? What's Richard know about housekeepers? What's her name?"

"Catherine."

"The last one was named Catherine."

"There can be more than one Catherine."

"Is she English too?"

"I think she's Hispanic of some sort."

" 'Hispanic of some sort'?"

"Don't get liberal on me," said Maddy, "you know what I mean."

"But not Catherine."

"Why not?"

"Catherine? What's her *name*. Katrina maybe . . ."

"Not Katrina. Her name's not Katrina. Wouldn't it be worse to latinize her name when it isn't even her name? To be honest I'm not sure the last one was named Catherine. I think it was the one before and I just called the last one Catherine out of habit. I call this one Catherine out of habit. I'll call the next one Catherine out of habit."

"But the last one was English!" he protested.

"Now who's stereotyping whom?"

He shook his head. "Is everyone in the world named Catherine?"

THE FOLLOWING morning Catherine managed to put the kitten behind her back just as Llewellyn Edgar walked into the service area looking for clean laundry. Llewellyn was athletic-looking like his wife; in a couple of years he'd be forty but he didn't show his age. He had light longish brown hair and a mustache. Catherine steeled herself to the impact of his regard.

His eyes fell on her for a moment, and then he turned away. He turned away too quickly to notice whatever she had hidden behind her; he walked out of the service area without even getting the shirt he had come for. He walked through the kitchen into the dining area where he met his wife. "Going to the studio today?" she asked hopefully.

"No. We can't afford a housekeeper," he said.

"What?"

"We can't afford the housekeeper," he said again. He headed toward the study. "I'm going to do some work."

"We're not paying her anything," Maddy said, "except room and board." He seemed funny to her.

"Uh"—he patted his pockets for his keys—"I have to go out after all. I forgot something." He went directly to the front door and opened it, leaving without any of his work or his papers, and in his undershirt.

"Lew?" she said.

"We still can't afford her," he muttered before closing the door.

AT NIGHT Catherine sat in her room in the back of the house, without a picture on the wall or a television or a radio or a book, none of which she missed, since none of them she knew to miss. There wasn't even a window. A small light burned on the chest. She was content to play with the kitten, who bounced across the room and the bed and insisted on perching herself at every precarious point, balancing on the side of the bathtub and tumbling into impossible corners. Both Catherine and the kitten were perfectly satisfied to be in this room with each other. Catherine sat on the bed for hours laughing at this crazy little white cat. She realized, watching the kitten attack her scarf ferociously, that except for her father this animal was the only actual friend she'd ever had, and for an hour after that she didn't laugh any more.

SINCE CATHERINE had no clothes and wasn't being paid a wage, Maddy bought her a minimal wardrobe: two simple light-brown dresses, some underwear which the girl seemed disinclined to use, and a pair of shoes half a size too large. Maddy didn't invest in a more extensive selection since by the end of the first week she'd decided Catherine wasn't going to be around very long. Someday she would learn not to listen to Richard, who wasn't exactly ringing the phone off the hook for progress reports on his new discovery.

One morning she decided to bring Catherine out of the back of the house and put her to work in the living room entryway. There wasn't any doubt that the girl worked hard, and Maddy had her own things to do upstairs. Jane was on the mend from her chicken pox and would be back in school the following week. "The mantel over the fireplace needs cleaning," Maddy said to Catherine, still manually illustrating every point, "and you can dust the tables. Use the window spray on the mirror." She squirted the spray as an example. "When you're through with that I'll show you how to run the vacuum. God, do you understand anything I say?" Actually, thought Maddy, she's not at all a stupid girl. "Jane," she said to her daughter, who was at the foot of the stairs, "don't bounce the ball in the house." Jane had a translucent red ball with glitter on it. "If you have that much energy you ought to be in school."

"I'm sick," Jane explained.

"Yes, I can see." She handed Catherine the dust rag and spray gun and went upstairs. In her bedroom she spent a few moments attending to the unmade bed before sitting on the edge of it, looking out the window to the drive, wondering if Lew would return today at noon or three or ten. He had come back at different hours the three previous days, out there driving around; she knew he wasn't at the studio, since he'd been leaving and arriving without carrying any work. Of course she considered the possibility that he was seeing someone, but she didn't believe it; she had the feeling it was something worse. How can it be worse? she thought. She sat on the bed with her hands in her lap, looking out the window about five minutes, when she heard a tremendous shattering in the room below.

She leaped up and ran down the stairs. In the living room she found Jane stunned and motionless, the translucent red ball rolling at her feet. The housekeeper stood at the side of the room in terror. In the middle of the floor was the glass of the mirror in pieces, its remaining edge framing a white gouge in the wall. "Christ!" Maddy exploded. She came down the stairs and took her daughter by the hand. "I told you not to bounce it in the house," she said in rage; the child, amazed, just shook her head. The mother looked at the mirror again and began leading the child up the stairs.

"No," Maddy heard someone say; it wasn't Jane. She stopped on the stairs and stared down into the living room. "No," Catherine said again, quietly, the first word Maddy had ever heard from her; and Catherine pointed to herself and pointed at the pieces of the mirror on the floor. She was shaking, struggling for composure. Then Maddy saw her hands. They were slivered with glass, small dots of blood turning to wild streaks down her arms.

With one shard of the mirror and her own bloody hands wrapped in the skirt of her dress, the girl ran from the living room out to the back of the house.

Maddy stood on the stairs several moments before she realized her daughter was watching her, looking up. "Go to your room," the mother said quietly, "it's all right. Just go play in your room awhile, okay?" Jane walked slowly to her room, and Maddy finally came down the stairs to pick up some of the glass. She watched in the direction of the kitchen, expecting to see or hear something unimaginable. Then she turned to the front door and said, "Lew?" as though he would arrive on command.

CATHERINE LAY naked on her bed, her hands wrapped in what had been her dress. Her white kitten dozed on her chest between her small breasts, and in her sink lay small pink pieces of glass from her arms. Occasionally she would hold up in front of her the shard of mirror and look into it several moments, for as long as she could stand it. When she didn't look in the shard she saw her face anyway on the wall in front of her. Over all the months between the jungle and Los Angeles, over the thousands of miles, there was no telling how many hundreds of times her reflection must have flown past her in a mirror, or a window, or on a bright metallic surface. In cars, in boats, in the backs of houses, in entryways and pyramids, in the passage of place and time, opportunities abound for those who know their own faces. She had never known her face. She was as unconscious of its existence as she was of her heart, of which one is aware only when one stops to listen for it. She'd never looked for the image of her face by which she blended into jungles and houses, by which she signaled ships and persuaded men to wager all they had. When she stepped before the Edgars' mirror, she saw what she'd come to know as the image of treachery and cowardice, by which her father had died, her village had been ripped asunder, and her life changed forever. That the image belonged to her, that it was attached to her hands and body, didn't alter what it embodied to her. That it was not a shivering creature in water, that the Edgars' large living room mirror placed her face in another context (when she raised her hands, the image raised its hands; when she gasped, it gasped) did not alter either the treachery or the cowardice but only attached those things to her. All those people, she thought bitterly to herself now, who've considered me a fool were right. I've betrayed myself with my stupidity, I've worn on the front of my head the villainies I loathed. She put the shard down on the bed and grabbed at her face; had her hands not been wrapped in the dress she would have torn at herself. Murderer of my father! she said to her face. She stumbled to the sink crying, to put her head under the water of the faucet, but when she got there she saw little pink pieces of her face staring up at her.

First of all, it bothered him that they called her Catherine when it wasn't her name. His wife thought he was being silly about it, but perhaps the housekeeper liked her real name; perhaps, more to the point, she despised it, as he despised his; and therefore changing it took on all the more importance. In a town that exalted self-invention one struggled to reinvent oneself properly; what dismayed and destroyed people here was to find they had no control even over their processes of self-invention, to find they created themselves all over again only to fuck it up the second time even more than the first, and with fewer excuses. Somewhere in the last twenty years Llewellyn Edgar, so named by his heartland American parents, who thought such a name would give him a head start because it sounded like the moniker of money and status, somewhere in the last twenty years Llewellyn Edgar had lost control of his own re-creation. It was a small defeat, as defeats in this particular city went, but it still struck him as fundamental: if he were to throw away the name he hated for something else, he would as soon have it something of his own authorship. Rather, it was an invention of accident, the lining up of letters like the lining up of stars in constellations, an amalgam of initials, Lee (his middle name was Evan). Only his wife called him Lew. The studios credited his scripts to Lee Edward, a name anyone could have, not calling much attention to itself. It was the idea in this town, it was an art and science, to call attention to oneself but not too much so and not before the public was ready for it. The industry was never really ready for it, even when it made them a profit.

At the age of seventeen Llewellyn Edgar received a poetry scholarship to Princeton, an occasion propitious enough, he would have thought, to convince his heartland parents that the name they gave him was every bit as good an idea as they had originally supposed. In fact his parents thought American children left the heartland to become tycoons. Llewellyn's new assignment in life led him to New York City, where he commuted to school in New Jersey and spent his time with other poets and the Village theater scene then in flower. It didn't bother him that the only time he could bear New York was at night when the dark swallowed up everything but the windows, which hung like boxes of light strung along the gutters. Everything was connected. Those that lived there dazzled themselves. They were stunned by their own explosions and pretended to understand them; there was no one else who understood enough to argue that they didn't. It was in a lower East Side drama company that Lew met Richard, who was well into his early thirties and, the generational ethic of the era notwithstanding, all the more impressive to Lew for it. Richard spent most of his time hustling Off Broadway work and trying to conceal his homosexuality; in fact, the only person he fooled was Lew, who didn't recognize it until long afterward. The friendship between the thirty-something-year-old actor and the young poet was cause for some titters around the Village. By the time Lew would learn to care, the others had stopped caring and the titters stopped; by then he had slept with too many women to fuel the rumors further. The friendship was also strong enough to blind Lew, for a while, to the fact that Richard was only a dependable and unextraordinary actor and would never be more; and Richard was just finding this out about himself and just beginning to admit it. Faced with the truth of his sexuality and talent, Richard learned his life didn't belong to him anymore but rather to his dreams, which had been repossessed by age. Not much later Lew realized this period in New York was the first and last time his life really belonged to him.

HE NEVER went through the moral dilemma of his friends in New York, which was whether to go to Los Angeles. They discussed this prospect with the urgency and irrevocability of those considering a journey of light years to another celestial system, understanding that if they ever returned everyone they knew would have grown old and died while their own lives passed no more than two or three months. For those going on such a journey there was the abhorrence of losing family, lovers, everything they'd known of their lives, while at the same time there was the unspoken thrill of immortality: returning to new lovers and new lives. Though the choice was theirs to make, they could still blame the outcome on outer space and relativity physics. Outer space would persuade them they were not who they were and they were who they were not.

When Llewellyn came to Los Angeles at the age of nineteen it was for a reason he thought had nothing to do with the real drift of his life, though in a funny way it did have something to do with poetry. Funny because that year a poet was running for President, funny because it was not the poet but rather the other man in whose cause Llewellyn had come to enlist while in New York. The climactic California primary was in June. Llewellyn's candidate won. Llewellyn stood in the ballroom of the hotel where the victor claimed the elec-

tion, and as the young poet went up to his room to pack for
his return east, the would-be President crossed from the podium to the hotel pantry where a man fired a shot that killed
him in a way protracted and bitterly inefficient. Llewellyn
waited the twenty-five damn hours or whatever till the man
died. I was a poet, he thought to himself one day at the end
of an altogether different decade as he was driving up Sunset
Boulevard, and I supported the man who quoted poetry
rather than the man who wrote it. If I'd supported the man
who wrote poetry, I would have been on the losing side of
that campaign, and while I would have grieved for the mar-
tyr, as did everyone, I wouldn't have felt compelled to stay
while he died. I would have gone back to New York and continued being a poet. Moreover, if enough people like myself
had supported the man who wrote poetry rather than the
man who quoted it, the man who wrote it might have won
the primary. This means the man who quoted poetry might
not have been at the podium that night claiming victory; he
might have come at a later hour or the next morning or not at
all. There's a strong possibility that he would not have been
murdered, and would have become President, not that year
but another year. This logic led Llewellyn to believe that in
choosing the man who quoted poetry rather than the man
who wrote it, whatever the political virtues of such a choice
might have been, he had changed his whole fate and betrayed
his own destiny. He never went back to New York. He was no
longer a poet. Who's to say, Llewellyn asked himself, how
many others made such choices and betrayed themselves, not
with choices that in themselves might have been meritorious
but with choices that were wrong for the individuals who
made them, with choices not in the spirit of those who made
them? A country is different today because of it, because I'm
different, and everyone is different.

It was on the day he died, the man who quoted poetry, that
Llewellyn first became a part of the city in which he now

lived. But it was not the city that made the choice, it was not relativity physics that chose who he was rather than who he was not. He chose to let them call him Lee but he did not choose the name himself, and almost any name he had chosen himself, even his own name he hated, would have been better.

He LIVED in Venice Beach two years, his only address a local café on the boardwalk to which his furious father sent a stream of letters. When Llewellyn's younger sister drowned that first summer in Lake Michigan, the tragedy reinforced both the son's alienation and the parents' burden of heartland dreams. Llewellyn found a group of poets at the beach who published a little magazine and turned their verses into rock-and-roll songs. He wrote his first movie with a local filmmaker who saw his work as personal exorcism; when he felt nothing left to exorcise, he committed suicide by wrapping himself in a bed sheet and lying on the southbound San Diego Freeway just beyond the Mulholland off-ramp. By the time someone got him out of the road he'd been hit by twenty-three cars in less than a minute; the obituary mentioned his ironically titled sixteen-minute movie, *Unmarked Graves*, which had no narrative or characters or dialogue but rather the hallucinatory images of martial nightmare that were the vocabulary of the day. The "screenplay" was credited to L. E. Edgar.

This bit of dilettantism notwithstanding, in four years Lew found himself, in large part through his proximity to a friend of a friend, working on a screenplay with an Italian director who'd been brought over by a major studio to make his American debut. The project had all the earmarks of disaster; the writer and director disagreed bitterly over a climactic section of the picture. The studios were wary of the director as a successful but mischievous maker of successful but mischievous art films, their wariness justified by the director's conflict with the writer, who fought for a resolution more in line with what the studios wanted. The director won the conflict because he was somebody and Lew was nobody; but the incident endeared the young man to the studios, who saw in him a possible "quality" writer with the right instincts, that is the studios' instincts. To Llewellyn this was a peculiar paradox. At that point he still saw in himself someone who might be an artist someday, if anything destined to be at odds with the marketplace; that he wound up on the studio's side of things in this particular picture was an accident, he'd opted to resolve this particular picture in this particular way because he thought the dynamics of the picture called for such a resolution; the embrace of the studios was quite unforeseen. At least that was what he told himself at the time. Later, in the midst of his ongoing paroxysms of self-doubt, in the midst of the crisis of integrity that was beginning to overwhelm him, he questioned that he'd ever believed such a thing at all. He questioned whether in fact his instincts were not those of the studios and the industry all along, and whether his new crisis was not one that found him at war with those instincts, trying to persuade himself he was not who he was and that he was who he was not.

THIS MOVIE, which opened in America as *White Liars*, was a success, the director's prevalent instincts to the contrary. It proved fortunate for all parties involved, even as none of them was on speaking terms with the others. The studio scheduled a festival of the director's films at a museum in Pasadena, to be climaxed by a screening of *White Liars* and a discussion of the film among its participants, warring director and writer included. Llewellyn sat through the event sullenly, barely seeing the movie and contributing nothing to the discussion. Only some months afterward, when he went to see the film in a theater still trying to figure out who was right and who was wrong about it or, more accurately, why he was right about it, did he note the screenplay was credited to L. E. Edward. He never knew if this was the director's final revenge—which was his immediate conclusion—or a bit of studio machiavellia, the industry having appropriated his soul as theirs and thus giving the ownership a kind of institutional reality by changing his name. He could have taken the matter to the Guild of course. I submitted to it so easily, he would come to tell himself; it absolved me of so much responsibility.

At the Pasadena festival he also met Madeline Weiss, a girl of nineteen who had grown up very much on the right side of Pasadena's tracks. It was indicative of Maddy's station and status that working for the museum archives was directed not so much at making an income as accumulating some "life experience," as her father called it: he considered it part of the business of maturation, somewhere between piano lessons and debutante nocturnes. Of course it had to be the right sort of life experience; she wasn't slinging hamburgers. Her family, of the upper crust, regarded writing for the movies in the same way as did Llewellyn's family of the lower crust; contempt for the profession was utterly democratic, crossing all boundaries of class and money. To Maddy's credit, she didn't wait for Lew's success to fall in love with him; she didn't even wait for his peak before she married him, though by then, when he was twenty-eight and she was twenty-three, he was on a definite ascent. Maddy had a cynicism that seemingly came from nowhere, an errant gene that might have been unattractive in someone else but was enough to keep her from appearing as superficial as most Pasadena girls; it also kept her at odds with her family's exalted plans, in the way Llewellyn's romanticism kept him at odds with his family's practical plans. It did not, however, prevent her from wanting the house in Hancock Park.

THE HOUSE in Hancock Park was too big for two people, bigger for that matter than was necessary for two people planning on being three, as was to be the case several years after their marriage. It was also beyond the means of even a successful screenwriter. It was barely within the means of a successful screenwriter whose Pasadena father-in-law contributed half the down payment. For Maddy this fact undercut her reasons for wanting the house: Hancock Park was not only *not* Hollywood, despite the residence of one or two aberrational rock stars, it was the only thing about Los Angeles that old established Pasadena respected and envied. Thus Maddy aspired to the house in Hancock Park to prove something to her father, only to have her father bail out the couple on the finances. By the time she realized that none of this made any sense, by the time she realized that her father had proven something to her rather than the other way around, they'd gotten the house.

Llewellyn didn't want to live in Hancock Park. Its history denied the ever-transitory truth of the city. He didn't want the burden of the expense either, meaning he didn't want the burden of Hollywood success. In his own way Hollywood success was something he wanted to live down, in his own mind it only ascertained his corruption. It proved he was who he really was, he was not who he was really not. He capitulated in the end because Maddy was adamant and because of the house itself: red brick with white edgings, smaller than most of the houses in the park, with a door right in the middle and two large windows upstairs; and though he wasn't a child, it reminded him of Christmas when he was and the family— Lew and his sister and his mother and father—got in the car at night to drive through the upper-class neighborhoods of the heartland, looking at the lights and decorations. A very similar house of red brick and white edgings, with a center door and two upstairs windows, was bedecked with a string of nothing but white lights that flickered on and off. Llewellyn and Maddy drove up to the house in Hancock Park twenty years later, and he sighed heavily knowing he'd regret whatever he chose to do. Perhaps he believed that his mother and father might relive some memory of their own; he imagined a reconciliation at the airport, and driving them up to the house and sitting there in the front seat of the car watching them, recognizing on their faces dreams the dreamers could not name.

TEN YEARS after *White Liars* Llewellyn had his greatest success with a picture called *Toward Caliente*. The picture had been conceived and written by Llewellyn, and in the early stages of the project he had made a bid to direct. This plan was aborted by what he saw as his own lack of temperament conducive to direction and also by the birth of his daughter, Jane. By the time *Toward Caliente* was released, Jane was two years old; Lew and Maddy had been in the Hancock Park house five years. *Toward Caliente* provided an experience for Llewellyn similar to that of *White Liars*, with the writer and director at odds over a crucial resolution. Since Llewellyn believed this to be his movie, with the director merely the pilot of a vehicle the writer had constructed, he warred heatedly for the resolution he favored. The fundamental difference between *Toward Caliente* and *White Liars* was that this time the studio sided with the director in the conflict. In a high-level meeting with the studio executives Llewellyn was gently admonished for what were now considered his "arcane" instincts; the director's position was praised as providing the audience with a "stronger emotional identification." Llewellyn said, "If I hear another word about 'strong emotional identification' from another idiot who's never written a sentence or directed a foot of film, I'm going to slug him." It said much about the talent of Hollywood executives for self-abasement that those to whom Llewellyn directed this outburst took it sanguinely; there was, after all, a good deal of money involved in *Toward Caliente*. "We've made our decision," the production chief explained. "We realize, Lee, you have your artistic conscience to live with in this matter. If you wish, we'd be willing to remove your name from the picture." Lew was aghast. "This is *my* picture," he said.

A woman named Eileen Rader was brought into the conflict. Rader was the head of the studio's script department. She'd been with the department thirty-five years, having begun in her early twenties. She'd become particularly adept at dealing with what the studios called their literary prima donnas, writers who had detoured through the studios on their way to careers as poets or playwrights or novelists. Only after these writers realized how far they'd detoured and how unlikely they were ever to return to the main thoroughfare did they become reasonable. Rader was successful with this kind of writer because she affected empathy with them; she was admired by the studio for her soft touch. While some complained that she coddled them, the evidence was the writers came around. She demonstrated to them, in ways they found irrefutable, how they could live with the studio's position and still consider themselves artists. Invariably Eileen reduced the problem to a single question. "Listen to me," she would say, "we both know these guys are bastards. We both know their taste is what they sit on. But ask yourself this. Will anyone be better off if this picture doesn't get released? Do you really want to punish the public, who'd be better off with ninety percent of a Lee Edward movie than none at all, in order to try and punish the studio, which you can't hurt anyway because it's too callous and bloated to feel pain? I'm not on either your side or the studio's in this," Eileen would say, "I'm on the side of this picture which, even slightly compromised, is too good to lose in a world of bad movies. I think that's the side you're really on too." Implicit in all this was the inescapable reality that the studio was going to win and the writer was going to lose. Once the writer accepted this, even subconsciously, it was a matter of time before he relented.

In the case of *Toward Caliente* the time was long and uneasy. *Toward Caliente* was Llewellyn's attempt to turn back the clock and win the battle over *White Liars*, where his name had changed and he had lost control of those things to

which he had once given passion. One night he went home,
to the house that reminded him he badly needed another success, and tried to convince himself there was something he
needed more and that it was still within his reach. He tried to
convince himself there was a way back to the main thoroughfare. Had he convinced himself of this that night, he honestly
believed he would have summoned the will for it: he'd have
gone into his bedroom and said to his sleeping wife, I'm going
to be a poet again, and if it means losing this house, if it
means losing my family, if it means losing everything, then so
be it. So he tried to be a poet again that night; he sat himself
in the study and went to work. All night he worked at writing
a single poem, there in the dark of the study with a single
light burning over the desk. At four in the morning, after sitting at the desk seven hours, he had written the following:

My love is like a red red pose

He looked at this "poem" and heavily, slowly, picked up the
telephone and made a call. "Eileen," he said, and to his horror felt a sob bubbling up from his throat. To cut it off he
croaked, "Give them what they want," and quickly got the
phone back in its cradle before it was too late.

AT DAWN a few hours later Llewellyn staggered into
his kitchen where Maddy was feeding Jane. She looked up
and was dismayed at the sight of him. "I gave them what they
wanted," he said in an abysmal voice.

"You couldn't help it," she said, "it's like that in this business."

"That's a lie," he answered. "That's what everyone says and it's a lie. Anyone can help it. It's not something they do to someone, it's a choice they give you and you take it or you leave it." He swallowed; the same sob had been bubbling up all morning. "I tried to be a poet last night," he explained. "I spent all night trying to write a poem and this is what I came up with." He handed it to her. "All night and what I came up with was, My love is like a red red rose."

He turned and left. She looked at the poem. "You wrote *pose*," she said to the kitchen door. She heard the front door close.

TOWARD CALIENTE was an impressive success in Los Angeles and New York and Toronto and Boston and did surprisingly well in such cities as Dallas and Santa Fe and Seattle. It got good reviews and, some months later, three Academy Award nominations for the performance of the lead actress, editing and screenplay. That his only Academy Award nomination should feel like such a stab in the back was beyond the understanding of those around Llewellyn, including his close friends and family. As with *White Liars*, Llewellyn found himself on the losing side of a creative conflict only to see the judgment of the winning side vindicated. The studio was not so heavy-handed as to call this to his attention. They thought it ungracious, though, that he didn't thank them for making his movie a hit. Part of him genuinely hoped he would lose the award, as though that would some-

how prove something to the studio and justify himself; part of
him wanted to win so that he might lambaste them from the
podium, though in such a triumphant context this action
wouldn't carry much logic, let alone appear particularly attractive. In fact the worst thing that could happen did: *Toward Caliente* won the Writers Guild award but lost the
Oscar, thus giving Lew's compromised script the esteem of
his peers while denying it the somewhat more tarnished sanc-
tion of the industry as a whole. "Don't you understand they
fucked with my script?" he railed at the members the night of
his honor, weaving drunkenly behind the microphone. The
writers burst into laughter. Since Guild winners usually went
on to win the big prize, it could later be assumed the rest of
Hollywood didn't find the spectacle amusing. After that there
was nothing like a palpable blackout of his career, it was just
that the phone didn't ring so much. The city assumed that
with *Toward Caliente* something of Llewellyn's career was
dying by his own hand, and they were right.

In THE two years after his Guild award and Academy
Award nomination he wrote and delivered one complete
script, a quite mediocre television movie, for which he'd been
commissioned. After that he wrote nothing at all. The mort-
gage on the house was salvaged by Maddy's father, who was
less interested in the property investment than in the contemplation of his daughter's unseemly pending reemploy-
ment with the Pasadena museum. Your father's absolutely
prehistoric, Llewellyn snarled at his wife, to which she an-

swered, God, are you so beyond gratitude? Gratitude! he cried.

THEN HE got a call one day from Eileen Rader, who offered him a job. He would be writing the sequel of a very successful picture of the previous summer, with a cowriter; this meant he'd do a treatment and first draft which someone else would then rewrite. It was the studio's way of protecting itself from any possible idiosyncrasies on Llewellyn's part. "Listen to me," Eileen said, "this assignment isn't art, Lee, we both know that, this is you getting back into action, this is you becoming a working writer again," and he read between all the lines right there on the phone: Eileen had pulled strings to get him this gig, she had swung weight. Accept it with good humor and a sigh of relief. So he did, with no enthusiasm. Among those around him there was enthusiasm enough: Maddy, his father-in-law, and his friends, including Richard, who was out from New York for the third time in five years, living at the Ambassador, a fifty-something-year-old actor who couldn't get so much as a commercial. "Write me a part," Richard said when he heard, and didn't even have the pride to laugh as though he were joking.

Now, IN the last years of his fourth decade, Llewellyn had found himself thinking about his life and everything it meant in the manner of a man who's at the end of that life. When I was a young man, he told himself one day, I fell in love with women who made my heart stop. When I became older, I fell in love with women who made my heart melt. That pivotal transition came with Maddy, whom he'd known at least a year before he loved, and it came one lunch when she pushed her caustic cynicism too far in his direction (now he couldn't even remember what it was she said) and he withered her with a look. The blood ran from her face. She was like a child, stricken by the way his gaze turned cold; and in that moment, having hurt her, his heart melted for her and he loved her.

On the day he saw the new housekeeper in the kitchen he heard the actual stop of his heart, a thump as though it had fallen from his chest onto the floor. He wrenched his eyes from her so that his heart might begin again; by the time he was in the other room he was suffocating. He ran into Maddy. "Going to the studio?" she asked, and he just answered, "We can't afford her." At the door he said it again, and got in the car and drove up Sixth Street to La Cienega, north on La Cienega to Burton Way, and out Burton Way into Beverly Hills, where he crossed Little Santa Monica Boulevard to Big Santa Monica and turned west. Not the beach, I can't take the beach today, he said to himself half a mile from the beach. He turned around. He paid three dollars to park in a lot in Westwood where he just sat in the car. On the street adjacent to where he sat beautiful women passed him by, dressed and toned and carnivorous. You're *nothing*, he whispered to them: don't you know what I've seen? He had red visions of The Beast mounting The Earth and fertilizing it, the soil splitting open and the housekeeper emerging, her hair a hollow black and her mouth the drooling purple of carnage. He sat five hours trying to remember the faces of his wife and child.

AFTER THAT he went out each day, driving aimlessly. Maddy kept telling herself he was going to the studio. Are you going to the studio? she would ask him on his way out. Yeah, he'd say, the studio. When his friends like Richard called, she said, He's at the studio. Richard said, Yeah but is he working? One day the studio called looking for him. He's in the study working, she told them.

On the day Catherine broke the mirror in the Edgars' living room Llewellyn was sitting in his car parked on Cañon Drive. A New Jersey photographer he knew named Larry Crow was walking up the sidewalk, and Llewellyn sank down into his seat so Crow wouldn't see him. He closed his eyes and the next thing he heard was the car door on the passenger side opening and closing; he could feel the weight and heat of someone sitting next to him. Crow, he said, his eyes still closed. Crow was a man of such odious self-assurance that no amount of hostility or indifference could discourage him. He'd been in Los Angeles eighteen months pushing very hard; unfortunately he was a very good photographer, and he was good at persuading the magazines and agencies for whom he worked what it was they really wanted and believed. He understood that he lived in a world where the arbiters of taste and trend and image had no idea what they wanted or believed; they were in a race to discover what their competitors wanted and believed before their competitors discovered it for themselves. Crow had been introduced to Llewellyn by Eileen Rader six months before at a party. The acquaintance of the two men had gone through three stages. The first was the stage in which Crow learned Llewellyn was the writer of *Toward Caliente* and had received an Academy Award nomination for it. The second was the stage in which Crow learned Llewellyn hadn't worked in two years. The third was the stage in which Crow learned Llewellyn had just gotten the *Nightshade Part II* assignment. The first and third stages found Crow very interested in Llewellyn, and the second stage found him not the least interested. If *Nightshade II* is a disaster, Lew thought hopefully, I won't have to put up with this asshole sitting in my car anymore.

Llewellyn opened his eyes. He was always disconcerted to find Crow a more pleasant-looking man than he appeared in Llewellyn's mind. Crow had a large envelope with him filled with photographs; they were all pictures of women. Crow had found working in Los Angeles exactly the same as working in New York except that there were more beautiful women in Los Angeles and the venality of the city was closer to the surface; in Los Angeles, Crow could identify more readily what he was dealing with. All the women Crow showed Llewellyn in the car were predictably gorgeous, in all hues and variations of gorgeousness. "Check this one out," Crow said. "This one here." He moved through the photographs. "This one. This one."

He looked at Llewellyn. Llewellyn looked back at him with something resembling superior benignity. "They're nothing," he said to him.

"Shit," said Crow in disbelief.

"I know a face that will crack your lens like a diamond."

"All right," said Crow, "let's see her."

Lew was disgusted with both of them. "I gotta go." He motioned to the door.

"Maybe another time," said Crow, out of the car and leaning in the window.

"I gotta go." Llewellyn pulled from the curb and headed up Wilshire.

I THINK you're right we can't afford her, Maddy said in a rush before he'd gotten in the door; her voice expanded and tottered. He saw the mirror. What happened? he asked calmly. She broke the mirror with her hands there's blood on the carpet: our good mirror, said Maddy. Forget the carpet and the mirror, Llewellyn said, what about the girl? Is that all you care about, Maddy cried; she could hear the sound of Catherine's blood in her voice. I think she's disturbed, Maddy said.

Then let this disturbance pass, he said, before we deal with it.

CATHERINE FELL asleep still naked on the bed, the remains of the dress unraveling from her hands and her white kitten asleep on her thighs. She was awakened in the middle of the night by something moving like a web across her eyes. It was several moments before she realized her face was alive.

It was inching slowly, almost imperceptibly across the front of her head, a large flesh spider attaching itself to her and spinning its web in her hair. She panicked, believing her own face would smother her. She wrestled with it and soon fell back in exhaustion from the effort. When she slept again she was aware of the face slithering off her and crawling across the bed and floor to the other side of the room. It settled over the fragments of glass still lying at the bottom of the sink, and there in the night she could hear it breed, until the room was filled with them.

In the mornings Catherine took a small bowl of cold water from the kitchen and dabbed at the blood on the living room carpet. Maddy found her doing this after two days of avoiding her completely. It doesn't matter, she said to the girl, the frenzy of her expression barely containing itself. Catherine looked up at her and continued what she was doing. Maddy began staying more and more in her bedroom upstairs and kept Jane upstairs with her.

Llewellyn would not look at Catherine. After years of knowing nothing but men's looks Catherine was now confronted with a new phenomenon, a man who always looked away. As Catherine spent her mornings slowly but surely removing the blood from the carpet, the entire Edgar family situated itself on her perimeters. Every day Maddy remained upstairs, every day Llewellyn went out driving. Two months had passed since he had gotten the film assignment from Eileen Rader. In the past weeks the studio had called each afternoon, only to be told by Maddy that Llewellyn was working. Llewellyn never returned the calls; he had not written a single word of the script.

The less he saw of Catherine, the more he saw of her. The less he saw of her in his life, the more he saw of her in his head. He took to seeing her around town, not as an actress or model or any of the beautiful women in town but as a housekeeper in a light-brown dress with no shoes. He saw her in the places where he knew it was impossible for her to be. He was hounded by her captivity in his house, though he began to believe it was the house held captive by her. Finally one night, after sitting awake in his study until four in the morning, he picked up the telephone, heavily, slowly, and made a call. "Crow," he said, a familiar sob bubbling up from inside; to cut it off he croaked, "The girl I told you about. Want to shoot her?"

On the other end Crow was barely cognizant. "Is it daytime?" he kept saying.

"Now, if you want to shoot it," Llewellyn said.

"What time is it," said Crow. "Lee Edward? Is this Lee?"

"Come *now*."

SHE WOKE to find two men standing over her, watching her. She touched her face. One of the men was Llewellyn and the other she didn't recognize, though she remembered the camera as a source of rituals at the pyramids of Mexico. The men were staring at her intently; they didn't see the glass still in the sink after a week's time, or the kitten sleeping in the drawer of the chest, or the outline of her naked form beneath the bed sheet. They motioned for her to come with them. She wrapped the sheet around her and went into the kitchen; she was surprised to see that outside it was still dark.

Crow set up the camera. Llewellyn was looking out the window. Crow looked back and forth from Llewellyn to Catherine with a strange expression on his face. These aren't exactly ideal circumstances, he said to the other man. Five in the morning in a kitchen, I don't know what I can make her look like. Llewellyn said, after several long moments, Don't make her look like anything. Crow spent thirty minutes moving Catherine nearer and farther from the wall, under his lights. He touched her hair to arrange it and she jerked away. Llewellyn said, watching from the corner of his eye, Don't make her look like anything I told you. Just shoot it.

Maddy came in. She was wearing a robe. She looked at Llewellyn and Catherine and Crow and said, What's going on? Her voice was little when she said it, as if it were the voice of only half of her. Llewellyn? she said, and he didn't answer. Her voice kept getting smaller, and when he finally glanced in her direction, he saw the look on her face she had the first time she made his heart melt. He turned back to the window, and she brushed her red hair from her eyes and looked straight into Catherine's eyes and backed out of the room silently, through the door, never taking her eyes away.

Crow took a long time. At five-thirty the sky was a shade lighter. Finally Crow took a picture and then set up for a few more. I think I fucked that one up, he said to Llewellyn, who realized Crow was procrastinating. He realized Crow was afraid, maybe for the first time he was ever afraid, that he had a picture he couldn't get. Llewellyn never turned from the window. The sky grew lighter and lighter, and after an hour Crow finished. In all the time he had taken the pictures Catherine just remained with her eyes open, in the same place; neither man understood she was sleeping.

Wᴴᴱɴ CROW returned late that afternoon Llewellyn knew he had something. If he didn't have something, Llewellyn told himself, he wouldn't have had the nerve to come back. Crow was moving around the room, excited; he'd come straight from the lab via an agency on Wilshire Boulevard. He carried an envelope which he emptied on the coffee table; he began sorting its contents. Screwed this up in development, he said, and this and this. He was throwing aside the misfires. Maddy, on the stairs, crept down several steps and stood watching them. Crow got to the last photo he'd taken as dawn had shone through the window. Llewellyn looked at it.

Took it to the Harris people on Wilshire, Crow said. "They flipped."

"Forget it," Llewellyn said.

"Forget it?"

"She's not modeling for anybody."

"What are you talking about," said Crow. "What did I drag myself over here at five in the morning for?"

"Sorry if you got the wrong impression." Llewellyn laid the picture on the table.

"The wrong impression! What's the right impression? What's going on here? You know, Lee," he said angrily, "this is a seriously weird scene you've—" He stopped, for the first time seeing Maddy on the stairs. Llewellyn turned to Maddy too. Maddy was looking at the kitchen doorway, where Catherine stood with her bowl of cold water for the living room carpet.

Not to be discouraged from what had become a point of honor for her, the excision of her blood from the Edgar house, Catherine came into the room and set to work. There she saw the pictures on the table. She stood up from the floor and went over to the table and picked up the picture Llewellyn and Crow had been studying. She looked at it and then looked at Llewellyn. He has taken, she said to herself, the image of my father's murder and made a map of it.

"Have it," Crow said to her. "I can print a zillion."

She crumpled it into her fist, still staring at Llewellyn.

She backed away from the two of them and something else caught her eye. It was one of Crow's discards, lost in the lab in a blur of light: it had come out a large black spot. Catherine picked it up and turned it from side to side, as though reading it. She looked back at Llewellyn and spoke to him in a language they'd never heard. This is the real map of me, she said, holding it up to them, if you're not too blind to see it. Then she took it to her room where she set it up against the wall by the bed, pointing out to her kitten its astounding sights.

T HAT NIGHT Catherine had the strongest dream of her life, in which the world of the dream was full-blown, independent of the gaps in sense that dawn and awakening reveal in dreams. She was running down a long corridor in a dark city. She could feel her arms wet with something, she could smell the thick redness of it, and in one hand she carried something; the feel of it was familiar and fatal. She turned a corner and went through two large doors out into the night, stone steps dropping before her feet. She stopped for a moment and there, at the base of the steps, was a woman she'd never seen before. The woman wore a spotted dress and had long amber hair. Catherine didn't think her dreams could invent someone so distinctly. The woman raised a camera and aimed it directly at Catherine, who turned and ran back the way she had come. A while later Catherine woke. There was a beginning and end to this dream she'd forgotten before she even opened her eyes. She was alone in her room with the kitten and the black map against the wall, everything just as it had been before she went to sleep. But she had the feeling she'd been somewhere else.

IN THE days and nights that followed, her face became more. Her eyes became more and her mouth became more. Her hair became more. Her beauty blossomed like the flower of a nightmare; it pulsed through the house. The throb of it kept her awake at night; the throb of it kept Llewellyn awake at night. They both lay awake feeling the throb and pulse of her face at opposite ends of the house. I'm caught in America, thought Catherine, where people know their faces and wear them as though they own them. Perhaps, she thought, in the beginning their faces were the slaves of their dreams. Perhaps, she thought, in the end their dreams are the slaves of their faces. At his end of the house Llewellyn thought to himself, It wasn't enough to capture her face within the boundaries of a photograph; it hasn't rid me of the vision. He got up and, for the first time in two years, went into his study. When Maddy woke in the morning she was flooded with joy to hear the sound of his typewriter.

MADDY WAS no less distressed by Catherine's presence in the house, but the sound of her husband working after so long was a welcome sign of normality. She rationalized to herself that the recent strange dynamics of the household were a kind of catharsis for her husband, some last bit of eccentricity to be dispensed with before he got down to serious labor. The studio still called every day and Llewellyn still stubbornly refused to return the calls; but now at least Maddy could sound convincing when she explained he was at work, and once she even held out the phone in the direction of the closed study so Eileen Rader on the other end could hear the telltale clatter. Maddy wanted Catherine out of the house but decided to forgo that confrontation a while until Llewellyn had gotten the new script well under way. Besides, a new plan of action had presented itself with Richard and one of his increasingly frantic phone calls. "He's writing, Richard," she said one day.

"At the studio," Richard said dubiously.

"Not at the studio. Here, in the house."

"Really?" There was silence. "Listen, Maddy. I have a rather large favor to ask. Some kind of bash is happening here at the hotel in June, some anniversary or other." A pause. "I may need a place to stay." Another pause. "Should the management decide to collect on any outstanding bills, in anticipation of . . . inviting some guests to leave."

"For God's sake, Richard," she said. Richard, she thought, living here? Along with the crazy housekeeper . . . and then Maddy realized the opportunity.

"It would only be for a while, of course," Richard said quietly, keeping his dignity. "I wouldn't make a nuisance of myself, honestly—"

"Richard," she cut in, "there's a room in back. It's not

much. As far as I'm concerned you're welcome to stay a bit. But there's the housekeeper . . ."

"Housekeeper?"

The one you brought here, you idiot. "The one you brought here, Richard. Remember? Almost a month ago?"

More silence and then he said, "Yes, I remember now."

"I think you should talk to Lew about this. Maybe you can come by this evening or when it's convenient. I mean, you're a friend. Surely you take priority over a housekeeper, I should think."

"I haven't been sure of Lee's priorities in a long time," Richard finally said. "Maybe we were never as good friends as all that," he added almost questioningly, hoping Maddy would contradict him. When she didn't, he said quickly, "I'll be by this evening."

She hadn't contradicted him because it struck her as odd that Richard, who'd known her husband some twenty years, since he was a nineteen-year-old New York poet named Llewellyn, now called him Lee, like everyone else in this town.

W HEN RICHARD showed up that night he'd had at least two stiff drinks. Llewellyn greeted him warily and Maddy had the feeling her plot was a mistake. The two hadn't seen each other in a while. Heard you're working, Richard said. Llewellyn answered as though in a trance. Richard, who was wary himself, and drunk on top of it, did not ask this particular evening if Llewellyn was writing him a part; he was afraid to. As do all people with no hope, these days he staked everything on a single hope that was bound to fail. Not despite the fact it was bound to fail but because of it. He had come to Los Angeles to fail, on the assumption that in Los Angeles it was an easier thing to do. "Maddy tell you why I came?" He got to the point directly.

"Because it's easier to do," Llewellyn said.

Richard blinked at Maddy, who decided to intervene. "Richard's afraid he may be evicted. I thought we might give him the back room for a while."

Richard hastened to explain. "Something in June at the hotel. Some anniversary or other."

Llewellyn nodded. "Twenty years," he said.

"Twenty years?"

Twenty years ago they shot a man who quoted poetry. "Back room's occupied," Llewellyn said.

"Surely," Richard answered acidly, as much to Maddy as to Lew, "a friend takes priority over a housekeeper."

Llewellyn sat in a chair in the living room corner, not far from the remaining spots of blood on the carpet. He rubbed his eyes with his hand. "Why don't we," he said in a monotone, "wait and see. You haven't been evicted yet have you? Maybe something will turn up at Eileen's party. We can ask around." He waved his hand in the air absently. He seemed to Maddy very distracted.

"Is Eileen giving a party?" she asked. She didn't understand how he knew such a thing, since he hadn't talked to Eileen in a long time, judging from the persistent phone calls.

"Some Academy Award nonsense," he waved his hand again.

"Am I going?" she said.

"Of course," Llewellyn answered. "You and Catherine and I."

She looked at him as if he had taken leave of his senses; she was barely able to repeat what she'd heard. "You and I . . . and the housekeeper?"

"I'm sure I must have told you," he said, rubbing his eyes again. Richard appeared absolutely befuddled. Maddy stared at her husband, head pounding with such incredulous fury that she was speechless. Slowly she turned to the stairs and then back to the two men, and then to the kitchen. She couldn't think what to say or do or where to go.

Richard watched her walk into the kitchen. He was still befuddled. "Don't want to go to a party," he mumbled after her, almost to no one. "I'm tired of the parties in this town. Don't want to see people I have to explain things to." He said, "It's a bloody fucked place with bloody fucked people. Eileen Rader and all the rest of them. My agent. Your producer. That awful Crow fellow. I like New York people better."

Llewellyn looked at Richard. For a moment he seemed out of his trance. "Your agent is from New York," he said through his teeth. "My producer is from New York. Larry Crow is from New Jersey. This whole city is full of people who came from somewhere else, and when they got here they looked at everyone around them and said, Isn't this a terrible place. Four months later they're still here and someone else has just gotten into town and is looking at them, saying, Isn't this a terrible place." He sighed. "Why are you *here*, Richard?" Richard stared back at Llewellyn glumly. He didn't know if Lew meant why he was here in Los Angeles or why was he here in this house; either way it didn't seem a promising question. He was trying to think of a promising answer when there was the sudden outburst in the kitchen, the sound of Maddy's voice, and the heightened incomprehensible language of the housekeeper.

When Maddy came into the room, her speechless fury of moments before had found expression. In her hands she held a small white kitten. Catherine was behind her in the kitchen doorway, clutching at her shoulder. Maddy turned and, efficiently and stealthfully, reached back and landed a blow across the girl's face. Catherine fell back against the wall and then came at the woman. Llewellyn jumped up from the chair and took her by the wrists.

"She's had this animal the whole time," Maddy said. "Since the first day she's been asking for milk and it's been for this animal and she's kept it in the room."

"Maddy," Llewellyn said.

"She must have had it when you brought her here to us," Maddy said to Richard accusingly.

"It's only a cat," said Llewellyn. Catherine was struggling in his grip. Llewellyn pushed Catherine through the kitchen door, back through the kitchen and into the service porch where her own room was; Catherine was screaming something he didn't understand. He pushed her into her room. He never looked at her face but stared into the background beyond her black hair. He pushed her onto her bed and closed the door of her room and locked it. She pounded on it from the other side.

By now Maddy, in the living room, understood she was directing her sense of violation at a simple cat. But she had no interest in stemming the tide of it. She gave the kitten to Richard. "You brought it," she told him, seething. He took it in his hands as though it were an infant. "What am I supposed to do with it?" he groaned.

"Richard," she said, trying to explain before her husband returned, "if I can get the damn cat out, maybe I can get *her* out too." This didn't impress him as much as she'd expected; he no longer seemed to care about the question of his residency. She went to the phone and called a cab and went to her purse and gave Richard some money. Take the cat, she said. Richard looked over his shoulder once to see Lew, his hands in his pockets, standing in the kitchen doorway, staring at the spots of blood on the floor of the living room.

CATHERINE FLUNG herself at the door of her room, pounded on it and clawed at it till it stood pitted and punctured, small flakes of paint like eggshells on the floor. Finally she sank to her knees and slept at the door's base. Coward, she cursed him, better the men who would look at my face than you who will not. That he and her face couldn't stand the sight of each other only confirmed to her that the two were conspirators. Without her small white soft friend her life became smaller and emptier than it had ever been. She sobbed herself to sleep and then dreamed she was walking on a beach on a moonful night, a strange but distantly known city on the horizon. Her arms were bare and clean but she still felt in her hand something she'd held from other dreams and another conscious place. Down the beach, in the light of the moon, just beyond the water's edge, someone knelt on his knees in the sand.

LLEWELLYN AND Maddy did not discuss the situation that first evening; in fact they discussed nothing at all. Llewellyn went not to bed but to the study; when Maddy woke in the morning it was to the volley of his typing. All day there were long periods of no sound at all, followed by bursts of it. Maddy dressed Jane for school. Jane ate her breakfast at the kitchen table and listened to the pounding in the servant's room. Is it Catherine? the child asked. Maddy hurried Jane to school. When she returned Catherine's pounding had stopped but the door was still locked. Maddy was afraid to open it. Llewellyn didn't come out of his study all day and was there long into the night after Maddy had gone to bed. In the night she woke to the renewed sound of Catherine's attempts to get out; she wrapped the pillow around her head. The same pattern repeated itself the next day. By the second night she had finally overcome her state of general mortification to knock on the study door. After a long minute the door slid away. The man who stood on the other side was barely her husband. He was unshaven and his hair was a tangle, and his jaw hung slightly, small streams of saliva glistening in the edges of his mouth. His eyes were pinpoints of color. They seemed to look through her. Yes? he said quietly.

She backed away from him. Finally she said, I won't have this. What? he said. Don't you think she might be hungry, said Maddy, don't you think she might need to use the toilet after two days and nights?

I've fed her, he said. I've attended to her concerns.

I'm going to call the police, she said, mustering her resolve.

Bad idea, he said, shaking his head. Nothing but trouble there. Girl's illegal, no doubt. They'd send her back.

Fine, said Maddy, they'd send her back.

You know what slavery is, Madeline? he said. You own someone and bend them to your will without compensation, locked in a room. . . .

You locked her in the room! Maddy cried hysterically, her control dissolved. She held her face in her hands. She heard the door slide closed. She looked up and stepped to the door and said through it, I'm not going with you to that party. She listened, and when he didn't answer she went on, Let them say what they will there. She listened, and when he didn't answer she went on, You're pimping her to that photographer and the rest of them. On the other side of the door she heard him begin to type. When she looked around, Jane was standing at the top of the stairs.

I'm not pimping her, Llewellyn said out loud, though she

would no longer hear him. I'm not pimping her, Llewellyn said to himself, I won't take money for it. Rather I'm like a man who can't bring himself to love her, and therefore offers her up to others that they may love her for him and he may watch. In this instance I'm a man who cannot bring himself to look at her, and therefore offers her up to others that they may look at her for him. I'm a voyeur, not a pimp, watching others in the act of watching her. There's a difference. One pimps for a profit. One voyeurs for a passion.

AFTER A week he came to her one night, unlocked the door and took her by the arm through the house. The house was eerily quiet except for the two of them until Catherine heard, just as they were walking out the front door, Maddy call his name from upstairs. Llewellyn put Catherine in his car and they drove. He said nothing to her at all. They went deeper into America than Catherine had ever been, crossing La Brea Avenue up into the Hollywood Hills. After ten minutes they came to Eileen Rader's house, where a party was going on.

It was a small elegant house. The living room shimmered with glass and light. In the center an enormous wax candle burned like a volcano on top of a glass table, and an antique music box played in the background. The room was filled with Jamaican actresses and German models and Austrian chanteuses and Australian actors hailed in the morning papers as the next Gary Cooper. There were girls from Chicago and Portland and St. Louis with small breasts and blue nipples that shone through silk tops. The only person

Catherine had ever seen before was Larry Crow, who was at
the bar. Richard was not there. The party gathered in pockets
of actors and editors and writers, with associate producers
traveling desperately among whoever would speak to them.
Llewellyn held a firm grip on Catherine's arm and seemed
propelled toward something; he was breathless by the time
they got in the door. He looked around at everyone and
Catherine watched the back of his head, her eyes on fire.

Then she saw they were looking at her.

The room did not exactly come to a hush, but conversa-
tions trailed off and there was left only the last downward
flutter of someone's laughter and the clink of glasses. They
were all watching, as though having willingly surrendered the
room's center of gravity to her: her more face and her more
eyes and mouth and her more hair, and the beauty of her that
pulsed. The room was wanton in its regard of her, women and
men both; it was like the times Coba had brought her before
the gamblers of the rivertowns. In her eyes Llewellyn became
all of them: sailors and governors and professors, gathering his
strength by the self-imposed celibacy of his eyes that would
not take her, by the rape of his hands that forced her on the
eyes of others.

He pulled her through the room to the bar on the other
side. Hello Lee, people said to him uneasily. He didn't answer. Soon the room recovered its composure. Llewellyn was
standing at the bar with his second drink, holding tight to
Catherine, when Eileen flowed by in an airy blue dress. Eileen looked at Catherine's light-brown dress and her bare
feet. Hello, she said to Catherine. Catherine watched her
mouth move. Hello Lee, Eileen said, turning to Llewellyn.
She asked how he was. He said he was fine. She asked how
Maddy was. This is Catherine, Llewellyn answered. I hear
you've been working, Eileen said. Yeah, working, said
Llewellyn. There was a pause between them and Eileen said,
Lee, let's talk later, all right?

Llewellyn had his third drink. He and Catherine stood at the bar with him holding onto her. When she tried to pull away, he held her tighter. He made no attempt to hide this behavior from anyone else; she kept looking around her. His face and eyes were still crazy, as they'd been for a while. People greeted him cautiously as they passed. They congratulated him on the *Nightshade* sequel; he didn't hear them. He only wanted them to look at her face. They all looked at her face.

He heard someone speaking to him and glanced over at Larry Crow. The photographer looked past Llewellyn to Catherine. "How you doing Lee," he said. "I hear you're working hard." Llewellyn ignored him. "I've been trying to get in touch with you. Phone rings and rings or your wife answers. Your wife sounds like she's not feeling well." He looked at Catherine again and laughed like a machine gun.

"What do you want," said Llewellyn.

Crow took a folded paper from his inside coat pocket. "I have good news, Lee." He handed Llewellyn the form. It was a model's release from a magazine. Llewellyn handed the form back. "They're nuts about that last shot. Remember? In the kitchen, your lovely lady here in the bed sheet."

"Forget it."

"Sign the release," Crow said merrily, swirling the ice in his drink, "and we all do well by it. I do well, your friend here does well. You especially do well. I mean, being the girl's . . . executor, so to speak. Handling her finances, that sort of thing."

"I'm not pimping her," said Llewellyn.

Crow went from merriment to annoyance very quickly. "They're giving it a hell of a spread, Lee. An art approach, basically." He looked at Catherine and then back to Llewellyn. "You see the way everyone looked at her when you walked in here? Two dozen aspiring nubiles in this place and it all stops for an Indian girl with no shoes and a dress from

Thriftimart." He lowered his voice. "The Harris people will sign her tomorrow, no questions."

"My name isn't Lee."

"What?"

"Come on," Llewellyn said to Catherine, but not to her, past her. He began to pull her away.

"Listen you crazy bastard," Crow said with anger, then gave a short laugh; he was trying not to get excited. "Lee or whatever your name is," he laughed again. "I want this credit. I want this layout. I want to take a hundred pictures of this girl, a thousand. It can be very much worth your while. This isn't another Hollywood airhead, you and I both know that," he said, pointing at Catherine. "This is a look here." He pointed at her eyes, her mouth.

"Come on," Llewellyn said to Catherine.

"Where's Chiquita's green card, Lee," Crow said angrily. He looked around and lowered his voice again. "What do you think you're doing." He put his face right next to Llewellyn's, practically snarling. "I don't want to ice your groovy thang here, Lee. But this girl's an ixnay immigration-wise, and I got a feeling otherwise too. You employing her in that house or what? And I don't mind telling you I'm leaning toward 'or what.' Her running around in bed sheets and all."

Llewellyn, in a series of very tidy movements, turned to Crow, opened Crow's coat, and pulled the document out of Crow's coat pocket. He set his drink down, took a pen from Crow's other pocket, signed the model's release on the top of the bar. He put the pen back in its pocket, opened Crow's coat and put back the release; and then gazed into Crow's face, sighing deeply. There was a dimple above the corner of Crow's mouth, on his left side, Llewellyn's right. Never taking his eyes from that spot above the corner of Crow's mouth, Llewellyn stepped back and brought his fist rocketing into its target. There was a crack and Crow literally flew across the room into the volcanic candle, as though the candle had been wheeled onto the set for just such a scene.

Llewellyn also did one other thing during this series of very tidy movements. He let go of Catherine.

Momentarily the living room came to a standstill. Streaked in light and shadow, the antique music box wound to a low groan in the background, and a woman at the edge of the room lost her balance slightly and froze in a stumble. The expressions on all the faces were suspended, the air turned to a haze in the explosion. The candle rose balletically. Crystal and glass and wax flowed upward and then cascaded down, the table splintering in a thousand fragments. The wax cooled in midair and rained on the floor in flakes. Crow moved on the floor in a slow thrash, and an actress from Portland in a silk top giggled a moment and then stopped, the look on her face becoming very curious. She stared down at the front of her silk top to find it mottled with ellipses of red. Only after this did something burst loose, an ugly offended roar imploding on the core of the room. Five men grabbed Llewellyn by his head and every limb.

In the downpour of the glass and the wax and the roar Catherine walked across the room, up the steps and out the front door, as though through a blizzard of arrows and jungle and fever.

BECAUSE THERE always existed at the bottom of Maddy's cynicism the cynic's usual sense of failure, she was all the less prepared to accept the devastating failure of her

marriage: it seemed too sudden and baffling, and she hadn't
seen the early signs—which perhaps justified her sense of failure after all. When Llewellyn took Catherine out the front
door that night, once again Maddy sat on the edge of the bed
upstairs with her hands in her lap, looking out the window
and wondering what to do. Slowly she removed a suitcase
from the closet and opened it on the bed; she began to fill it
up. By the time she had carried the process as far as Jane's
room, however, where the scenario would have her gather the
child in her arms along with a favored toy or two, she had
balked, reminding herself, I'm not really going to do this. Not
really.

She had a glimmer of an idea, which was to go to Llewellyn's study and read the script in progress; and for the moment she balked at this transgression too. Instead she put
Jane back to bed and went to bed herself. She seemed to toss
endlessly, and thought, I'm fooling myself if I think I'll sleep
tonight. So it was a shock for her to wake, sometime early in
the morning around three, and find she must have slept after
all, since her husband was passed out on the bed next to her
and she had no idea how he'd gotten there. He smelled of liquor. He also looked bruised and cut, and what instantly and
inevitably flashed through Maddy's mind was a scene in
which the bruises and cuts were received at Catherine's
hands, never mind everything leading up to it. Downstairs, in
the part of the house with the housekeeper's room, things
were quiet.

Thus transgressions now seemed appropriate. Maddy got
up from her bed, put on her robe and went to the study. She
slid open the door and went to the desk with the typewriter
and several yellow pads of paper. She turned on the small
desk lamp; there wasn't a sound in the house. She opened up
the folder in which her husband kept his script, except that
there was no script. Instead she found a thin collection of
fifty or sixty poems, and by the time she had read a few, she

understood they all had the same subject: she could recognize her immediately, the hair the color of night and the rage to match, and her mouth the color of blood. Her eyes, he wrote, had the opaque rushing depthlessness of the blind, like the color of white skies and seas meeting at some point in the distance. They were poems about a face that was ignorant of its own image, and a man whose cognizance of that image divided his life in two. She closed the folder and shut off the light on the desk and thought to herself, The surprise is that I'm surprised.

SEVERAL TIMES the next morning, as she lay in bed in a stupor of despair, she heard the phone ring and go on ringing many times before it stopped. About nine-thirty she looked over and Llewellyn wasn't there, and the phone was ringing again. When she got to the top of the stairs Jane was playing with her toys; she looked up at her mother in confusion. At the bottom of the stairs she saw Lew, not in the study where she'd expected to find him, but sitting in the living room staring, as he had before, at the spots of blood on the carpet. The phone had not stopped, and Maddy picked it up. On the other end was Eileen Rader, who began speaking before Maddy had gotten out a word. "Listen to me, Maddy," Eileen said. She sounded very cold. "Lee's fortunate I'm not calling the police after last night. A couple of other guests still may, and why Larry Crow doesn't I don't know, unless Lee's got something he wants. Whatever is going on in your house is none of my business, but how it affects Lee's work is. When Lee's ready to face things, I want to

talk to him, and it had better be soon if he's still interested in
a career."

"Police?" said Maddy. Eileen hung up.

Maddy walked into the living room and looked at her husband. "Lew," she said quietly, "we have to talk now."

"I have this poem in my head," he whispered. "Not the
last poem but the poem after the last poem: I keep trying to
find it. I keep writing closer to it, because I know when I get
there I'll be at the point of no return. If it means losing the
house, if it means losing my family, if it means losing everything, I'm going to find this poem."

"Lew," said Maddy, "we have only one more chance before it's too late."

He nodded. He got up from the chair; he walked toward
her and then past her, out the front door. She went over to
the chair where he'd been and sat down in it. While she contemplated the blood on the carpet her daughter called twice
from the top of the stairs. When the phone began to ring
Maddy looked up at the kitchen door, struck by the huge silence from the back of the house. Slowly, timidly, she finally
entered the kitchen. Slowly, timidly, she finally entered the
back of the house, where she came to the open door of Catherine's room and saw no one was there.

LLEWELLYN DROVE past La Brea up into the Hollywood Hills, the way he had taken Catherine the previous
night. Then he drove back along Franklin. He kept his eyes
open for Catherine everywhere he went. After hours of
searching for her futilely, up and down side streets and main

boulevards, he went home. When he got there, something about the house seemed odd. He wasn't certain exactly what it was, but there was no doubt the house was different somehow. Then, after he had gotten out of the car and started up the small walk to the door, he looked at the red brick front with the white edgings, looked at the door and the two upstairs windows, and saw, distinctly, that one of the two windows was not where it had originally been. It was at least several feet over from its usual spot. Extremely annoyed, he went into the house and slammed the door and marched up the stairs. He started to go into his bedroom and, sure enough, it was not where it had been before but rather a door down. There Maddy was sitting on the edge of the bed with her hands in her lap. She looked up at him expectantly. What's going on here anyway? he said.

OVER THE next week Llewellyn left the house every morning to drive past La Brea up to the hills and back down Franklin, looking for Catherine. He continued to take every side street and boulevard in between. Every day that he returned to the house, something about it had changed. Inside Maddy and Jane were always in their places but the places were different. The telephone was always ringing. Shaking his head and muttering with irritation at this turn of events, Llewellyn walked into his study only to find it was now Catherine's room, with the bed in the corner and the bare walls and pink bits of glass in the sink. He walked out into the entryway of the house and, just as the phone stopped, announced, This has gone on long enough. Madeline? Jane?

They didn't answer, and after several minutes the phone began again.

HE TOLD himself he was inching closer to the poem of no return. If I can just find the study, he thought, I'm sure I can get it, it's nearly in my grasp now. The telephone came to be an outright nuisance. Once he answered it and it was someone from the studio; he hung up. Once he answered it and it was Eileen; he hung up. Once he answered and it was Richard: Good news, old man, said Richard in that way of his. The hotel may not evict me after all. Guess assassination anniversaries don't exactly pack them in; it appears, said Richard, that everything will go on being *exactly as it has been*. Beneath the affectation of triumph his voice rang with abject terror. Llewellyn hung up. Richard is mad, he said to himself.

THE LAST straw came when Llewellyn returned home one afternoon to find the front door moved a good five or six feet from its proper place. The correct placement of the door, neatly centered between the two upstairs windows, was in-grained in a memory that rooted itself in childhood; now Llewellyn's patience had run out. He came inside to find

Maddy at the bottom of the stairs. She was shaking as she held the banister. She's losing her grip, Llewellyn said to himself grimly. He was determined to put things right, to take command. You have to call Eileen, she said choking, it's urgent, they want you to call tonight. Llewellyn looked high and low for the telephone, finally locating it in the fireplace. He dialed a local construction company.

Maddy went upstairs. She didn't come down until several hours later, at which point she found part of the front wall of the house lying in a rubble on the lawn. Several carpenters were at work. What . . . is happening? she asked her husband, who stood supervising the carpenters with his arms folded. I am having the door, he coolly replied, restored to its proper place. She looked at him, at the huge hole in the house and the carpenters at work, and then went back upstairs. She removed a suitcase from the closet and opened it on the bed and filled it up. She went into Jane's room and gathered the child in her arms along with a favored toy or two. She carried the suitcase, the child and the toy down the stairs, past her husband and the carpenters. She put the suitcase, the child and the toy in the car and left.

ONE APRIL night the Hollywood division of the Los Angeles Police Department received a report from a city utilities commissioner who lived in Hancock Park that he had found a girl with wild black hair staring at him through his bedroom window. Had this incident not involved Hancock Park or a city utilities commissioner, the Hollywood division of the Los Angeles Police Department would have dismissed it. As it was, they sent out a single patrol car to circle the area ten minutes; the patrolling officers found everything quiet and in order. Two nights later the division received a similar report from someone else who lived in Hancock Park, and the very next night there were two such reports. In all cases a girl with black hair was staring through someone's window. Subsequent calls reported she wore a plain dress and no shoes. She was seen only at night, never in the day. By early May the Hollywood division of the Los Angeles Police Department was receiving an average of eight reports a night, all in the same area. Half a dozen patrol cars were prowling the streets, with the residents of Hancock Park in a veritable snit that such a state of siege should be necessary at all.

THE NAME of the lieutenant overseeing the Hancock Park investigation was R. O. Lowery, a towering black mountain of a man who'd been with the force twenty-two years. By the middle of May people in City Hall, most particularly those who either lived in Hancock Park or had Hancock Park constituencies, were complaining to Lieutenant Lowery about the progress of the case or, more precisely, the lack of it. Lowery regarded the whole matter with contempt. Someone's assaulted or murdered every five minutes in this city, he thought to himself, and I have to baby-sit *these* assholes. His contempt intensified when he realized he'd have to involve himself in the case personally. This realization came on the evening the girl in question hurled a rock through the window where she was looking. When Lowery walked out of his office he found his men reading the city map as though it were the writing on pyramid walls. He sighed. "Check this out, gentlemen," he said, drawing his fingers across the map, "you got her walking right up Fourth from Rossmore. Arden Boulevard, Lucerne Boulevard, Plymouth Boulevard: sweet Lord, she's sending us satellite reports." His men looked as disgusted as he did. Lowery lowered his frame on the edge of a desk. He said quietly, "Now I know you're good cops. I know you all understand we have a duty to protect the citizens of Hancock Park who work very hard so they can stay in the upper brackets and avoid paying the taxes that provide your wages. I'm going to have eight damn units out there tonight. Next report that comes in on this girl I want full response—sirens, lights, screeching tires, everything short of a SWAT team. Wrap this up so we can get down to dealing with the serious criminal element in our society like fifty-year-old whores and teenagers who wear their hair in cones." The room cleared as he lumbered back to his office to get his gear and coat.

WITH AN accompanying detective, Lowery drove down Wilcox to the edges of the Wilshire Country Club, then east on Rosewood to Rossmore and Fourth. Arden Boulevard, Lucerne Boulevard, Plymouth Boulevard: only in Hancock Park, Lowery thought, do shitty-assed little streets like these get called boulevards. They patrolled the park three hours without a single report on the radio. At two-thirty in the morning the lieutenant finally decided to post a unit outside the house that had been vandalized, leave another unit for all-night duty, and go home. The rest of the evening was quiet. The following evening Lowery went on patrol again and it was also quiet.

He'd nearly determined the Hancock Park trouble had run its course when another report came in the next night. Lowery and his detective got in the car and headed for Fifth Street between Windsor and Lorraine (both, of course, boulevards) where someone had seen the girl, not staring in a window but gliding across the grass. "Gliding" had been the caller's word, and the officer who had taken the report repeated it. Lowery was fed up. "I presume," he answered dryly over the unit radio, "you mean she's on roller skates." Next thing, he said to himself, they'll be seeing stigmata. Then, when they got to Fifth and Lorraine and the lights of the car swung across an oceanic lawn, against a brick wall that ran through the yard he saw her too.

Rather he thought he saw her, at first. So did the detective at the wheel. "Got her, Lieutenant!" he said, and then stopped the car, the headlight beams staring into space. There was no one at all. What they had taken to be her eyes were simply the large fiery insects that buzzed among the bushes. What they had taken to be her mouth was simply the red wound of a departed animal. What they'd taken to be the form of her face was simply the bend of a bough. What they'd taken to be her hair was simply that part of the night where there was no moon.

"Sorry sir," said the sergeant sheepishly, "thought we had something." Lowery didn't tell him he thought they'd had something too. "Well let's look around," he said, and they got out of the car. An hour later, driving back up Rossmore, they got another report of the girl over the box, and Lowery reached down and flicked it off.

IN THE downpour of the glass and the wax and the roar, Catherine walked across the room, up the steps and out the front door as though through a blizzard of arrows and jungle and fever. She left Eileen Rader's house and started down the hill. In the dark she saw the fog rumbling in from the sea like a herd of white horses. They trampled a path through the middle of the city, separating its roots from the spires that rose from the back of the fog like hooded riders. The black stone rivers of the city stood dry and hopeless, stitching America to the rest of the plains. She got to the bottom of the hill and walked east. She crossed a lone river of lights and walked south. At one point she came to an abandoned fair, where the empty mechanical rides were poised in silhouettes. She went into a tent to sleep and caught the whine of the white herd from far away.

SHE SLEPT in the tent nearly a week, venturing out each day to pick fruit off people's trees. Occasionally the people who owned the trees would run out of their houses, having glimpsed the theft; but they always wound up standing on their back porches deciding they'd seen nothing at all. Finally she resolved to head back to the border of America, via a final act of justice. In the middle of the night she came to the edge of the Hancock veldt. She followed a wall of fog around till she came to an opening where, inside, she saw the mansions in their gorges, elephantine and languid. She walked into the first valley and up the first hill and then into the second valley; balconies floated above her like boats, as though she were at the bottom of a lake looking up. The lawns were blue and cool. The air smelled of wine and clocks. In the days, she slept in a part of the maze no one knew.

She looked for his house, that she might inflict her final act of justice. She made her way up and down the gorges of the Hancock veldt; it's a matter of time, she told herself, till I find him. Behind the windows of the mansions people danced like the cartoon characters of music boxes. Several times she peered in; often they saw her. She continued looking for his house but to no avail. Once she thought she'd found it, a red brick house with white edgings, but it was all wrong, all different, the windows and the door in the wrong places. She continued looking until she was beginning to recognize houses passed before; and when she came to the red brick house again, about a week and a half later, it was even more different. The faces of the houses were changing, she realized: caught up in an America where people knew their faces, she now attributed to those faces the very chameleonlike qualities that others attributed to hers. Before I leave America, she told herself, I'll replace the face of my treason with the face of my destiny. Only when she saw her reflection one night in the window of another house did she understand both faces were one and the same. This was the window through which she hurled a rock, shattering glass and reflection and peace of mind and the patience of local law enforcement, everything but her futility.

Then she had a dream: she again walked a beach on a night of moon, a peculiar and vaguely felt city ribboning the edge of the earth, her hands filled with what she now knew to be the knife with which Coba peeled fruit on his boat. Down the beach in the light of the moon, just beyond the water, Llewellyn knelt on his knees in the sand. As usual he would not look at her as she came to him. As usual he would not look at her as she stood right before him. Had he raised his face to her, everything would have been different. Had he raised his face to her, she couldn't have done it. Instead he turned away, and she said to herself, Your turning from me is more obscene than all the faces that never turned; it's a denial by which you believed you might own me. It's an ownership by which you believed you might save something. It's a salvation by which you believed you never betrayed yourself. Not another moment will I be the sacrifice by which America pretends its dreams have never changed. My knife chimes in the moon.

She was watching his head sail off into space when she saw a boat drifting by and on its deck another man watching. He looked rather like the man who lay at her feet. Before she woke she said to herself, My life, it's nothing but sailors.

SHE WANDERED the Hancock veldt two months of nights. On the evening she decided to leave America she woke to a red sky alive with a thousand flesh spiders. From horizon to horizon they spun silver webs that shivered with pain. Beneath these strange skies she left the veldt and traveled the road east to the border. She crossed Western Avenue and soon came to the swirling map in the sky that read Ambassador Hotel, where she remembered the morning she met Richard. On this evening the hotel was bustling with more activity than usual: a line of limousines stretched along the northern wall, and near the lobby were the white holes of television lights and the chrome and black of cameras. Guests shuffled with hotel management. Several security guards dashed back and forth. Catherine walked up the long drive

and resolutely through the throng, through the doors she had
passed before.

SHE WALKED with the throng down a long corridor
lined with shops: ticket agencies and barbers, boutiques and
small post offices, rental services and magazine stands. She
went up the stairs at the end of the corridor into the lobby,
where many chandeliers glittered above a fountain of water in
the middle. There were also two elevators, a dining hall and a
lounge. At the front desk the management was coping with a
flurry of check-ins. To the left was a cavernous ballroom. No
one danced in the ballroom, and the sullen dark was scarred
with candlelight; across walls that held no windows hung curtains that reached the ceiling. The bar in the corner aspired to
near invisibility. Only a few people were present but more
brushed past Catherine in the doorway, and as the room
filled, nothing changed but the presence of silent faces; no
laughter was raised or discussion exchanged; people groped
for facsimiles of discretion. The candles were kept burning as
though to mask the smell of decay. When a flame went out it
was urgently relit by someone in a hotel uniform assigned to
no other purpose.

Catherine turned from the doorway and went back into the
lobby. A number of people were noticing her and looking at
her, including the manager behind the front desk. He kept his
eye on her as she walked the entire length of the lobby toward
the elevators. Madam, he finally said, a conceit meant to flat-
ter the hotel more than Catherine, since in her plain dress
and bare feet she appeared nothing like a madam. She an-

swered him with a look of her own and stepped into an elevator; the door slid closed as she watched him come from behind the desk. She stared at the panel of lights to one side of
the door, remembering how they had flickered the day Richard took her to his room; she tried to remember how many
times they had flickered and which small map lit up when
they stopped. Another couple was in the elevator with her.
They moved to the other side. At the third floor Catherine
got out.

She went to the place where she remembered Richard's
suite had been and found the door open. Inside a maid was
changing some towels and turning down the bed; she stared
at Catherine over her shoulder. It took Catherine a moment
to realize this was not the room she was looking for. She went
back to the elevator and waited with a man in a suit who
whistled aimlessly; every few moments his eyes would rest on
Catherine and he would stop whistling. He kept pushing the
button on the wall. Finally he got into an elevator going
down, and when he was gone Catherine pushed the buttons
as she had seen him do. An elevator arrived, empty, and she
got in and got out at the next place it stopped—the sixth
floor. She went to the place where she remembered Richard's
suite had been and knocked. A strange man in a bathrobe answered the door. She backed away and returned to the elevator.

For an hour she traveled up and down in the elevator
knocking on people's doors. After a while she began to understand the numbers of the floors and took them systemati-
cally, one by one; rather than wherever the elevator randomly
let her off. She had eliminated all the other floors when she
decided to try the fourth. She went once again to the place
where she remembered Richard's suite to have been. There
she heard a sound, like a baby crying. She knocked on the
door and no one answered. She knocked on it again and the
only response was the sound of the baby's cry. Some people

in the other rooms were peering out into the hall, aroused by the sound of her pounding. After a while a bellhop arrived to investigate a reported disturbance. When he came up the hall the guests were still leaning out their doors; the bellhop seemed a little uncertain how to handle it. He said something to Catherine. She grabbed the knob of the door and shook it.

He would have pulled her from the door except that he heard it too, the sound of crying. He took her arm and she shook him away, pointing fiercely at the door. The bellhop looked around at the other guests. She's been making a racket for twenty minutes, said one lady. The bellhop nodded and listened to the sound in the room and sighed, then he took a key from his ring and put it in the lock. He opened the door.

Inside, the suite still displayed Richard's fastidiousness. The only thing about it not fastidious was Richard. He was lying on the living room floor in his underwear. An open bottle of liquor sat on the table, a glass overturned in the midst of a stain. There was also an empty pharmaceutical bottle on the sofa. Catherine stood behind the bellhop, who softly called to Richard and then bent down to gently shake him. At the frigid touch of Richard's body he jumped back. Oh shit, he said.

He nearly ran over her trying to get out of the room. Catherine remained staring at the body. She heard the sound like a baby from the other room and, not taking her eyes off Richard, she stepped around him. In the other room she made the discovery. Trapped in the window was something that had once been a white kitten. The kitten had been trying to get out the window; she was moving, animated, but not really alive, caught rather in a last nervous reflex, like something that continues to move several seconds after its head is cut off. The window in which the kitten was caught had several long horizontal panes of glass which opened to an angle by a latch on the side. At some point the kitten had maneuvered the latch, squeezing between the panes of glass and pushing herself toward a crack at the side of the screen. So desperate had she been to get out, so frustrated had she been by how securely the window was fastened, that she became determined to escape at any cost. Now Catherine saw the side of the kitten's head pressed flat against the pane of glass and its emaciated body twisted in the window; she had no idea how long the kitten had been like this. She might have been this way before Richard's death; she might have grown from a kitten into a cat within the panes of this window, and he might have sat on the sofa drinking and taking his evil medicine as he listened to her howl. The last sun of this June night was gleaming through the glass at this moment and the new angle of each pane cast a different hue while the trees of the Hancock veldt cried hideously in the distance. The cat was drowning in the colors of the glass and the noise of the trees, and when she moved, the glass moved and the colors changed. The more hysterical her capture, the more vibrant the light, until she was writhing in the dark red of the spidersky that was caught in the window with her. When Catherine put her hands on the cat, the creature was crushed in the light and din. Both girl and animal made a low and barely audible sound, this low hiss of refuge, like the familiar glint of refuge Catherine had seen in the animal's eyes.

Dazed, she took the kitten in her hands and walked back out into the other room where Richard's body lay. Several of the guests from down the hall were standing there watching. The bellhop had not yet returned. Catherine moved toward the door with the kitten; the others moved out

of her way. In the hall, momentarily disoriented, she began
going in the wrong direction, then turned around and headed
back. She got to the elevator and stepped into an empty one
going down just as another arrived coming up with the bellhop, a security man and two medics.

In the lobby Catherine stepped out of the elevator, still
holding the kitten. The manager behind the front desk saw
her immediately and signaled to a man across the room.
Catherine crossed the lobby toward the ballroom where it
was shadowed and hushed and stung by candle fire. Two men
came up on each side of her and grasped her arms. She
flinched and they held her firmly. For a moment they were
deciding which way to take her; they decided against the
lobby and started her along the wall of the ballroom toward a
back entrance.

Later, during the police investigation of the matter, the
various accounts of what happened would all differ. It was
agreed that there was a man, apparently in his thirties, with
brown hair and a mustache, milling aimlessly around the ballroom. He had, according to those who noticed, gotten there
some thirty minutes before, and those who watched him for
any amount of time at all found him odd. He said odd things.
He didn't weave as though drunk or drugged, but he seemed
lost and disturbed. At any rate the strange girl with the black
hair stopped dead in her tracks when she saw him, and he
dead in his tracks when he saw her. One of the security men
tried to move him out of the way. The other security man insisted he heard the man speak to the girl in a way that was
familiar even though it was prefaced by no sort of salutation
or cordiality. I have this poem in my head, the security man
heard him say.

You know this woman? the security man asked him.

I have this poem in my head, the strange man went on.
Twenty years ago tonight I became a man who quoted poetry

rather than write it, here in this place where they kill such men.

The security man placed his fingertips on the strange man's chest. Uh, excuse us, buddy? he said, pushing him slightly.

Then, according to various accounts, the girl dropped something she held in her arms, tore control from the two men who held her, and seized from the wall one of the burning candles. She flashed it before her across the strange man's throat as though to send his head soaring to the ballroom rafters. Of course the candle did nothing of the sort; the man touched his neck and looked at the cooling wax on his hands. The candle broke in two, its end flying behind them, where it fell at the foot of the curtains. For several moments there was only a harmless flicker.

Everyone—the security men, the girl and the man with the mustache, men in dark coats and women in vanilla gowns—watched the flicker, immobilized. And then, like a wave very far on the horizon that rushes forward faster than anyone can imagine, the curtains were a wall of fire that stretched from one end of the ballroom to the other in a bare moment. The air was gauzed in smoke before anyone thought to even scream, and then, like the fire, the reaction was roomwide. Catherine looked around her and the men were gone. Llewellyn was gone. On the other side of the room the doors flew open, and the floor was a swamp of blue flames. In less than a minute the ceiling above became shimmeringly hot, like liquid. Beams of the ceiling began to collapse.

She ran for the doors. Colliding with the other people, she could hear the fall of the ballroom behind her. She reached the lobby to see the carpets smoking and the chandeliers dripping like the colored ice of a cavern. Around her were the molten lines of people consumed and displaced by small eloquent puffs, dark glows left where the forms had existed moments before. Either there was remarkably little shrieking from those trying to get out or it was drowned by the fire's roar, but the silence was tomblike and malignant; there was a dreadful smell. Only when Catherine reached the street did she hear the sounds of a world outside: footsteps, voices, sirens, wheels. She fell on the long grass outside the hotel with other people, and got up to run and fell again; it was impossible to get away from everyone else. The sirens came closer and closer and still seemed as if they would never arrive. The first of the fire trucks pulled up the drive by the time Catherine had crossed the lawn to the west knoll. Near the end of the hotel's west entrance she heard the crash of a milk truck that had just arrived with the night's delivery; the hood of the truck was burrowed into the corner of the building. Someone was caught between the building and the truck. Milk gushed out over the lawn; people ran through puddles of it and their shoes left white tracks gleaming in the firelight. Hoses were hoisted from the fire trucks and Catherine could feel the spray of the water turning to steam.

By now the upper floors of the hotel had caught fire. Flames coursed up the sides of the building like veins. People were streaming out onto the fire escapes in nightgowns and pajamas, women carrying furs and men holding briefcases. The bottom level of the hotel shone a brilliant gold. Catherine heard a terrific crash and screams from the lobby, and through the glass doors she could see the hotel's chandeliers crashing to the floor. From around the corner came a sharp dry crack and a resounding rumble and then a gush of white light and from the crowd its first and only collective outcry. When the air cleared, half the hotel had disappeared. Those who could still run ran everywhere. Catherine jerked from the electricity in the air, and around her people began running into each other and into the sides of limousines and fire trucks. They held their hands in front of them and called for directions. The firemen began aiming their hoses wildly, showering the dark with water. More fire trucks rolled up the drive, blasting their horns at the people who were holding their hands over their eyes and howling from the flash of the explosion. More women and men poured from the hotel, wandering down to Wilshire Boulevard in white robes, black soot falling on them like snow. Many people were perched high in the windows of their rooms. They shouted down to the firemen to tell them where to jump, and the firemen stood at the base of the hotel with a canvas in their hands listening to the cries above them. Finally the people just began dropping from the windows. Everything went silent, mute firemen and people dropping quietly from the windows. High on the sixth floor a woman clung to her window, gray hair blowing and her sightless eyes glittering like ice. Catherine watched the woman spread her arms and take off like a bird.

At the bottom of the knoll on Wilshire Boulevard scores of police cars flashed red and blue lights; troops crawled up the hill as though in an invasion. In the middle of the drive Catherine saw a group of children in nightclothes screaming and crying; a tall thin woman with her hair in a bun was trying to calm them. They kept groping in front of them. Moving blindly in a group, they left one behind, a small blond girl who reminded Catherine of the Edgars' child. Catherine picked the girl up and carried her in the direction of the group. Who is it, the girl said, where are we going? Catherine said something in her own language, and the girl reached for her eyes. You can see, the small girl said; and then, to anyone within earshot, she cried, This one can see! Catherine felt the child reach for her eyes again, as though she wanted to take them from her head. This one can see! the child kept screaming, and then someone else reached for Catherine's face too. This one can see! yelled a man with black gnashing gums. Catherine pushed him away.

Someone else had her nails near Catherine's eyes, and someone else pulled at her; she felt a pain shoot from her

elbow to her shoulder. It didn't matter now that Catherine
was possessed of a chameleon face; the only force her face
could deceive now was the blinding explosion of moments
before. She can see, she can see! they were all screaming at
her, running into each other in order to get her. Catherine
flung the child in front of her and struck back. People tried to
tear from her head the face she had despised so long. Someone had his hands around her neck, someone had his arms
around her chest. Backed against something solid and cold,
she turned to hoist herself up onto it while people wailed beneath her. Where is she! they were screaming back and forth.
She could barely stay on her perch, her arms and legs shook
so badly. She had no idea how long she could keep from beng
pulled down. People around her were shoved and trampled;
the children among them were laughing and chattering, their
fingers wet with blood. The tall thin woman with her hair in a
bun stood in the distance sobbing hysterically; none of her
children paid her any attention at all. Then Catherine saw
that the thing onto which she had crawled for safety was a
police car: she recognized it from her nights in the Hancock
veldt.

The door of the car opened.

It opened with enough force to throw many of the people
on the ground; in the throes of hysteria, some of them
laughed. Getting out of the car was a towering black mountain of a man, who turned to look at Catherine on his roof-
top. "Come here, girl," he said quietly, and took her under
her arms and lowered her from the roof, and then put her in
the front seat of the car and got in, locking the door. He did
it as though it were a picnic at the beach. She sank into the
seat, looking at the faces of those outside, most of whom
didn't know or no longer cared that she was inside the
car. The black man turned on his unit radio. "Lowery here,"
he said to someone. "I got myself caught in a mob on the
drive."

"We'll come in," came a response.

"No," said Lowery, "this bunch has spent itself, I think. But we've got a disaster here, and we can use more paramedics and ambulances. People in extreme shock, also apparent loss of vision among most of them when the hotel generator blew. That includes the fire fighters and people jumping from the upper floors. I got a girl here, they were trying to tear her eyes out of her head." He snapped his fingers in front of her face and she blinked.

"How'd she get so lucky," came the other voice.

"Good question. Maybe she didn't see the blow. Maybe it didn't see her. Anyway I have a few other theories about this one."

"Yeah?"

"Remember," said Lowery, "the Hancock Park business a few weeks ago?"

"No kidding."

"Well, it's a theory," he said. He cut off the radio, and when he looked at Catherine again he sat up straight. Her eyes were still open but spinning in her head; he snapped his fingers again in front of her and this time she didn't react. "Don't flip out on me now," he said to her, "I've got some questions for you." He didn't believe she had suddenly gone blind; he knew it was something else. He didn't know that she was asleep with her eyes open, but he might have figured from the movement of her eyes that she was dreaming. He wouldn't have any way, sharp detective though he was, of investigating where she went, of following her back through the hotel, which stood in her dream husklike and black, a mammoth tunnel ripped through the ceiling and starting toward the stars, lit only by a fire in the far lounge where a tall middle-aged actor waited for his last shot against failure while the other haunted incarnation of the poet approached her from out of the dark. "It . . . is you?" R. O. Lowery heard her say in awkward English.

"It's me," he said, still snapping his fingers and waving his hands before her eyes.

But it wasn't to him she spoke.

CATHERINE WAS treated for shock in the emergency room of General Hospital, then taken after several days to a sanitarium in Malibu. There she had a bed on the second floor, next to a window that looked toward the sea. Her eyes were always open and moving in a dream, and she answered to no one who called her. Doctors who examined her found nothing wrong physically. Psychiatrists, speculating on what might have happened to her, were at a loss to account for her condition. The police had no idea who she was or where she had come from, except that for two months prior to the Ambassador fire she'd been reported walking at night in Hancock Park, looking in people's windows. There were witnesses who saw her start the fire in what appeared to be a dispute with an unidentified man in the ballroom of the hotel, and there were also witnesses who had seen her just prior to the fire on the fourth floor of the hotel, in the room of a man who had succumbed at some undetermined point to a toxic overdose, perhaps by his own choosing. The "Wilshire Holocaust," as the papers called it (several other buildings in the proximity of the Ambassador had also burned), was one of the worst disasters in the city's history. Catherine, a Jane Doe to the police until they determined differently, was charged with arson and one hundred and sixty-seven counts of second-degree murder.

LOWERY'S CASE was at an impasse before he began. The logical starting point was the man found dead with the bottles and pills in his room on the Ambassador's fourth floor; the statement of a bellhop and other guests on the floor put the girl in that room ten minutes before the fire began. She'd been carrying what looked to be a dead animal. But the body and identity of the man had gone up in smoke along with the hotel records. Two maids said the description given by the other guests sounded like that of a man who had been at the hotel a while—tall and fiftyish, polite but recently reclusive. The manager of the hotel, who was aware that two medics had been sent up to the fourth floor a few minutes before the fire, thought the man might have been one Richard Dale, who lived on that floor and had been in the hotel long enough to have not paid his bill in some time, which was the only reason the manager remembered his name at all. Over the course of a week Lowery's detectives couldn't find a single person in Los Angeles who knew or had heard of Richard Dale.

The case didn't break for another week, during which time the papers diligently reported the degree to which the police were stymied. Each day Lowery drove up to Malibu to see his suspect, to the disapproval of the doctors. None of these trips was fruitful. He'd returned from one such trip one afternoon and was sitting at his desk trying to think of all the ways one leaves tracks across the landscape of one's life and how he could find those tracks and follow them, when his door opened and the tracks led to him. Bingo, Lieutenant, said one of his men.

Lowery lowered his feet from the desk. The detective came into the office and laid an open magazine before him. Lowery found himself looking at a picture of Jane Doe in a bed sheet. For several minutes he sat gazing at the picture and the photo credit with it. When he closed the magazine he said to his man, Then let's locate Mr. Crow and have a talk.

AFTER THAT things fell into place, up to a point. Larry Crow sent the police straight to Llewellyn Edgar's house, which they found with several walls missing, two new doors six feet off the ground, and a window erected out by the curb. Edgar himself was in the only part of the house still intact, a servant's room in back, where he was trying to fit together a hundred bits of shattered pink glass over a black photograph, as though all the pieces of a puzzle had fallen out, leaving an empty hole. Over the next forty-eight hours the police also talked to Madeline Edgar, Eileen Rader, the guests at a party given by Eileen Rader three months before, and several workers at a local construction company who had, around the same time, done some curious work for Mr. Edgar on the house, the results of which were now so unmistakable. In return for a promise of immunity from prosecution Mrs. Edgar made a statement. Lieutenant Lowery asked for medical reports on both Llewellyn Edgar and Catherine, and received the preliminaries the next day in a phone call. "Don't know that I have much for you, Lieutenant," the doctor said. "You know the mental state the girl's in, and Edgar isn't exactly bowling with ten pins either. At this point it's tough to make a case against him for assault. Also, molestation's out."

"Yeah?" said Lowery.

"Girl's a virgin. Of course there might have been some other form of sexual contact, but somehow I don't think so."

By now the press had gotten the photograph and were running it incessantly. When more details of the story came out, the district attorney's office settled for slavery charges against Edgar and reduced the second-degree murder charges against Catherine to a hundred sixty-seven counts of manslaughter. Lowery drove up to Malibu to see her again on a shiny blue fin-de-June day. Sitting by her bed watching her dream, he said, Wherever it is you are now, girl, don't come back. You won't like it here if you do.

WHEN SHE opened the door of the cell he was hunched on the floor asleep. She stood beside him and waited for him to wake. He stirred and opened his eyes; he looked as though he didn't believe he saw her.

She knelt and watched his hands. He held them open before her and then dropped them and said something to her she didn't understand. Somewhere behind her a door closed, and there was a wiry little man with red hair outside the bars who appeared very startled to see her. He said something and approached the door and then turned and left.

She looked at the prisoner; his face was bathed in the purple light of the sun going down. He moved toward her slowly: he's afraid he'll frighten me, she thought to herself—as though anything can frighten me now. He was very near her, and the shadows of black bars rose through the purple light on his face. Looking at him closely, she realized he didn't seem so much like the other one. He was tired and gray and his eyes hummed with something sad; he looked at her in a way no man had ever looked at her, not held by her face but rather as though he was the poet of a different destiny, of a different choice made long before, who had never consumed so easily his own vision. His eyes said, I was born in America. They said, I believed one was guiltless as long as his faith was true; I thought the act of treachery was beyond those who did not know its name. I never thought treachery was like a face. I never thought it was something one wore whether he knew it or not.

Better, she wanted to say to him, that faith betrayed you rather than you betray it.

For a while he held her, just by the arm. Then he let go, and she realized she'd been cold from some ocean breeze through some open window. She pushed the cell door and walked to the dark end of the hall, where she turned to look at him once more. The cell door swung back and forth but he didn't move from his place. She heard footsteps. Lieutenant, she heard someone say. Lieutenant?

"LIEUTENANT?" LOWERY shifted in his chair, opened his eyes. Catherine was still lying on the bed in front of him, her eyes still moving. An orderly was touching him on the shoulder. "I think you nodded off, Lieutenant," he said. Lowery rubbed his brow with his hand and said to himself, I thought I could investigate where every sharp detective would like to investigate. But the only place I went was cold, from a Malibu ocean breeze through an open sanitarium window.

Lowery returned two days later. Nothing had changed. A week later, after the story had finally dropped out of the papers, he came back. Catherine was still lying on the bed. "If anything," said one of the doctors, "she seems to have slipped further." The dreams? said Lowery. "Her eyes are going a million miles a minute," said the doctor. He looked spooked.

Lowery went to sit by her again. He loosened his collar and examined her a long time, exploring her countenance for a clue. The sun dropped into the sea and, as had happened before, he dozed. When he woke it was dark outside and the bed before him was empty.

He jumped to his feet. He called an orderly and the orderly came running into the room. Before Lowery said a word the orderly took one look at the empty bed and disappeared. In twenty seconds he was back with two other orderlies, a nurse and the doctor. "I fell asleep for about fifteen minutes," said Lowery. "She was gone when I woke."

The two new orderlies took off. In the hall the lights went on and another troop of nurses arrived. The first orderly went to the window by the bed and looked out. "Ten-foot drop," he said. "She didn't go this way."

Lowery wasn't so sure. He went to the open window and stood in the Malibu ocean breeze looking at the edge of the Malibu cliffs. After a moment his eyes narrowed. "There's someone out there," he said.

THERE'S SOMEONE out there, she heard someone whisper, and she ran down the path of the cliffside to watch a ship not foundered on the reefs of her childhood but rather sailing past, teeming with the blind of paradise. When she reached the sand she found it empty, but she saw his form in the water, swimming to shore. The night was dashed with waves. If he were to crawl onto the beach and collapse on his face she would run to him and say, But nothing swims in the dust. But he did not crawl and he did not collapse. He sailed to her; he knew the water; he strode from the sea. She hid the knife in the fold of her skirt and walked out to greet him.

THREE

THERE IS a number for everything. There is a number for justice. There is a number for desire. There are numbers for avarice and betrayal. But when the scheme becomes utterly one of avarice and betrayal, then there are no more numbers other than those that quantify what we possess and lose. It is in the land of dreamers, it is in the land the dreamers dream that dreams of justice and desire are as certain as numbers. It is in the land of insomniacs that justice and desire are dismissed as merely dreams. I was born in the first land and returned to the second: they were one and the same. You know its name.

❧

He was born in the northern heartland of his country in the year before the outbreak of the first world war. His name was his father's, Jack Mick Lake, three cracks of gunfire that suited the father as the publisher of a small newspaper outside Chicago. For the son the name was apt less for its explosiveness than for its symmetry. When he was six, the year after the war ended, he discovered the family tree, reaching back to a great English grandfather on Jack Mick Senior's side, and including two uncles who lived across the state line in Wisconsin. Though too young to understand the thrill felt by a peddler's daughter named Jane Shear when taken in a London alley by an ancestral nobleman at five-thirty in the morning before the dawn of the Victorian era, Jack Mick Junior could still compute the *equation* of the illicit moment.

As he was staring into the family scrapbook on the afternoon his seventh autumn lapsed into his seventh winter, his mathematical genius found its first expression. After that he closed the book and computed the equations of autumn and winter themselves.

≈

His mother's past eluded recorded history. She was born to a woman of the Potawatomi tribe, also known as the Fire Nation, or the People of the Place of the Fire. Originally rooted in the northeast of the country, they migrated southwest. Jack Mick Junior's maternal grandfather, by what accounts existed, was a white trapper or sailor, perhaps from Europe. Thus there was bastardization on both sides of Jack Mick Junior's parentage, though it was surmised the union involving the Potawatomi grandmother lacked the thrill that marked the one involving Jane Shear. Precocious enough to compute a number for sexual thrill even though he did not yet understand the experience, he would nonetheless need several years to find a number for rape, let alone humiliation, let alone subjugation. As with avarice and betrayal, once these experiences became a part of the scheme, the scheme became so utterly bankrupt as to defy numbers altogether. Thus his mother, who assumed the name Rae in place of a Potawatomi name for which there were no English sounds, remained to him a woman of mystery as well as strength and depth, until she died at the age of forty-one or -two, when the son was twenty-two or -three.

≈

She was forty-one or -two. I was twenty-two or -three. I know I saw her on the tracks that night; the moon was too full for my eyes to play that kind of trick on me. It would

have been better, I suppose, if we had found some remains,
some body; yet no one particularly regretted that we didn't.
It had been a troubled time for my father, the ten or twelve
years that preceded that night, and it seemed there was
nothing left to happen to us.

❧

First his uncle died when Jack Mick Junior was ten. Jack
Mick Senior was the youngest of three brothers: the middle
brother, Dirk (a family of gunfire names, this was), had gone
west in 1915, venturing back once the next year and then disappearing for good. Eight years later Jack Mick Senior and his
oldest brother Bart got a wire on a night when, as it happened, they were returning to Jack's home together from a
card game in Chicago, where Bart would sleep off the bourbon before going on to Milwaukee the next day. It would
later strike Jack Junior how the influence of bourbon on this
particular night was a harbinger of things to come. Of course
Bart did not go to Milwaukee the next day but, looking
odiously green, accompanied Jack Senior in his motor car out
west where they would either bury their brother or bring him
back. For three unnerving weeks no one heard from them,
either at the Lake home or the newspaper office. The ten-
year-old Jack Junior waited hours by the dirt road running
along the railway tracks, watching his own shadow shrink before him in the mornings and slither out behind him after
noon, until finally one day he rose from his bed and came on
his father and uncle sitting in the family room before an
empty fireplace. His mother was standing in the doorway of
the kitchen; she had found the two men the same way. She
asked if they wanted coffee. She made them coffee. She asked
about the west; she asked about their brother. They only
stared before them with their mouths slightly open. Jack
looked at his mother and his mother looked at Jack; he looked

out the window at the car crusted with dirt and there flashed
across his mind the image of these two men sitting in the
car and looking just like this all the way back from wherever
they had been, never saying anything. By that evening Jack
Senior had gotten out of his chair and built a fire in the
hearth, which he watched until the flames died. He did not
look like a ghost anymore, but he did not talk about the
west. He did not talk about his brother Dirk. Bart went to
Milwaukee.

~

The boy was a bit of a runt, compared to his father and uncle,
both barrel-chested and filling rooms. It was supposed his size
derived from the Indians on his mother's side. His hair had
the coarseness of his mother's and the lightness of his father's. His temperament was his mother's stony inscrutabil-
ity, into which, as his father said, one dropped words and did
not hear the splash for days. When the boy was seven the father noted, as did Jack Junior's teachers, that his eyes were
bad; the parents drove him into Chicago on a Saturday to get
him glasses. As they left Chicago the blur that had accompanied him on the way in was transformed into a panorama of
revelations: the blast of the lake in the distance and a great
hubbub in the streets on behalf of a newly ratified constitu-
tional amendment. Women carried on as men watched in silence from the doors and windows of the shops. Young Jack
looked to his mother who smiled to herself. He looked to his
father who looked to his mother and said something to the
effect that he hoped her first contribution to democracy
would not be the election of Harding. In her way she turned
from the window with her knowing smile and answered without saying a word; in his way he smiled too, once she had
turned back to the window. Jack gazed at it all through his

heavy glasses, gladly bearing the burden of their weight in exchange for a thousand distinctions, colors that cut.

≈

He had eyes of a blue that vanishes with infancy only to return a lifetime later with old age; in all the years between, the blue journeys to some unknown place, presumed dead and, upon homecoming, is received with some resentment as it lays out a treasure of sights the eyes can never understand. That the eyes of the boy retained the blue didn't mean the blue never journeyed, didn't mean he more sensibly deciphered its treasure; but it may have explained the numbers. Behind his large thick glasses the blue took the form of dual spheres, as though his eyes were two moons that had always been in the sky but had never been seen because they were exactly the sky's color, and now they had fallen to hover before the face of a child. He was also a little hard of hearing. This may have explained the music.

≈

I was out in the fields behind the house and I heard it. I don't know how old I was, twelve or so; it was after Pop and Bart came back from out west. Part of the field was ours but a lot of it was no-man's-land, where lived a few Indians the country tried to run off until my father made a thing of it in the paper. Not my mother's people at any rate. It was early in the evening. The sun was down but there was still a cold light left, and from out of the ground came a music, cool and hazy and windy like the light, and in the music were a hundred numbers, sixes and sevens and threes waving back and forth in the sound of the light. It was the music and light of a person's sleep, as when you

dream in the morning and everything is very sharp except
the background, people's faces sharpest of all against backgrounds that go nearly blank. There was a big burly Negro
man who ran a mill down by a creek a couple of miles over
the ridge, and in my dream when he laughed his Negro
face was sharp and clear and the room behind him fell
away utterly: he laughed a five. A deep full five. The light
now in these fields was of that kind of sleep and the music
of that kind of light. But no fives. Sixes and sevens and
threes. Honestly I don't think it was a dream when
I heard that music; but honestly I have to say no one else
heard it or admitted to hearing it. My mother and father
hadn't heard it. I asked Bart once and he hadn't heard it.
They didn't laugh at it when I told them; I had never made
up such a thing before. They knew about my numbers.

❧

It was true he didn't make up such things. Even as a child he
didn't imagine things; he never feared the dark. Moreover his
talent with numbers was already clear; he mastered the basics
of mathematical deduction by the time he was six, geometric
principles by the time he was eight. By the time he was
"twelve or so" he moved into the realm of calculative theory,
with the fledgling University of Chicago watching him
closely. His other intellectual capabilities were above average
but not spectacular. He read occasionally but not feverishly;
geography interested him but not history. So mathematics
was his genius, and that he heard numbers in music and
music from the earth did not alarm his parents. They didn't
wish to make his talent any more of a chasm between them
than it already was. Therefore he did not ask them and they
did not ask him to take them to the fields where he heard the
music; if they were to go together and he were to hear it while
they did not, the chasm would only be wider: they did not

need to confront each other's distance. Fully aware of his
son's genius, Jack Senior, who in all other ways encouraged it,
did sometimes wonder at its usefulness and remark to his
wife, "Be nice if he lived in the real world now and then."
She gave him that look, like in the motor car in Chicago on
that day of her suffrage. She knew (he knew) the numbers
came from her, from a place back beyond her being born,
traveling up through her to the son as though she were an underwater cave, the sunken burial ground of the Potawatomi
tribe, the Fire Nation.

❧

It is interesting, given his proclivity, that everything in Jack
Junior's real world happened when he was "twelve or so,"
"twenty-two or -three." Later it drove his father a little crazy,
a perfect example in the father's mind of the exotic futility of
the son's abilities; this was a man who, every day of his life,
checked the exactitude of the date on every page of his newspaper, who numbered his achievements by such dates, every
memory recorded by a number of significant intractability.
Ten. Thirty. One thousand nine hundred twenty-nine. On
that date his newspaper announced the pending economic
collapse of a hundred million lives. "Yes," Jack Junior would
remember later, "I was about sixteen."

❧

*He and I were different in a lot of ways, and as we got
older he got more and more like who he was and I got
more and more like who I was. He always needed people
around him, he was always taking them into his orbit; down
at his paper he'd be mixing it up with the printers or
whomever, his sleeves up to his elbows and his hands black
from ink and blue from the metal filings beneath the first*

level of flesh. He put up with things for which, from his
own family, he wouldn't have had the patience; sometimes
I thought he had more patience with those he employed
than with those he loved. By the time I was nearly twenty I
felt as though I had no patience for anyone.

≈

If you'd called him a reformer or liberal he would have
stared at you aghast. If you'd called him a crusader he
would have been disgusted. Later after my mother was
gone, close to the second world war, I'd hear people in bars
call him a crusader. When they called him this it wasn't
meant as a compliment. But when I was younger, after I
began hearing the music in the fields, I woke one night to a
red glow over the ridge down by the creek; the Negro's mill
was afire. The Klan had come over from Indiana at the
news that a woman in Gary had been affronted by a colored man in broad daylight. Given the broad daylight, you
might have thought they'd have a better idea of who it was,
but it probably didn't matter; they picked on the first colored man they came across and the fact that he was in another state just made it all the more inconvenient in terms
of legal prosecution. The Negro got out of it roughed up
but alive. Pop ran about seven or ten stories on it and got
copies into Gary. He shamed two states into extradition
proceedings. He was always running stories about the Indians too. But call him a crusader, he had no use for it.

≈

In fact Jack Senior considered himself rather a conservative,
in that his values were unabashedly traditional, and his self-
identification, when asked about his politics, was simply "Pa-
triot." This in an age mesmerized by the convulsions of the

East, in which the vanguard held hopes that had nothing to do with countries. "Prattle," said the father to one-worldism.

Still, in the son Jack Senior saw an inner withdrawal that struck him as luxurious and irresponsible. This triggered an argument. It was late in the day and they were driving back from visiting Bart and his new fiancée in Milwaukee, and from Chicago where Jack Junior had applied for admission to the university. The road curled above them like a blue vapor and across the valley in the wet rust of twilight the wheat silos of the farms, burning moments before, were doused to silver. When the valley went dark the sky went riverblack, houses and barns cauterized in stabs of gold and slash-red. Into the dark father and son drove angry and speechless. Finally the father sighed. "I know you're not like others. I know you hear things others don't hear, I know you hear your music. But all the more reason, you know. All the more reason. You're curt sometimes. You're abrupt. You ought to think about other people sometimes."

"I don't give a damn about other people," the boy said.

The older man was crestfallen. They got home and parked the car. The boy had a lump in his throat; hating himself, he said to his father as they walked to the house, "I didn't mean that." He had meant something else. He had meant he felt alone next to his father who knew people so easily. He had meant that no matter how hard he tried, he could not be who his father was, his father who got more and more like who he was. The father barely heard him. "I didn't mean it, Pop," the boy pleaded. At the door Jack Senior nodded.

When he was admitted to the university, the month before the economic collapse of a hundred million lives, Jack Junior filed his papers under the name of John Michael Lake (no junior), which was a fiction, not so much to mute the gunfire of the father as to escape the symmetry of the son.

~

Bart first married in the last years of the nineteenth century, when Jack Senior was still a boy; for that matter Bart was still a boy, barely twenty. By the time he was thirty the marriage had ended, the young wife having met a saloon keeper about whom she made no secret of her excitement. Jack Senior would later conclude Bart's drinking started in those days as he wandered saloon to saloon looking for the man who had stolen the wild Mrs. Lake. One night he found the saloon, with the man, with Mrs. Lake, upon which confrontation the new couple demonstrated to the abandoned husband the full extent of their crashing passion, in a kiss that couldn't begin to match the demonstrations Bart had seen in his mind time and again. Bart ordered another drink. He left only after the keeper went off his shift and took Mrs. Lake with him. Bart and his wife had had a daughter who was well into marriage and motherhood herself when he met his second wife; the daughter was two years older than the prospective step-mother.

The match was even more curious than this. Bart was now in his late forties, the edge of his masculinity dulled in a previous decade, a man of some ascendant means, and a large man of height and girth that bespoke recent fortune. Melody was a pretty blonde. She had much humor and was not wild like her predecessor; she didn't want or need wild things. Given her own childhood, it was enough that she had a man who would care for her, it was enough to have an affectionate love rather than a passionate one. They lived in Wisconsin, a Wisconsin couple. It never occurred to Bart when he met her that he had a chance with her; when he got the chance it never occurred to him he could actually keep her. They married in 1921, quietly. Jack Junior knew nothing of it until it was over; later in his life he couldn't even remember a ceremony, at which his father was best man. Every month or two Jack Mick and Rae and Jack Mick Junior drove to Milwaukee to visit; sometimes Bart came down alone, as on the night they got the wire about Dirk. After the marriage the drinking did not abate but became worse as Bart waited dreadfully for the new wife, blond and pretty, to get wild and leave like the old wife. That she did not, at least not until life became intolerable for her and her love for Bart was rendered so clearly inadequate, only tortured him more.

～

This business with my uncle and his second wife went on over some time of course. I was growing up through most of it. I never understood anything was wrong anyway, the insurrections and dashed treaties of the bedroom were beyond me, and mostly I remember Melody laughing all the time. Also I was at the university. Also I was in my own world, as my father always complained: I barely saw the soup lines, the liquored amber flash of gangland nights. I don't think it occurred to me something was wrong in the country until one evening in the door of a flophouse I recognized a man from my bank, a man who'd been sitting behind a desk nine or ten months before, deciding whom to give money to. Then I noticed every road off the college grounds seemed to be an alley of sleeping men, and the yellow lights of the flophouses were dim not because the houses were closed but because they were so full that men inside were sleeping against the windows one atop another, the light from the bulbs barely seeping out between the fingers of their hands. I think one day I said to myself, Life's different now. Meanwhile my family was coming apart too and I didn't know it. In my third year, when I was nineteen or so, a couple of things happened. I met Leigh. I found The Number.

～

I was computing an equation one night in my room at my desk when everyone else was sleeping, and there it was. I shouldn't have been startled: it was the twentieth century. Mathematics was new. It shouldn't have startled me that there was this other number no one had ever found. It was there between nine and ten. Not nine and a half or nine and nine-tenths, not the asteroids of ten or nine's missing moon, but a world of a number unto itself. For the next year I tried to compute the moral properties of this number: it was not the number for justice or desire, or avarice or betrayal. It was the number of an altogether different promise made from an altogether different place. No field or plain had ever sung it. No dream or memory had ever known it. I told no one of it, not yet.

❧

Young "John Michael" fell in love with Leigh the second time he saw her only because he was incapable of so unequivocal a response to anything the first time; it was also one of those rare instances when he remembered a real life event with such statistical certainty. Jack Mick/John Michael had never gone with a girl, discouraged by his wiry slightness and the dark Indian quarter of him which he supposed would frighten the creamy girls of Chicago. Leigh was in fact attracted by this Indianness. She was the creamy daughter of a district judge and had scandalized her family by becoming a Red. Her cadre worked out of the shack of a newly failed boat-building operation on Lake Michigan. Jack/John saw her distributing leaflets one morning to eight hundred laborers in line for three jobs who watched her with open mouths. It wasn't what she said to them, they had heard that before, it was the gold of her, as though in the windblown flame of her hair was the transience of their luck, the flight of their futures. They would have ridden her hair to other births, somewhere out west, where there was no history. "Ah, utopia," the boy said when she handed him the paper, and he nodded knowingly. "Go back to your books, college boy," she answered, and took back the leaflet. But it meant, of course, she knew who he was.

≈

He asked her out twice and twice she refused. The third time she said, "I want to drink whisky tonight. Come if you'd like." He said, "It's not legal," and she laughed and walked away. He followed and she led him to a blue speakeasy down a back flight of steps where the patrons drank and danced to Louis Armstrong and Earl Hines playing "West End Blues," and she barely paid attention to him. She got a little drunk and the two of them stumbled down the street under the eyes of the cops until they arrived at the brownstone of her father and mother. He had assumed she no longer lived with her father and mother. "I assumed you wouldn't get along with them," said Jack, "on account of the politics." She laughed again. "They decided I'd only be wilder on my own," she said. "Besides Daddy has a soft spot for his princess." She leaned into the front door beneath the light of a gas lamp; up the street the iceman dropped a white glassy block from the back of his truck. She looked at the Indian virgin in hot silence. "What now?" he finally said, his mouth dry. "Utopia," she answered, and opened the door and pulled him in. "But your parents," he said, and she curled her lip and sneered, "College boy." The seduction took place at the bottom of her father's stairway, her claws predatory and her moans provocatively unrestrained. When it was over she laughed, "You do it like a bourgeois. Tenderly."

≈

Nothing but trains. I moved into the far wing of one of the outer dormitories and stared out my window at the convergence of tracks. I went with Leigh to her political meetings and met her political people. "This is a college boy," she told them. For utopians who espoused a brotherhood of man, they had impressive reserves of contempt. Later she asked what I thought of them and I explained I wasn't a political person. Everyone's a political person, she said. I attended the speakeasies, new subversive that I now was. Sometimes Leigh made love with me and sometimes she didn't. Let's say she never did me any favors. She got it when she wanted it. She took it till she was full of my Indianness, till she had drunk the quarter of my juices that came from the underwater cave of my mother. I went mad for her. Sleeping alone I slumbered into Leigh-madness and woke one night to the black roar of trains and the knowledge that this madness, it was my new number, beyond desire. Beyond justice. The communication of the maternal blank of my past with my most passionate dream, the most untouchable part of my integrity. What I felt for her was the new place beyond nine; when I entered her I was on a far journey into what I was capable of being. I was the anarchist of passion in an age when passion was a country.

~

Pop and I got into it one night in the city. We were supposed to meet at Gene the Wop's for supper, off Clark; I was late and didn't arrive until he'd finished his meal. He glared at me as I walked in. I also smelled of bourbon. "You've been in a speakeasy," he whispered. "I thought you'd changed your mind about prohibition," I answered, and all he said was, "Law's still the law." Then he saw some of Leigh's handouts I had with me. "Oh you're a bolshevik now," he said. "No," I said, and forlorn pain shot

through me because I thought of her and wished I was a
bolshevik, I kept thinking I'd gladly be one if it got me
Leigh, and yet the fact was that, for some reason inside me
I couldn't understand, I wouldn't be one, glad or any other
way. From there on Pop and I just began yelling at each
other across the table, and the more I thought of Leigh the
worse it got. Finally he just pushed away, stood up and put
on his coat, and walked out without a word; it was the last
conversation we had in a while, until my uncle died.

∼

In the face of the Depression, as he struggled to save his
paper, in the face of his estrangement from his son as he
struggled to save his family, Jack Mick Senior received a letter
one day from Bart's wife, Melody. By now Bart was nearly
sixty. The early sexual disappointments of the marriage had
come to be, after ten years, profound failures as his wife, past
thirty, lived in the late afternoon of her fertility. "These
things never mattered to me," Melody wrote, "but he doesn't
believe this." She was frantic. He drank all the time. "There's
one soul prohibition never saved," Jack said bitterly to Rae.
"I can't continue with this much longer," Melody went on.
"I don't know what to do." Two months later she left him.

∼

The last time Leigh and Jack made love it was at twilight on a
cold May day down by the water, where she unzipped and
straddled him, her coat pulled around her neck and a flurry of
revolutionary announcements flung from her fingers. "Damn
you," she snarled in his ear when they had finished, and he
knew by the way she looked at him as she left that he would
never have her again. In the subsequent nights he continued
to wake to the black roar of the trains and the despair of an

irretrievable connection with her; and he would throw the
sheets from him and go to his dark window naked, erect and
aroused, standing in the window and pressing his whole body
against the glass so as to freeze the black roar of his veins. He
supposed he could put out the fire this way. To the tracks
below, to the country beyond them, he called her name, and
the hardness burst beneath him, the wet white of him rivering
off into the beyond country; and he called her again. Later he
could not remember how long he stood there or how many
times he said it.

～

On the day of John Michael's commencement Bart died,
some six months after Melody had left him. The father and
son accepted a mutual truce long enough to journey to Milwaukee, where they and Rae spent the afternoon with Bart's
daughter and her own children. Most of these hours were
taken up with a general discussion among members of the
family about the tragedy of Bart's end and his awful second
wife. Bart's awful first wife—that is, his daughter's mother—
went unmentioned. Jack Mick Senior did not comment on
any of this except once when he interrupted a rather euphe-
mistic autopsy report to say, "Medical complications due to
kidney disorder hell: the man drank himself to death." After
that the entourage traveled to the mortuary together amidst
the continuing castigation of Melody Lake. The mortuary
was small and filled with light; the open casket was at the
front. The family filed in and there in the corner of the room,
in an empty row, Melody sat sobbing with such a spastic grief
that John Michael couldn't imagine she would ever stop. Her
face was invisible in her hands and she choked with desolation, gasping. The family stood watching in cold mortification.

～

And I was looking at her, and I was thinking that someone crying like this could never stop, and then I saw my father walk over to her and touch her gently on the shoulder
and just rub his hand back and forth on her arm, over and
over. I guess my cousins were stunned. My mother's eyes
had that way-back look in them. And my father stood there
a long time, rubbing her shoulder over and over, not saying
anything as she clutched the bottom of his coat and held
on. It was the greatest thing I ever saw anyone do for anyone. He didn't care whether the family liked it or not. It
didn't matter that the last of his brothers was gone, well of
course it mattered, it mattered in that he'd lost everything
of his childhood, but it mattered a little less than the fact
there was this stricken woman alone in an empty row who
needed the mercy of the living to survive the judgment of
the dead. And my father stood there alone with her, and all
I wanted was to know that sometime in my life I would do
something as good. "She gave him the worst moments of
his life," someone said to him later. "She gave him the best
too," he answered. That night we sat in our house by the
fire where I had found the two brothers so stunned on that
morning years earlier, returned from the west; and my father remembered all the nights they had sat there, back to
when I was an infant sleeping in a bed by the heat, and
they talked about the war and whether we'd be getting into
it or not and how Jack Johnson lost the heavyweight cham-
pionship of the world. Now on this night he said to me
gently, "Go easy on the drinking, son," thinking I guess of
our argument in Gene the Wop's and how I had smelled of
bourbon. I flushed with shame. "I will, Pop," I said. We
had fights to come; we were still different. But not on this
night.

❧

On the last morning of her life Leigh got into an argument
with Jack about his father. She dismissed the stories Jack Senior had printed in his newspaper about the Klan and the Indians as mere bourgeois reformism, the last throes of a dying
society trying to resurrect itself. "My father," the son answered, "is worth three of you." Walking away she said, "Go
do it to yourself, college boy." She said it without her usual
malicious gaiety; the scorn was bottomless.

He wasn't in college anymore anyway. He was in town
trying to get a job. Since everyone was losing jobs, he
didn't have much luck. There had been a riot at the market
two days before with people nearly killed by the police; on
this morning there were rumors that unemployed workers
were building a barricade of blocks pried from the brownstones along the street. All Clark Street was brownstones
with holes. Men passed the stones down a line to those mor-
taring them into a wall in the middle of the road. He could
hear the pickaxes chiming all the way up the block; by
that afternoon the wall was a man's height and ten feet long.
For a while he sat on some steps with other passersby and
watched.

At some point he looked up and there was nothing but police.

The sun was burning and rows of police stood snapping
sticks in their hands, and the men building the wall in the
middle of the street began raising their heads, looking up at
the police and dropping their arms to their sides. There were
many people just watching, children with their faces between
the rails of the fences along the walkways and old women
with yellow sashes around their waists, stopped in midstroll.
Jack had an idea that there was some zone where the police
couldn't touch them, those like himself who weren't political.
But there wasn't any zone like that. The police sealed off the
street and everything stopped, the air itself stopped; and

when Leigh suddenly appeared in the middle of it, it was as though her auric flash was a signal for everything to begin.

~

Years later he had a vision that, right before the fall of the stick across her head, she turned to him there in the street where she stood and called to him. "I love you," he heard her say in this ludicrous vision. Then there was the splash of her hair on the ground and the gush from the deep red well of her face.

~

There is a number for everything. There is a number for defiance. There is a number for the lethal vertigo one feels when a bash of brain matter floods the inner ear. Once I would have supposed that the number of every demise was nine, including the demise of the New World. But then I became older, and found it wasn't so.

~

And she was forty-one or -two; I was twenty-two or -three; and I saw her on the tracks that night, the moon too full for my eyes to play any sort of trick. For a moment he thought he was back in the college dormitory, looking out the window at the trains of the city; he woke many nights this way, gripped in the six-month fever of Leigh's death: the fever hadn't stopped when he came home. Absently he reached his fingers to his brow to feel the bandage that hadn't been there for at least four months. Absently he clutched his nose and his mouth so as not to taste or smell the smoke of the riot. Then he remembered he was in his father's house, and that was when he looked out the window and saw his mother on the tracks that ran by the road down which Bart and Jack Senior had returned from the west many years before. She just stood on the track staring at the fields; and out of the red moon of the east, as though it were a tunnel, the train was suddenly there, insidious and silent. John Michael screamed to the glass. The train screamed back.

She must have heard it, he thought later. But then perhaps she hadn't. Over the following three days, as men paraded up and down the rails looking for a sign of her, while his father stood devastated among them, hands in his hair, the son crossed the rails to gaze out at the same fields that had entranced his mother and, with a chill, every bit of the down on his flesh standing on end, considered the hush. The hush. Where is the music? he thought to himself: The music's gone. Did she come out here that night to hear it? Did, in the face of everything's decomposition, she wish to hear the music of dreams, when no one could dream anymore? The son's guilt was immense. Had I only kept it a secret, he anguished; had I only never spoken of it. Then he wondered if she had heard it; and wherever she had gone, back through the underwater cave of herself, he wondered if she had taken it with her.

~

He came to the field every day after that, but the music was gone for good. His father languished awhile, then slowly took himself back to the tasks of the newspaper. The fervor of the past was gone for good; but John Michael didn't ask that everything be the same as it was: he would accept it that anything could even be similar. He thought of changing his name back to Jack Mick Junior and decided this would somehow make it worse. His father, as he had done in the case of

Bart upon comforting Melody the prodigal wife, would not insult or demean his tragedy by calling himself a victim. For his father the concept of victimization would always belong more appropriately to others of even more unfathomable tragedies. Intuitively Jack Mick Senior understood that the greatest tragedy was not the loss of Rae but of the music she had taken with her, even though it was music he had never heard or perhaps even believed. In the sense that she was the last to hear the music, John Michael thought one day, my mother was the last American. In the sense that he must now survive never having heard the music at all, John Michael thought, the last American is my father.

~

One day in 1937 he had walked from his house a mile down the track to catch a ride on the same train he had watched from the dormitory window of his Leigh-madness, the same train he had watched take his mother. He rode it across the state about a hundred miles, which was ninety-nine farther west than he had ever been before. He came to a wide river that ran to his left. He believed he should have come to this river about ten years earlier. He walked down the beach looking to the river's other side.

He fell asleep on the banks of the river in the last light of the sun and woke that night to a sound he'd never heard. He couldn't tell if this sound came from the sand beneath his head or from the river, or from the other side of the river or the very air itself. The night was cold and, pushing the palms of his hands into the sand, he shook his head slowly to the sound, rousing himself and saying, or perhaps someone said it to him, Nothing swims in the dust.

~

Or perhaps someone said it to me; and I looked up and
there were men carrying torches, and debris scattered over
the sand, and the dark form of something in the middle of
the river. Its sail draped the beach and the remains of the
ship washed to shore bit by bit: there's been a wreck, he
told himself. And then, standing there by his head, he saw
the little girl gazing at him intently, a little girl who seemed
to belong to no one. She wore no shoes and had a tangle of
black hair that fell over her face; she was a very serious little
girl, three or four years old, and she didn't smile. She
looked as though she might be Indian. I don't know if she
saw me looking at her in the dark, I could barely open my
eyes. I managed to say, "Did you speak to me," but when I
opened my eyes again she was gone. I felt the weariness of
this far journey and slept some more.

When I woke again none of it was there, no men with
torches, no ship in the river, no sail on the beach. I was still
exhausted. I finally shook myself to consciousness in the
earliest hours of the morning; I felt a rush of anxiety about
Pop. I can't be worrying him like this, I thought to myself,
he has nothing but me to lose anymore. The red moon was
out, its tunnel gate having shifted to the other side of the
river. In its red light I was surprised to see small footsteps
leading across the beach to the water; I had figured the little girl for a dream like the rest of it. But there were definitely the steps, and I followed them to the river and at the
edge I heard it again, the music I'd never heard before. I
had figured it for part of the dream too. It was right there,
coming from the other side of the river; and with the same
chill as when I'd stood staring across the tracks that morning after my mother had gone, with my hair standing on
end just the same way, something occurred to me. It occurred to me that this particular music was the music of
The Number, the number and music of the black distant
part of me beyond desire, beyond justice. This number was

no mad fancy then, no theoretical conceit, it was out there,
beyond the river that stunned the fathers and uncles of
America into incommunicable silence; and it also occurred
to me, standing where the small steps of the Indian child
vanished, that my mother had heard this music too the
night she left, and that at this very moment I was very close
to that which had taken her. Confronted by it, courage
fled. Before I bolted I listened once more to the farthest
beach where the red tunnel ran to the end of the night; and
it sang to me. It sang.

~

When the country declared war he was nearly thirty years
old. Because his sight and hearing were poor he was not en-
listed to fight. For a while he was a military engineer, and his
facility for numbers and mathematical theory took him to
Washington. He became a secret part of the dour devoted
days of the country, secret even unto himself. He had been
working three months on a special project when he requested
an interview with the project director. He did not receive it
till after a seven-week period of infuriating his supervisors by
insisting that what he had to say was for the ears of the director and no one else. Late one sweltering September Friday he
was ushered into the director's office. He was seated in a chair
before the director's desk by a window that looked out to the
sun setting behind a pool of water and a monument. He was
there alone for ten minutes when a man he had never seen
before came into the room and sat behind the desk, folding
his hands on top of it. Mr. Lake, the man said. Are you really
the director? John Michael asked. Yes, the man said, I really
am. He waited, and John Michael cleared his throat and
pushed his heavy glasses with his invisible-moon eyes up the
bridge of his nose. He began slowly, trying to sound as sane as
possible. Like everyone else, he said to the director, I do not

know the exact nature of this project. However, I thought I might have information that would be helpful. The director waited as John Michael continued. There is a number, he said slowly, that we have never known. It is a number between nine and ten; not nine and a half, not nine and nine-tenths, not the asteroids of ten or nine's missing moon, but a world of a number unto itself. I discovered this number some time ago and have tried in the years since to calculate an equation that proves the number, beyond the primary equation that led me to discover it. I have to tell you that I have so far failed to develop such a proof. I must also tell you, how-ever, that I have been unable to disprove this number. More-over, if one hypothetically presumes the existence of such a number, heretofore unforeseen possibilities come within our grasp. He stopped to see if the director was having a reaction to this; the director was not. John Michael sighed and pro-duced a sheaf of papers which he offered the director, who took them. The director glanced over the first several and then laid them on his desk. He looked at his hands a while and then up at John Michael. He asked John Michael why it was nobody else had ever found this number, and John Mi-chael said, Because it isn't to be found over there; and he pointed east. It is rather, he said, to be found out there, and he pointed out the window to the sun setting behind the pool of water and the monument. I know it's out there, said the young man, because I've heard it. It's across the river. The Potomac, you mean? the director said. John Michael shook his head. The Hudson, you mean? the director said. Of course not, the young man answered in disbelief. The river, he said: it's across the river. The director, after watching him a while, asked if he'd told anyone else about this number, and John Michael said no, and then the director said, Of course there is no such number, Mr. Lake. We have all the numbers already. We know all the numbers, we found them hundreds of years ago. If that's so, answered the young man across the table, then tell me why the Old World came to the New; and the director smiled a little, quizzically, and dismissed the young man. Thank you for your interest, he said formally; he did not return John Michael's papers. John Michael continued to work for the project another month, when he was transferred to an accounting bureau in the Pentagon where he added numbers of tanks and divided them by numbers of platoons. On the seventh day of August in the year 1945 he was released from service and returned to Chicago, where his father was dying.

∼

My father sold the paper during the war, and when the war ended he sold the house, which was too big for him and too small for his memories. He got a room in the city. I set up residence with him. I didn't have much and I think he was happy I was there. I got a job in the payroll department of a business down on Clark Street. Pop asked when I was going to find a woman and marry and I told him I had no plans. Leigh had been dead over ten years. Pop reprimanded me if I stopped at a bar on the way home. I never drank much but it was always too much for him. "You've been hanging out at the speakeasies again," he said. "It's legal now, Pop," I'd point out, "it's been legal a long time. They're not speakeasies anymore." His eyes would look hurt. "Take it easy with that stuff, son," he'd say. The doctors didn't give him long, a year or two.

∼

Of course he fooled them: he was around another five. But he wasted away the last half of it, becoming more dispirited and living just for the arrogance of it. "I don't know where I am anymore," he'd say, reading the newspapers. One day not long before the end, some government men came to see me. They asked allusive questions, referring vaguely to this or that. My involvement with the war project was of some interest. They asked about Leigh and the people we knew. "She knew them," I said, "I knew her. What is this anyway?" I finally told them I would explain anything they wanted to know about me but not about anyone else. They told me I knew some things that could help my country, and I said I didn't know anything about Leigh that would help my country. You don't know that, they said. You just said I did know it, I answered. Do I know it or don't I know it? We know, they said, what it is you know and what it is you don't. I'm not a political person, I said. Everyone's a political person, they said. I finally told them, You want to arrest me, then arrest me; I haven't done anything except fall in love with a girl who's been dead ten years. Is that a crime? Could be, they said.

❧

They didn't arrest me. I continued with my job and put some money away; some nights I would go to a bar and listen to a baseball game on the radio. My father got smaller and smaller until he was smaller than I. That was what I couldn't stand, that he was smaller than I. He read the newspapers over and over about congressional committees and counterfeit confessions, nothing but committees and confessions. "Something's wrong," he said in confusion, shaking his head, "it's different." Forget the papers, I said. One night I tried to wake him and could not; I called the doctor. I sat with him two days and at the end of the second day he woke, desperate eyes in his small white face searching the ceiling. Pop, I called to him. "Something's wrong," he whispered. "It's different." Pop, I said. He dug

*his fingers into my arm and lunged for his last breath. "My
God," he cried, "where did my dreams go?"*

❧

In the autumn of 1951 a small dark American who styled
himself John Lake arrived in the seaport of Penzance on the
far southwestern tip of England. This was a time when the
tide of GIs that had flooded the island during the second
world war had long since ebbed; the summer flux of tourists
was gone as well. After disembarking Lake made his way up
past the civic promenade and took a room at the Blue Plate
Inn on the northern edge of town. A Mrs. Easton ran the inn.
For two pounds a week Lake received room and board. In defiance of a proud national reputation for disastrous cuisine,
Mrs. Easton cooked well enough. After several weeks Lake
applied for a job loading crates down at the docks; it was a
position for which he was singularly without qualification.
The man in shipping explained this to the American with
quiet tact. At a year or two shy of forty, Lake was rather old
for such a job when he had never done any physical work in
his life; he was also overeducated, something the man in
shipping could deduce without knowing anything of Lake at
all. Eventually Lake found himself attending to the company
books. He had dreaded this inevitability, wanting nothing to
do with numbers; but the numbers found him.

❧

Mrs. Easton's daughter Anne Bradshaw came to the inn each
day to work in the kitchen. She lived on the other side of
town, which in the case of Penzance meant a twenty-minute
walk, in a small cottage with her own seven-year-old daughter.
She had moved into the cottage twelve years before as a girl

of nineteen, with her husband, Thomas Bradshaw from London, who had met her while vacationing on the coast. The husband did not come back from the war. Now Anne earned money cooking for her mother and running errands for people in town. Several times in the passing years she had considered selling the cottage, but she clung to those things of an earlier life which she still could hold onto. It was odd to be barely thirty years old and to have had an "earlier" life, but in many ways this was true of England in general and the Old World it belonged to. Anne had dusky yellow hair and a weary generous smile, and she noticed the new American in town on the stairs of the inn as she was leaving to take some weekly groceries up the road to the only other American left in the area, an old man who lived out on the moors.

~

Lake had a good view of this road from his window, which was on the third floor of the inn and looked out to the north and the expanse that stretched from Land's End on the left to the Bodmin moor a couple of hours in the distance to the right. At first he thought he would rather have a view of the sea, on the other side of the building. But the guest room downstairs had such a view, and after a week or two he became drawn to the desolation of the moors, their chrome light dribbling over the heath. In the flash of the storms the land disappeared altogether, leaving the window a square of rain. After a couple of months of walking the coastline Lake exhausted his attraction to the bay and the ships and the castle of St. Michael's Mount; but the moors, which on the face of them offered much less to see, never bored him. It's true that for a long time he went out into them to listen; the wild brush and hidden ponds seethed with their own life and, he might have thought, their own sound. It's true that he thought he might hear some kind of music there. When

he didn't he thought he was disappointed, until he realized
that what he mistook for disappointment was immense relief.
That he loathed himself for such a surrender seemed a small
price to pay.

~

*As I understand it, my great-grandfather and -grandmother
came here once, about a year before Victoria became
queen. My great-grandfather, Edwin Lake, was married to
another woman. My great-grandmother, Jane Shear, was the
daughter of a peddler. The affair between the two lasted
three minutes and took place in the alley behind a sweat-
shop off King's Road, and it wasn't nearly enough for her;
she pursued him as he vacationed with his family in South-
ampton and, the story goes, was walking up the street to his
hotel one morning when he saw her through the dining
room window. He set down his tea, patted his mouth with
his napkin, and excused himself from breakfast; his wife
asked if he felt well. Quite well, he told her. He explained
he would return in a few moments. He walked from the
dining room, out the back door of the hotel, and to the
train station. He took a train to Exeter. By now of course
he knew everything was over, he had already passed the
point of no return. He had made the mistake of toying with
a girl who did not understand that passion was a country
where there were definite borders. She did not see the borders; she crossed borders as though crossing an empty avenue at midnight. In Exeter he contemplated his ruin for
several days until Jane Shear showed up there as well; then
he took another train. This time he crossed the Tamar
River from Devon into Cornwall; he crossed, then, into the
final no-man's-land of the Old World, he went as far as the
Old World could go. She followed without a second
thought. I have had the miserable misfortune, my great-
grandfather thought ruefully to himself, to make love to a*

woman who will pursue her passion to the edge of her
world and perhaps beyond. At Land's End he jumped into
the sea. She might well have followed except that while her
passion was such as to transcend borders and worlds, her
maternal instinct was not; she watched pregnantly from the
rocks of Land's End and turned around, going back to London where she bore a son, giving him the name of his father. The son in turn would go to America and bear three
sons, Bart, Dirk, and Jack Mick, names that were in spirit
rather the antithesis of Edwin. Thus my great-grandfather
and great-grandmother lived in a country they each called
passion but which was in fact two different countries; each
crossed into the country of the other without knowing it.
When they did not honor each other's borders, they believed each other to have committed treason; for each, treason was the same crime by a different law.

❧

Lake had casually noticed Anne many times before he saw
the similarity with Leigh in appearance. In fact the Englishwoman seemed almost softer to him, though he decided later
it was the person who was softer rather than the face. As he
watched her wandering up toward the inn through the streets
of the town that tumbled back down the hillside, the wind of
the bay lifted her hair in a way that the wind off Lake Michigan would lift the hair of a judge's daughter. On the other
hand, Leigh was now of so long ago he couldn't completely
trust the memory this new woman resembled. In every other
way Anne was utterly different. Sometimes Lake could barely
hear her when she spoke to him, and she flushed slightly and
looked anxious around the corners of her smile. Her heart was
different, bound in a tourniquet and fighting to live.

❧

Rather dully, he took even longer to understand her interest in him, since she wasn't the kind to express it directly. By now the long sexual death to which he'd committed himself almost twenty years before was no matter of steely will but willful resignation; for a while he hadn't realized it was happening. A year passed after Leigh's death before it occurred to him he hadn't had another woman since; but the resolution of this abstinence became apparent not with Leigh's death, not with his mother's death, not with any other death at all but rather with the night on the banks of the river when he heard the sound of his own number and followed the small footsteps to the water's edge. With his retreat he put something of himself behind for good; in Cornwall he had retreated out of his world altogether.

❧

He didn't know what she saw in him, a small dark man with heavy glasses. Perhaps she wasn't sure herself, unless it was the pain of his retreat and that he was a man who had sealed himself off from any more loss. She didn't need another man who flung himself into the thick of things. She was insightful enough to know that what some were unimaginative enough to call passivity might be a wounded stoicism, a life bound in a tourniquet and fighting to live. Then also maybe she was a little like Leigh after all, though drawn to his Indianness not for its exoticism but for the rooted depth of it. Anyway, she wasn't one to flirt. But every way she could find to pass the inn wherever she was going, she did; and one day, forwardly, she brought him lunch down at his office on the docks. It was roast beef and potatoes and a fruit cobbler, with a pint of ale. "It's so English," he said smiling at her, spreading it out over the desk. "Imagine," she laughed.

❧

I worked four days a week with the other three off. Sometimes I'd go with her onto the moors on Saturdays when
she took old man Cale his weekly groceries. Her daughter
would stay behind at the inn with her grandmother; the little girl was the very image of Anne. I tried not to think of
her as yet another bit of Leigh; I tried not to think of them
as Leigh in different stages, the little one innocent and new,
Anne older and sadder. Of course Anne was not really an
older sadder Leigh: if Leigh were still alive Anne would be
eight or ten years younger. I knew that. I knew they weren't
the same at all. I knew Anne was a better woman than
Leigh in a hundred ways I hadn't even seen. She laughed
without calculation. She was kind to the old people in
town. She did more for more people than a hundred of
Leigh's revolutions. She seemed a part of the moors, she
was like the moors, exhaling silence and sending forth the
inner light of her. On the way to the old man's house we'd
find ourselves caught in the sudden storms of the country,
where it is the land that seems to rain on the sky rather
than the other way around.

∾

The old man lived in a stone house that had been built a
hundred years before by a farmer who grazed cattle on wild
moorish grasses. Some in Penzance speculated that maybe
the old man grazed on wild moorish grasses too. He was
going on seventy but looked eighty-five: stooped and utterly
white, with a long beard, like a troll that lived beneath a
bridge. He didn't say much when we came with the groceries, just nodded to Anne, but we heard him talking up a
storm when we left. He obviously believed the only person
who understood what he said was himself, and no one
would have contradicted it. He had been in the house alone

nearly thirty years, since the day in 1923 when I was proba-
bly standing in the dirt road waiting for Pop and Bart to re-
turn from out west and the old man, then about my age
now, was washing up on the beach near Land's End where
there's barely any beach at all. They found him caught in a
thicket of trees bashing back and forth against the coast,
not a few trees but a whole woods of them, as though
someone had sailed the forest to shore, guiding it from the
highest perch. Though they found him alone, they said he
constantly called through a fevered night for a nameless girl
with a deathless face.

~

Lake and Anne borrowed a car one Saturday and, at her sug-
gestion, drove out to the tip of England. Also at her sugges-
tion, they took the old man with them. "He's a fellow
American, after all," she said, "you two can have a grand
talk." Lake answered that the old man seemed to have his
grandest talks with himself, to which Anne replied, "Then
you may each have your own grand talk."

In fact the two men did have an interesting talk, but only
after an hour of riding in silence, when they got out of the car
and slowly made their way to the edge of the rocks that overlooked the blue sea, not far from where the old man had been
found among his tangle of trees on the beach three decades
before. Clearing his throat and expecting nothing, Lake said
to the old man, "I was born in America as well, you know."
For a moment he thought he hadn't been heard.

But the old man slowly turned to look up at him, a wild
comic look in his eyes and his mouth parted in both skepti-
cism and anticipation. Then he said something curious to
Lake. "America One," he asked, "or America Two?"

"I'm sorry?"

"America One or America Two?" the old man said again.

Lake shrugged in confusion. "Uh . . . just America." He tried to smile, and shrugged again.

"I never could get that straight either," the old man said, nodding confidentially. He added, "I was also born in just America."

Lake looked past the old man to Anne, who was trying to keep from laughing. "Exactly where in America," he said, "are you from?"

The old man waved at the sky. "Beyond it," he said. "Where the annexes run out." He turned to Lake. "You been out there?"

Lake shook his head. "No, I don't believe so," he said slowly. He thought for a moment and said, "I'm from Illinois," with the sinking feeling this would explain nothing. For a moment the old man narrowed his eyes as though Illinois was a name so unremembered as to be alien, but then he nodded and just looked at the sea. In the distance was a lone lighthouse and for a while the three contemplated it, Anne pointing out that it had been deserted for many years, unmanned and unlit. Sometimes the old man seemed unsteady where he stood; there was always a gust from the sea against which Lake and Anne had to support him upright, taking him by his arms. When they were ready to go Lake said, almost whimsically, "So this is the end of the Old World. What will the end of the New World look like?" And the ancient by his side raised his white face to the younger man and whispered, "I know what it looks like. I've been there. I've been there."

❧

I watched autumn pass. The Penzance winter was surprisingly mild. There were the constant sheets of rain but not the marrow-chilling cold of Chicago. The tide was in nearly all season, sealing off St. Michael's from the rest of the city and keeping the boats docked. I'd go down to the water to do the books twice, maybe three times a week, and the rest of the days I'd sit in the guest room by the fire looking out to the Channel. Sometimes Anne would sit with me. She was waiting for something from me. She never regarded me with reproach, but the hope was unmistakable.

≈

Sometimes I would nap in the afternoons, up in my room under a quilt Anne's mother had given me, with a candle burning on my table. More and more I was drifting away from myself; beneath the lids of my eyes I could see out the window the black smoke and blazing green grasses of the moors and the dazed barricades of rain. I barely heard her when she came in one day, standing at the foot of my bed; only at the last moment did I find the presence of mind not to call out Leigh's name. She was shaken and breathing hard; she thought I was sleeping. She slowly pulled off the sweater she wore, looking at it in her hands for several moments before she laid it down and unfastened the rest of her clothes. As though just thinking of it, she went to the door and locked it, but with no haste; she didn't actually expect to be interrupted. The whole inn was quiet. There were no sounds from the kitchen below, nothing from outside, just the falling walls of rain. Soon she was naked and standing at the foot of the bed. Her body was fuller and browner than I would have expected of an Englishwoman. It was a long time since I'd seen a woman this way but now it didn't seem so long, it didn't seem long enough. A distant part of me wanted her but the heart I lived with these days couldn't find its own door to beckon her in. I knew that for her to have done this was courage beyond fathom; she was struggling to continue looking at me, to not lower her eyes, though to have lowered her eyes would have been to confront her own nakedness, which was another courage too. I could not find the door for her. I sat up and tried to explain it to her.

❧

"I'm thirty-eight, thirty-nine," she heard the mathematician say with his usual imprecision concerning personal statistics. He pulled back from the light of the candle on the table as though to hide behind his dark Indianness in the darkness of the room. "I look in the mirror sometimes," he said, "and I think I'm fifty or fifty-five." He shook his head. "I don't know how I got so damned tired. When I was younger I despised anyone who gave up so easily, but that was when the world sang to me, that was when there was a number for everything. I couldn't imagine I'd ever feel this old and this tired." Now he leaned into the light of the candle. "It isn't your fault. It isn't that you're unbeautiful, it isn't that you don't deserve what you want. The humiliation is mine, not yours. In a musicless moor at the end of a numberless world all I can manage now is to grieve for what I once felt and for how much I felt it. How is it I'm so old now and I don't hear the music anymore, I don't find the numbers anymore?" He said, "Please." She watched him pull the quilt from around him and offer it to her; fighting back her tears, she picked up her clothes and put them on. It seemed to take her forever to pick up her clothes and put them on as he sat watching her. Then she went from the room, taking curious care not to slam the door behind her; she was the kind who would never slam even the doors that others were closing to her. She got her daughter from the hearth in the guest room below and the two made their way through the drizzle back to their cottage on the other side of town. Sometimes she would see him in the weeks and months that followed but they didn't speak anymore and they didn't walk on the moors. In the spring she sold the cottage and moved to a town in Devon.

~

After that the long distant part of who he had been drifted so far it was out of sight. He held to it in the way of a man who holds the string of a kite that is so high he can't see it anymore, knowing that any moment it may break and the only way he will know it has broken will be by the sudden ripple of the string as it dances slowly groundward. Then he stands watching a fragile white line winding across the country before him and wondering if the end lies in a pool or a bush. There seemed no way to draw back in the long distant part of who he was. He was terrified by the prospect that some current in the air would thwart him, he was terrified he would draw it in and nothing would be on the other end. Better to risk a sudden collapse of the line on its own. Of course something in the cordiality of Penzance changed when Anne Bradshaw left; though no one blamed him directly, the people of the town couldn't help the sense of violation, the sense that this dark Yank had divided the town's present life from its future life, England and events having already divided present life from earlier life. Mrs. Easton became flustered in his presence. Lake considered leaving the Blue Plate Inn and then wondered if this would compound the insult. If I had compromised her, he thought of Anne, I'd be wildly popular; he told himself this with sardonic indignation. But he knew the sardonicism was false and uncalled for, let alone the indignation.

~

In the spring I began walking out onto the moors every week to see the old American. What with Anne gone, someone needed to take him his groceries, which the town contributed: some bread and a couple of meat pies, some potatoes. He did a little gardening out in front of the stone house. Feeble as he was he did all right for himself. He'd barely speak to me when I first arrived, but if I stayed long enough he'd finally talk. It became pleasant in the spring when we sat in front of the house until nine or ten in the evening without feeling the chill, in little chairs that seemed made for children, rocking back and forth. Across the moors could be seen the lights of church steeples, churches not even there in the silver sheen of the moordays, as though they were beneath the earth and their lights shone up through the ground after dark. He watched the lights very intently, counting them in his head. Twenty-eight, he reported, I got twenty-eight. What do you get? I counted. Twenty-eight, I told him. He nodded in disappointment.

❧

I couldn't vouch for it that he wasn't a little out of his mind. He was certainly confused about things: time and dates and places. I told myself I should become more careful about time and dates or I would be confused too when I was older. One night he asked me the year and I actually had to think a moment. Nineteen fifty-two, I said; he shook his head peculiarly. It was as though he didn't understand the very number itself: No, no, he said, that can't be it. He understood the numbers of churches but not the numbers of years. I could never get a straight answer out of him; I asked if he'd been to Chicago. Again he looked peculiar and shook his head, as if Chicago were Asia or the Antarc-

tic. I asked if he'd been in New York and that seemed to
ring a faint bell. Once I think, he said, nodding. Very long
ago, before I went to prison. Prison? I said, startled; and he
answered, Out in the annexes. Montana. Saskatchewan.
And then I went to a city, he said, where there were a hundred canals, and storefronts that wept in the distance, and
whores that slept in the lagoons. His whole little white face
struggled with the memory of it. He said, A terrible music
came from the earth. He said, A boat circled day after day,
and she was on it. He said, In this city I died, over and
over.

Music came from the earth? I said.

~

It's you, isn't it, he said. He said it in my presence but he
didn't say it to me. It's you I hear calling over the songs of a
zombie city. I cast myself in flight for the decapitation of my
own guilt, to live where I once died, to resurrect my passion,
my integrity, my courage from out of my own grave. Those
things that I once thought dead. By the plain form of my delirium I'll blast the obstruction of every form around me—
Mr. Cale, I said to him—into something barely called
shadow. I sail. Mr. Cale? I swim to you. I reached over and
shook him roughly by the shoulder. I know the water. Mr.
Cale, I said again, shaking him.

~

He turned to look at me, and I pulled my hand away. I saw
her there waiting for me as I came out of the water, he said. It
was dark there on the peninsula, nothing else around; but I'd
been wrong about one thing, and that was the light. The light
that had called me across the bay. I thought it was the thing

she hid beneath the folds of her skirt (as though at this point she could actually deceive me). But it wasn't that at all, it was her eyes, they were the fire that had warned a hundred sailors.

Perhaps they were meant to warn me. I stumbled onto the beach, falling down on one knee but then getting up, and she walked up to me in the same dress, her feet bare as I'd always seen her, and her black hair and bloody mouth. She still held her hands behind her skirt. We stood inches from each other and she gasped slightly when I wouldn't take my eyes from hers, when I held her stare with my own; I knew if I looked away, if I turned away, she would have done it to me, as she believed she had done it before, in other places, on other beaches.

Done it?

On other beaches, in other places. But I looked at her and she finally said in her bad funny English, "It is you, but it is not you." I said, It's me but it isn't me.

&

We slept on the beach, not together, warmed by no fire because I knew the feds would come if I made a fire. Several times I woke in the night to see her leaning over me, right above me, her face in mine, and I could feel the thing she held against my neck. I'd look in her eyes a long time and soon she'd pull back. Several times I think she tried to work up the nerve for it. I didn't care. I'd died many times in the city; there was nothing with which anyone could threaten me anymore. There was nothing that could be done to my life that had not been done already to my conscience or honor. Finally, after everything, the prison and self-torment and the larceny of my dreams, I was beyond the touch of every fear other than the fear I would lose her. I was in this place out beyond America One or America Two or as many Americas as they supposed they could invent. I knew she knew it. I knew she saw it in my eyes and understood I was not whoever she had believed me to be. I would not be surprised that men cowered before the things her face once dreamed, before the dream that destroys what is not fulfilled; but I wasn't like them, and finally she left me undisturbed. When I woke she seemed to be watching me, sitting in the sand with her hands in her lap. But though her eyes were open, she was only sleeping.

~

Off in the distance I could see the boats coming. I could see him standing by the side of the boat, his black size diminished. I shook her until her open eyes blinked and lifted to me, and I told her we had to get away from there. We made our way up the side of the hill. By the time we reached the plateau I could see the cops pulling their boats up on the sand; he walked steadily across the beach looking up at me, even from atop this plateau I knew he was looking at me. I've long since forgotten his name. He was not a bad man. Circumstances made us adversaries but I don't believe he was a bad man. He clung to his reference points. He lived in silly times. She and I continued into the hills and finally came to a cave.

~

We went into this cave that was clearly dug by men. At first I figured it as a shelter for the nomads of the area, or perhaps a mine. Thirty feet in we found old railroad tracks that came out of the ground, so we followed them for a while. I couldn't see the end of the tunnel but cops were behind us, so it didn't matter, there was one way to go. In the bare light, growing dimmer by the moment, the tracks before us rose and fell, and there was the hushed roar of a distant wind. I could make out graffiti on the walls. We were tripping over the tracks and the stones, making the best time we could, and at some point we were aware of another tunnel running on our left, parallel to us, and another tunnel running parallel on our right. Every few seconds we could peer through an opening to see the other tracks on each side of us, and running along, we could feel the wind of these other tracks. We were running among these three currents and I lost a sense of something. I don't know. It was just a sense of something I lost, as though she and I could step into either of the other currents and be swept somewhere and somewhen else. It wasn't that I'd never felt this way before. Rather it was that I'd been feeling this way all along, it was a wary exhilaration that I'd come to the geographical and temporal longitude where and when anything was possible, and that the accompanying latitude was in me: I was a walking latitude, finding its conjunction with the world's last longitude, out there beyond America. After we had walked a very long time, after I had lost track of the when of it, we came to the end of the tunnel.

～

We were on the other side of the peninsula. It was gray twilight now and the cove was plain except for a group of trees down by the water. The railroad tracks shot out over the water suspended by old wooden pillars; in the distance they disappeared into the fog billowing in from the sea. We made our way down the tracks to the bottom of the hill and then crossed the cove to the trees. In the trees we decided to rest. Any moment I thought I'd see cops coming out of the tunnel in the hillside, but they never came. As we had done the night before, she and I watched each other a long time, her full gaze never changing beneath her black hair, until I fell asleep among the heavy forked branches where we waited.

～

When I woke it was morning. I remembered right away I was in the trees of the cove on the north side of the peninsula, and I dozed a while until I thought of something. I was thinking that the cops had never shown up, and as relieved as I was about it, it surprised me a little; and I turned where I'd been sleeping to look at the mouth of the tunnel. And that was when I saw the mouth of the tunnel wasn't there. Actually, not only was the tunnel not there, the hill wasn't there. The peninsula wasn't there. The railroad tracks over the water were nowhere to be seen. I sat up in the tree and looked all around me and saw the cove wasn't there; the tree I was sleeping in was the same, the small forest in which we'd camped the night before was the same, but the beach was altogether different. It was straight and flat, and the hills in the distance were green. I looked up to the top of the next tree and the girl was there with her eyes wide open; I called to her until she woke. I asked her where we were, what had happened to the cove and the peninsula. She gave no indication that she understood me, but when I motioned to the landscape with my hand she smiled slightly and then stared off to the ocean; after a while she went off to pick some fruit. I walked a little way down the new beach to see if anything was familiar, but of course nothing was. Finally I came back. Our small forest bobbed on the water like a boat. A single vine tied it to shore.

～

Every morning when I woke up, we were somewhere else. Sometimes we would be on a barren beach, sometimes on a rocky coast with a little fishing village in the distance. Sometimes there were towering mountains with snow on the crests. Sometimes we were on an island. Our forest went with us, or rather we went with it. The previous day always seemed beyond recollection, as though it were in another age; sometimes I would look at my hands to see if, in the course of the night, they had grown old. But I was not growing old; my memories were growing old. My memories were becoming my dreams. The only difference I felt physically was a little seasick.

Every morning she would be perched in the highest tree from where she could see all around her; her hair had grown longer and longer and sometimes I'd find she had tied herself to the trunk. Exhausted from the nightsailing, she would still go to look for food. During this time nothing happened between us. I guess we had decided that whatever was to happen between us had to wait until we arrived where we were going. Once I climbed up to her place in the highest part of the tree and sat there watching her, tied by her hair; I reached to touch her, as I had touched her once before in a far cell in a far jail in a far city. But I didn't. I drew back my hand and slept another hour next to her, precariously sitting in the mast of the forest, and when I woke she was awake and looking at me.

I was in love with her. I had fallen in love with her long before, though I'm not sure when. I don't think it could have been the first time I saw her, but it might have been the second, one night when I realized she was in the same room with me and looking at me, even as twenty other people were there, never seeing her. I don't know what she felt for me. I don't think she loved me, I have to say that. But we were bound by a dream that destroys what is not fulfilled. The closest we got was on one afternoon when I came back from exploring the landscape and there she was, out on a limb, looking into the water at the reflection of her face, as though she and that reflection were bound too. Without a shudder, without a sound, with no sigh of grief or rage, one long tear slid down her face to her mouth, to drop slowly onto the mouth of the face in the sea, salt water to salt water; and I reached over and brushed her cheek. And she looked at me sadly, and I turned and climbed to my place to sleep, wondering where she would take us that night. Before drifting off I looked down at her once more through the branches, just at twilight among the limbs of the trees, watching the sea. That was the last time I saw her, thirty years ago.

~

The next thing I knew, the cold sand was beneath me and I felt as though every bone were broken inside, as if I'd been thrown somewhere hard. I lifted my head to see our forest scattered across a stretch of cruel coast, jagged and strange; men were lifting me up and carrying me to the top of a ridge. I tried to tell them about her. I told them there was someone else, she was out among the trees, tied by her hair to the tallest one; I told them and passed out. When I came to, we were on the ridge and I could look down and see the remains of the forest sinking into the sea.

~

I was taken into town and put in the back room of someone's store, then moved to an inn for a couple of months. The people of the town were very good to me. I don't think I ever extended much of anything resembling gratitude. I kept asking them about her, and when they humored me, as I knew they were doing, I accused them of callous disregard, these people who had saved my life. I know they thought I was crazy. I don't wonder why. In my delirium I talked of the nightsailing and the forest; soon I stopped talking of that. After almost a year I stopped talking of her too. I could have left, gone back to my country. Perhaps I should have returned to the city where I first saw her, assuming I could ever find her again. But I waited instead for some sign of her, because I was afraid that if I left I would sever forever the possibility of seeing her. It got to the point at which I would have settled for her body washing up on the beach; then, at least, I would have known my dream was over.

~

I moved out onto the moors with the twenty-eight churches. Time passed and I became the old man I am, hobbling up and down the overgrowth waiting to come upon her. Sometimes someone comes out to see me. There was a young woman who came, blond hair and widowed; they tell me there was a war a while ago. She brought groceries and took me for rides in a car, down to the place not far from where they found me once. Then she stopped coming. I heard she'd left. People in town still think I'm crazy, I know that. But they've taken care of me more years than I've deserved. I am sixty-eight, sixty-nine.

Then this American started coming, I had seen him with the woman a couple of times. A curious fellow, but then he thinks I'm a curious fellow. Dark, with sad blue eyes that his glasses magnify; there are ways he reminds me of me, but all old men are reminded of themselves by all young ones. When we talk of America, we . . . I don't know what he's saying. The names are . . . I don't know the names. Anyway, we talk of America. He tells me things about himself without realizing it; I think he doesn't believe I understand anything at all. He doesn't feel compelled to be careful about what he tells me. I told him about the city I knew, I told him about the nightsailing. He nods in that way that says he's going along with the cracked things an old man says. He has a few cracked things of his own. Not so much the story about his mother on the railroad tracks but other things. He made a mistake once. I don't know if he knows it. He was standing on the banks of a river listening to something from the other side, something he had never heard but had always *known*. And instead of crossing the river, he listened for as long as he could stand it and then turned his back and returned the way he had come. And he's never heard it again. He should have crossed that river. Little bits of his life come out the nights he comes to see me, sometimes the bits are cracked and sharp. Off they fly into the moor skies, and we watch them go. Tonight the moor skies are filled with rain and light, and he has driven through the heath in a truck he borrowed from town, dashing from the truck into my stone house. Tonight he said the only thing he's ever said that's made complete sense to me. When he said it, it got me crazy; I got this terrifying feeling that all these years something had been right under my nose and I hadn't seen it. Something that only I could have seen, the way I saw it from the window of a tower one night in a city thirty years ago. Tonight the young American told me about The Number.

~

One night I told him about The Number. There's a number out there, I said, pointing to the west, another number they never found. For a long time he didn't seem to hear me; the rain was blasting the roof and the sky was filled with sound. And then he looked at me as though he understood perfectly what I was saying; and I wasn't sure what to tell him, I hadn't thought of it in close to fifteen years because I didn't believe in it anymore. Another number, he kept saying, another number, and the more he said it the more excited he became; and I was sorry I had told him, because I hadn't thought he would become so excited. He

just kept saying, Another number! over and over. The Old
World, I tried to explain, is just a number off. Yes, that's
it! he said, and soon we were talking about church steeples
and lights. The Old World's just a number off, he kept re-
peating, and there are twenty-seven churches in the moors
rather than twenty-eight, because here they're a number off.
I nodded and smiled; I didn't see that it made any difference. But he said it made all the difference, because he and
I had counted twenty-eight lights and that meant there was
another light out there, the twenty-eighth, that wasn't a
church, and it had been there all along.

～

Then he had me in the truck driving him out into the bitter storm, heading to the point where the land ran out; the
rain splashed against the window and there was no heat in
the truck, and the moors were treacherous, a thousand invisible lakes. I should never have done it. Later the townspeople would say, An old man, and you took him out into
the storm, it's not enough that you drive our women from
town. But they hadn't seen the way he was, almost crazed
by the idea that this other light had been there all along
and he hadn't understood it. We drove toward one light
after another; we would get a hundred yards from a light
and then lightning would flash over the terrain and in the
momentary white glow we could make out the dim form of
an old gray church rising from the waving grass. Then we
would make for the next light, counting them down. We
seemed destined to spend the night going from one church
to another except that the old man was right, the twelfth or
thirteenth or fourteenth light was not a church at all but
rested out over the sea half a kilometer or so off Land's
End: the lighthouse that Anne, the old man, and I had

watched and talked about that first time we drove out, the one she said had been deserted for decades. Someone was certainly there now.

≈

A boatman lived down on the rocks above the water. I parked the truck and got the old man out the other side, and we made our way down the walk to the boatman's house. I still remember the light from the sky swaying across the old wooden door and the knocker in the form of a cat's head gnashing at us. The boatman was short and round, with hair puffing above his ears; he wasn't happy about being awakened and he was less happy when we told him we wanted to go out to the lighthouse. He told us we were both off our bloody nuts. He pointed out that in case we hadn't noticed, there was a rather violent storm taking place at the moment. But the old man, blue and quaking with cold, was out of his mind to get to that lighthouse. He wouldn't hear of it any other way. The boatman said the lighthouse had been deserted forever and the old man literally pulled him out into the rain by his shirt and pointed him toward it. The boatman discounted the light as some kind of optical illusion. "I'm tellin' ya, there's no one out there," he said. I offered him twenty pounds and he still wouldn't go for it: "Not till sunrise anyway," he said. Then we will wait for sunrise, said the old man. We would have stayed in the truck the next three hours but the boatman said that we could sleep in the house, assuming the twenty-pound offer still stood. I had just begun to doze when dawn came through the window and the old man was shaking me by the arm, telling me it was time to go.

≈

The storm had passed. I wanted to get to the lighthouse and back, since I had my work in Penzance and a truck to return. As we motored across the water the boatman kept advising us that this was a waste of time and our twenty pounds. "Don't be complainin' to me when there's nothin' out there," he said. Personally I didn't doubt he was right. In the sun over the cliffs the old man looked ghastly there on the deck of the boat: white as rock and chattering fitfully. Repeatedly I tried to get him down in the boat out of the wind, but he was mesmerized by the long white tower before us, and when I tried to shake him from his obsession he looked at me as though he were rabid. We crossed the water in a quarter of an hour; we hadn't gotten the boat up onto the island rocks before the old man was scrambling for the door at the lighthouse base.

The door was all splinters and holes, sodden from years of the sea bashing it. We didn't so much open it as pry it apart. The boatman was down by the water tying up the boat. When we got into the bottom of the tower, the old man flinched, looking up the stairs that wound to the top; he knew, he knew what was up there. Now I wasn't sure if the convulsions were fever from cold or another kind of fever altogether. Slowly he started up the steps before me. The rail shook in our hands, and above we could hear the wind crying through the broken windows. Once he stumbled and fell back against me, almost sending us both tumbling to the bottom. When he reached the top I heard a gasp, and he stood in his place a long time until I pushed him the final step. Behind us the boatman was climbing the stairs too. I pulled myself into the observatory and found a bare room of wooden plank floors and pale blue walls, flooded with sunlight through the shattered glass and the roof torn partly away. Through the floor and to the roof extended the pillar around which the stairs had curled from

*the ground. There, tied to the pillar by her black hair, was
a girl.*

≈

She had a face like none he'd seen. He stood agape, gazing
from the girl to the old man to the girl again. The old man
was frozen, his eyes narrowing in distrust now that he had
found what he came to find. The boatman peered up over the
floor and his jaw dropped. Immediately Lake's impulse was to
turn from her face, the beauty of which struck him as uncivi-
lized; finally he found the presence of mind to free her from
the pillar where she slumped. Her hair was in impossible wet
knots. He had to cut her away with the boatman's knife. Her
dress had been made a rag by the storm, her feet were bare.
Like the old man she was chilled deeply; her eyes were open
but she showed no awareness of what was happening. Lake
shook her hard as if to wake her. She blinked slowly and
raised her face to him; she watched him a moment, then
closed her eyes and fainted again in his arms.

≈

Lake concentrated on getting the girl down the winding stairs
and into the boat while the boatman attended to the old
man. They headed back for Land's End. All the way the girl
slept, bundled in blankets the boatman had pulled from a
metal box. The old man just sat staring at her. Sometimes he
would lean his head back and shut his eyes, then sit up again
expecting her to have vanished. He was still convulsed with
fever but his gaze was somewhere past fever. The boat
reached Land's End, and Lake drove the old man and the girl
back to the stone house on the moors, where a man from
town was waiting, furiously, for his truck.

❧

Lake did not feel equipped to nurse a young girl and an old man. He settled them both in the cottage, the old man in his bed and the young girl in bedding on the floor. When word got out, Mrs. Easton showed up with a doctor. Lake was trying to cook soup on the stove. Neither the woman nor the doctor said anything until just before they left: "I don't believe Mr. Cale's going to make it," the doctor told him. He asked who the girl was. Lake said he didn't know. He said she was an acquaintance of the old man. "A relative?" the doctor asked. No not a relative, Lake said. "Of yours, I mean," said the doctor. I said I didn't know her, the American answered.

❧

The old man fell in and out of delirium, muttering. Sometimes he spoke of her. The girl had a senseless resiliency; by the second day she was sitting up awake. Lake watched her many hours during the time she slept; and afterward, when he spoke to her, he made himself meet her eyes. She did not answer. She gave no indication of understanding him though he was convinced she did. He asked who she was, and she made no reply. He asked if she knew the old man, and she only looked at the corner where the old man lay. After a while she went to sit by the old man's bed, and as more time passed she came to touch the old man's head and hold his hand. Of course Lake understood there was no way this could be the girl of whom the old man had spoken: that girl, if she had ever existed in any place other than his derangement, had lived over thirty years before. This girl wasn't twenty. Yet the old man had known someone was in that lighthouse, marked by a light Lake couldn't determine; and this girl was nothing if not the image of what the old man had described, tied by raven hair to a tower as though bound to the highest tree of a woods that sailed as its passengers slept. That night Lake had many dreams. He woke amidst them, trying for the life of him to remember the name and face of a blonde he had once loved, and why in the world he had loved her.

❧

Then it seemed all he saw was her, black-haired manifestation of an old man's invention. He became dismayed at the pathos of it, a man nearly middle-aged who in his life had known one woman half a lifetime before, and who by choice had known no other, who by choice had committed himself to bury his passion deep in the heartland of his years. Now he was ignited by a girl born the moment of the previous passion's interment. There wasn't much chance he would approach her. He had buried faith with passion. There was moreover the old man; Lake could not take from him the last dream that fired him, in either his frantic sleep or waking dementia.

Sometimes, when Lake looked at her, she looked back.

❧

The old man slipped. He filled the room with his rattle till it quavered the flame of the candle on the sill by his bed. He was wide-eyed and thrashing toward death. The interludes of slumber became brief. The girl watched without expression, staying by his bed constantly, holding him and wiping his face. The old man burned when he looked at her; when he touched her face he saw the old white flesh of his hand against the pastless red glow of her brow. His eyes did not deny their confusion. With no conversation between them, Lake and the girl came to take shifts watching him, one sitting as the other slept.

☙

Mrs. Easton brought some food at the beginning of the third day, when the old man rested better than he had the previous two; Lake slept in the afternoon. He woke just after dark as another spring rain scattered across the roof; he woke in the way dogs wake to a tremor in the earth that hasn't happened yet. He lay there less than a minute on his side, facing the girl who sat dozing in a chair by the bed. Her eyes were closed. Then the old man began to wheeze. She opened her eyes and looked at the old man and then at Lake with the first sign of alarm he'd seen in her. He leaped from where he slept to the side of the bed.

The old man dug his fingers into his arm as another old man had done only the year before, though it seemed in an utterly different life. "You made a mistake once," he croaked to the young American.

"I know," said Lake.

"Should have crossed that river," the old man said.

"I know." He looked at the old man who was beseeching him for an answer, and tried to explain: "I had never gone so far before. Sometimes you come to a road or a ridge or a river and it seems as far as you can go." The old man moaned and shook his head. He slowly turned to the girl, holding his other hand, and then stared between them a moment at the ceiling as though into a tunnel that ran to the sky. Was it for the sake of the dying man or the living witness that Lake cried desperately, "That beach was as far as I could go."

"No," the dead man said, "there is one farther."

☙

She did not cry. But he knew she mourned the old man, as the dream that finds itself left full-blown and stranded and subject to the antibodies of mundane dawns mourns the dreamer that dreamed it. She helped Lake dig a place in the moors. That morning the smell of the rain lashed the air. When they had moved the dirt into the grave, the two of them looked up at each other, there together on their knees hidden by the high grass, and it was as though the rain smell would choke them; the color of her eyes dropped out altogether. With the death of the old man something in her face seemed to spin; the long-stunned inner clock of her finally began to tick again. Clasping his hands, he reached back to pull the last of the soil into the spot, and his heavy glasses fell from the bridge of his nose onto his lap; when he had picked them up and wiped them against his shirt and put them on again, she was gone.

She was gone. He thought for a moment he saw her, there in the grass against that bottomless sky; but what he'd taken to be her hair was a once white wind gone mad in a caged place, gathering the smudge of the place's darkness; what he'd taken to be her mouth was the clotted snarl of the pale plains. What he took to be her eyes were only recollections, psychic mementos, talismans of distance: tones across the bank, a red moon of aspirations, small footsteps that lead to the water and vanish forever. "Hello," he called, as though she would step into view. But she had never answered before in all the times he watched her. "Hello," he said again, without hope.

❧

He went to town to look for her. She wasn't in town. He went down to the docks to see if anyone matching her description had booked passage. They had seen no one like her. He asked about her everywhere; he was driven back to the moors by their reproach. He partly walked, partly hitched out to Land's End so as to be there when the sun fell; he sat all night on the cliffs watching the lighthouse for the sight of her telltale eyes. The lighthouse was dark. He went back to the cottage and now turned the place upside down, what there was to turn upside down: a chair here and there, a deathbed. She was not to be found beneath chairs or beds. She was not to be found behind the walls or beneath the floors. He scoured the moors for the next week, and then a month, and then many months. He didn't find her, and no one knew of her. He went back to the stone cottage again and waited there in the nights, foolishly trying to blot her from his sleep; sometimes he believed that if he slept long enough he would wake to her. Sometimes he believed that if he stayed awake long enough, he would tumble into her unconsciousness, wherever she had taken it. Those footsteps that once led to a river's edge haunted him; he loved, as does every man who is born to a vision, that unseen future that his courage once failed. He hated, as does every man who is born in America, that irrevocable failure that his heart won't forget.

~

On the stone walls of the cottage he added things, he subtracted them. He divided things and multiplied them. Sometimes he used chalk, sometimes coal, scrawling the equations the length of the room. After a couple of weeks the entire inside of the cottage was filled with additions and subtractions, multiplications and divisions; he then moved to the outside of the house. When the outside of the house was covered, he began writing equations in the earth. When he went to work at the shipping company, he began filling the company books with this arithmetic and then the top of his desk. Soon the moors where he lived were filled with arithmetic; he then took to adding and subtracting on the roads leaving Penzance, down on his knees with his back to the end of the island, adding and subtracting himself into a corner of Cornwall. The townspeople noted this behavior. They consulted among themselves and wondered what it was about this part of their country that attracted such preposterous Americans, one more preposterous than the other. Months passed, and when the spring gave way to summer, and the summer to autumn and winter, and when the year gave way to the next, Lake was still writing equations, new ones in the spaces between the old.

❧

His was not aimless adding and subtracting, however it might have seemed to the native people. He had determined to disprove, once and for all, the existence of The Number. He had determined to show that ten followed nine after all, that the only presence between the two was the debris of fractions and percentages, nothing more, and that The Number was only a terrible delusion, a personal fable he had told himself, and that there was no reason to follow the music across the river that night years before because there was no music: that The Number did not exist and the music of The Number did not exist and the passion of the music did not exist. In this way he would justify a private collapse. While he had tried once before to so disprove this thing, he had hoped then not to succeed; he had attempted to disprove it only in order to affirm it. Now, however, he laid siege to it.

He failed. He could not disprove his number or his music or his passion. He disproved everything else. He disproved the existence of the very walls of the cottage on which he wrote the equations; he disproved the existence of the books and the desk at the company where he worked. Under his employer's bewildered watch, he disproved the existence of the employer. He disproved the existence of Penzance. He disproved the existence of the sea and the boats on it, and the castle in the middle of the bay. He disproved the existence of the moors and the sun in the sky. He disproved the sky. He mathematically and empirically disproved his memories, one by one, all the way back to the blonde he had loved whose name and face he couldn't remember. But what he could not disprove was the love itself and the huge reservoir of hunger of which it was a part. In the end he hoped to disprove his own existence and the huge hungry place of which he was a part and which was a part of him. But he could not. When he had disproved one, two and three, when he had definitely ruled out four, five and six, when he had banished from all conceivable reason seven, eight and nine, and every exponent thereof, there was still his awful number left, the last number in the world, The Number of No Return. The next year passed into the next, and the next into the next. Five passed into ten, and he hurtled through his middle ages past his half-century mark. People around him came and went. In this time the company for which he worked declined and failed, a new company flourished and vanished. The Blue Plate Inn changed to some other inn, which did not matter because he had proved, certifiably, there was no such inn. All the things that he had proved to himself never existed passed in the manner of things that never existed.

When fifteen years had gone by, and the mathematically disproven end of the empirically disproven Old World was mad with his numbers, he had no choice but to believe that which he had spent a life trying to disbelieve. One morning he woke, closed the door of the old stone house behind him for the last time, and went down to the sea where he bought a ticket for home.

～

There was a number for everything once; there was a number for justice. I remember men half-crazed with it. They counted to it in their sleep and went no higher because there was nothing higher. It was a number that couldn't be divided by any number other than itself even though every other number was a component of it. Mathematically this is impossible but that's the sort of number it was. That's the sort of place it was, where dreams had the precision of numbers and passion was a country, and the country was called . . .

It doesn't matter. It doesn't matter what it was called. It's like forgetting the last line of a joke and trying desperately for a lifetime to remember; and then it comes at the end, right before you go, and it isn't the same. It isn't the same because in the forgetting of it, it has changed to something else. It's hard to decide what's the worst thing, whether it's that justice does not have a number anymore or whether it's that those who lived where passion was a country forgot their dreams and so scrambled to invent the memory of insomniacs, the small stingy arithmetic that counts no higher than avarice and betrayal.

I'm going back. I'm sorry it's taken me this long. I don't pretend to be strong enough for it. I don't pretend to have the passion my dreams once had. I don't pretend I'll hear the music I once heard or that I'll even reach the place where I heard it. Entering the last half of my life I could feel myself tire; entering the last quarter I feel myself succumb. I've tried every way to disprove what, in my heart, I knew to be true; I suppose it's in the nature of most men to spend lifetimes trying to do this. I cannot watch, sitting on the shores of the Old World, the ripples of my country going down for the third and last time. I would rather know, when I die, that faith betrayed me than that I betrayed it.

~

In the mornings, as Lake was shaving, he would look up from the white round sink to the blue round hole in the wall which was the sea; the boat slipped slowly to America. Sometimes at night he woke with the urge to fill the walls and ceiling and floor of his cabin with equations; he resisted this. There were no equations left, and he didn't want trouble with the ship's crew; he imagined being put in a small boat with a compass as the captain pointed vaguely back in the direction of England. So he simply sat on deck facing the west waiting for the sight of land and always listening carefully, should he hear something.

~

He spent no time in New York except what was necessary to cross town and get a train out of Penn Station heading west. Within the hour the train was past Newark. During the night the train came to Pittsburgh. The train continued across country; the morning of the third day Lake arrived in Chicago. In Chicago he found the buildings painted with pictures of human parts. On the side of a store would be an open hand and on the back of a gas station would be an open eye. There were human parts set against backgrounds of rainbows and ocean waves, desert plains and outer space. Walking to his old room between the railway tracks and the university, Lake went down a street of mouths painted in wilted colors, and from every mouth came bright splotches of sound like electric word balloons. None of what he heard was the music he was listening for; none of what he saw that he remembered was anything but a trapdoor for him. An old store sign, a familiar archway, the perennial sound of a bus stopping at a certain corner, the smell of beer in the wind, sometimes even a long-forgotten face now many years older: these were all trapdoors, opening beneath him and sliding him down a chute to 1934, 1935. *I should have been more careful about time and dates.* Crossing an old bridge, he would feel the falling black rush and find himself standing where he had stood thirty years before, Louis Armstrong and Earl Hines playing "West End Blues," and a dead blonde lying at his feet.

~

He went back to the station. He asked for a train west. They gave him a schedule for Rockford. They gave him a schedule for Peoria. Pressed, they found a schedule for St. Louis. I said west, he told them. Finally they gave him a schedule for the West. One train that left at no particular time; one had to wait for it at the station. One train with no signs of destination on the side; one had to know the particular train. On the fifth night he saw it, a white eye roaring out of the dark from somewhere above Lake Michigan. At first it seemed very far away, rising and falling; then suddenly the rhythmic huff of it became an overwhelming howl, barely stopping at all. Just before he jumped on he had this funny light-headed feeling, right at the end.

~

The train flew west. Lake stood in the aisle of his dark empty car watching the passing small towns while the cold air came through an open window. There was a field in a flood of stars; he had known it once. There was a house beyond the field; he had known that once too. The train flew past all of it. For a while he heard the sound of a dog on the ground below; it ran along barking until the train passed a wooden fence by a road and then the dog was left behind. Soon they were at a river; he knew this river. As the train flew past, as he turned to look toward his destination, he parted his lips as if to say something or cry out or simply breathe a little. The train wound its way into the open red mouth of the moon.

≈

He fell asleep in his compartment by the window to the sight of the black river beneath him. When he woke several hours later it was morning, and the river was still there. He decided they had stopped a while on the track during the night; he looked back in the direction they had come and strained to see the banks of the river behind him. He wasn't sure whether he saw them or not. The train hurtled on, a moving tunnel unto itself, the space of the west clearing before it and collapsing behind it. Lake fell asleep again; occasionally he would wake with a start, only to determine the train was still moving and had not yet reached the other side. When he woke again at dusk, he sat up abruptly to stare out the window; the river was still beneath him. He was certain the train had not stopped for any significant period of time. The horizon looked utterly different from the way it had looked that morning, and now Lake was sure the riverbanks behind him were far out of sight. The train seemed to him to be moving fast, though it was difficult to tell since there was nothing but river and sky against which to measure.

≈

He languished in and out of a stupor, overwhelmed not simply by the weeks and months of his journey but by the fifteen years he had lived on the moors disproving everything of his life except for a sound he had heard once long before from the other side of the river he was now crossing. As he dozed he dreamed only of the river and how he would wake to the white banks of the other side. People went west all the time, he reminded himself in his sleep; this is not unusual. It's in the nature of the times to go west. But when he woke the next morning the train was still moving and the white banks of the other side were still not in sight. Lake explained to himself that it was one of the world's major rivers.

≈

Sometimes an islet would appear or something that resembled the early stages of a marsh. By the end of the second day there were more islets; the water was magenta and the clouds were low and rumbling, barely a hundred feet above him and rushing ahead like rapids to the edge of the earth. On one of the islets he spotted a red windmill spinning against the sky, and then on another islet another windmill; within the hour there were waves of them as far as he could see, red windmills slowly spinning against the sky on a thousand islets spotting the water. The clouds rumbled on. We are approaching the other side of the river, Lake told himself with some relief. But within another hour, before darkness fell completely, the islets began diminishing, the windmills began disappearing, until there were only a few left on their outskirts, and then just the river again, as before.

≈

He sat up through the night, dread weaving a cocoon inside him, and collapsed at dawn into exhaustion. When he woke that afternoon the larva of dread had burst forth into full-blown terror. The river was still beneath him and the sky sagging onto him closer than ever. The sun was white in the west; and as he sat watching it, he saw a geyser erupt from its middle, first a small spittle of black, then a trickle in slow runnels up over its face. My God, he said, and raised himself feebly into the window of the train and held himself there, as he had held himself in the window of his college room many years before, thinking of her and contemplating before him the very track on which he was now stranded. He did not consider going to another car of the train to find someone else; he did not want to find that there was no one else. He didn't want to walk on looking for someone until he got all the way to the front of the train, to find no one was even running it. He didn't need to discover this. It was no wonder, he told himself, his mother had disappeared without a trace, standing on these tracks, riding this same train into the dream of America. It was a wonder, he told himself, his father and uncle had ever returned at all, had ever returned to look aghast into the empty fireplace. He was thinking all this and watching the black geyser of the sun when he heard the door of his cabin open behind him.

He whirled around. There, in the door, was a conductor. It was a rather common thing to see a conductor on a train, but Lake stared at him in astonishment. For a moment he closed his eyes, then opened them. The conductor was still there, looking at him questioningly. "You all right, sir?" the conductor said. He had a white mustache and a blue conductor's suit with red cuffs.

Lake closed his eyes again; he opened them again. "Yes," he smiled weakly, "I guess I am all right."

The conductor nodded and stepped back out of the compartment. "We'll be pulling in before dark," he said.

"Yes?"

"Angeloak is the station."

"Angeloak?"

"Before dark," the conductor repeated, and tipped his hat.

❧

I still could not see the end of the river. From both sides of the train I looked for it in vain. But as the sun set fast into the sea, its geyser continued to spew higher and higher,

*black and coiled, branching out beyond the star's outline
until the sky filled with it. Even after the sun was gone the
eruption grew larger and more powerful. Then I saw it
wasn't a geyser at all. Then I saw it wasn't from the sun at
all but out of the river: a colossal oak that spread in all directions against the billowed ceiling of the clouds, the
waves of the water pounding its massive scorched-black and
bleached-white trunk. As we came closer the tree became
more and more huge. Its top was mostly naked in the wind;
on the water below I could see passing leaves, bits of bark.
In the frail pink glow of the sun-stained west there was only
this tree webbing the horizon until the sky seemed a seashell curling to its middle, the roof of it beveled gray; and
there was this roar, the dull sound of the sea they said
when I was a child. . . .*

~

Soon the train began to slow. A blue fog drifted over the
river. By the time the train came to a crawl it had reached the
monstrous tree; the trunk was some forty or fifty yards wide.
Lake could see it from both sides of his car. A tunnel was cut
through the middle and lanterns hung from the archway. The
train reached a complete halt inside the tree; it was no surprise at all to Lake that he was the only passenger to step onto
the station platform. A wet wooden smell was in the air, and
through the trunk roared a gust off the water. The platform
beneath his feet still had a rhythm; he wasn't certain if it was
the sensation of the train in his legs or the tree buffeted by
the constant crash of the waves. A porter came up to him and
asked if he could take Lake's luggage. "I have no luggage,"
Lake told him; the porter nodded and touched the rim of his
hat. He looked at Lake in a way that was a little off-center. In
the light of one of the lanterns Lake could read a carved
wooden sign: ANGELOAK.

Lake stared through the tunnel toward the front of the train. Through the smoke of the engine and the fog off the river he could see the railroad tracks continuing on over the water into the dark until they vanished from sight. "Will we be pulling out again soon?" Lake asked the porter.

"Not for a while, mister," said the porter, still not quite looking at him. "You got time to get a hot meal upstairs if you like."

Lake cleared his throat a little and said, "How far to the other side of the river?"

The porter pursed his lips and after an uncertain moment answered, "Oh, still a ways."

Lake nodded. "It's quite a river."

The porter got a look on his face of almost vicious delight. He began to laugh. "Quite a river indeed," he said. He kept laughing, "That's it, all right, it's quite a river." He continued laughing as he turned from Lake and walked on down the platform.

❧

Lake walked up a series of winding steps to a level constructed above the tracks. In the hollowed core of the oak was a small cantina and inn: a few tables and a bar in a dimly lit wooden cave, with misshapen gaps in the trunk staring out into the night. Hanging on the inside walls were several odd pictures, all of them the same; behind the bar hung a calendar. The inn consisted of half a dozen very small rooms perched on individual tiers in the most formidable of the upper branches; these tiers were reached by four long rope bridges that draped the branches from the trunk. The innkeeper was a friendly fat man with ruddy skin, clear-eyed but looking at Lake the same way as the porter had, as though he was not quite in focus. He asked if Lake wanted a room. Lake said no, that he would be pulling out with the train, but he would like something to eat. He asked the keeper if many people came through and the innkeeper said, Not as many as there used to be. The innkeeper asked Lake where he was headed and Lake said west, and the innkeeper nodded agreeably to this, but he seemed to nod agreeably to everything. Finally Lake said if it was all right he'd just sit over on the edge of the cantina next to one of the open knotholes where he could look out over the river. The innkeeper said this was fine and to let him know if Lake changed his mind about the room. Lake sat over by the window of the tree and for a while studied one of the odd pictures on the wall: it was nothing but a black spot, framed and lit by a nearby lantern. The other pictures on the wall were exactly like this one except for variations in shape and size. Lake decided he would just as soon get on with his journey. He closed his eyes and listened to the seashell roar, which pulsed and expanded around him. Somewhere in his slumber something struck him, and he suddenly jumped to his feet to see that the roar was not that of any seashell but that of the train, which had just pulled out of Angeloak and was slithering off into the fog.

~

I watched in disbelief as the train went off without me; cursing, I went back to the bar and began berating the keeper. I ran down the steps to the platform below and stood there as though it would somehow bring the train back. I simply could not get it through my head that I had missed the train. The porter was still there and I berated him too: it wasn't, after all, as though there had been a throng of passengers. I was the only one, and both the innkeeper and the porter knew I meant to take that train out. The innkeeper assured me I would have a room until the next train came through. I told him I didn't want a room, I wanted to be on that train, and I asked when another

would arrive. He said he didn't know, that the trains didn't
follow a precise schedule and I must have realized that
when I got on. All the more exasperating was the way neither the innkeeper nor the porter would look right at me
when I spoke to them, and finally I got rude and snapped
my fingers in front of the innkeeper's eyes. And then I realized he didn't see me. Then I realized the porter didn't see
me either. Neither of them saw anything.

≈

I was given the room on the highest tier of the oak. There
was no key; the porter directed me to the third bridge and
smiled broadly as I went on my way. I expected to tumble
off the tree into darkness as the railing in my hand ran out.
A lantern hung from the branches; I took it with me. In
fact the bridge did indeed lead to a room, where the night
was warmer and the wind softer than it had been in the
tunnel. Hanging in my room were two more pictures that
didn't show anything. There was a single bed and a basin of
water on a stool. There was a contraption for bringing
water up from the river that hadn't worked in a long time. I
slept restlessly.

I woke early. I looked out my window and just began saying to myself, Oh no, oh no, over and over. I turned a complete circle, going from one window to another, gazing to
the north and the south, the east and the west. There was
nothing out there. I could see for miles and there was nothing at all to see: there wasn't a sign of land, not hill or
beach, and in the west nothing but fog, and nothing on the
water but the long gleaming zipper of the railway tracks.
The clouds weren't more than fifteen feet from the reach of
my hand.

≈

I made my way down the swaying rope bridge to the cantina. The innkeeper brightly bade me good morning but I still wasn't in the mood to be civil. I demanded to know when the next train was coming; he explained I had to be patient. He begged me to have some breakfast. I left the breakfast sitting on the counter and went down to the platform, where I found the porter. I insisted that he tell me when the next train would arrive. "Can't say," he answered. I stepped out onto the tracks; the planks between were wide and solid. I can walk the rest of the way, I was thinking angrily to myself, staring down the tracks into the fog, when the porter on the platform said, "I wouldn't think about walking if I were you. Tracks are strong enough but what if the train comes? Nowhere to jump but in the drink." For someone who couldn't see anything he certainly saw a lot.

The train did not come that week. It did not come the next week or the next. The April page of the calendar behind the bar was torn away; nothing changed. I sat in the window of the oak looking at the fog at the end of the tracks; May came, but the train did not come with it. Exasperated by my exile, I finally asked the innkeeper one day why it was anyone would be living high in a tree. "We could never find," he said, laughing, "the trunk of the sky." I nearly said, Would you have found it even if there was one to find? before I was answered by the soundless silver gaze of his eyes.

∾

One night early in June I woke in my room at the top of the oak to a ringing in my ears. It was high and sharp at the beginning and then trailed off for a long time, like the sound of someone firing a gunshot. The sound didn't stop, as though the shot was always traveling closer and closer.

*All the next day I heard the ringing. It didn't fade but
rather grew, gradually, almost indiscernibly.*

❧

On the next day, with the ringing still in his ears, John Lake
woke to a head full of sixes. It was the first time in a long time
he had thought of numbers at all. He got up and washed his
face, then went down to the cantina. At some point he asked
the innkeeper the date. The innkeeper told him it was the
sixth of June and that the year, at least according to the calendar, was 1968—that is, Lake realized, it was the sixth day of
the sixth month in the sixth year of his sixth decade since his
birth in 1913. It was the first time in a long time, and one of
the few times ever, Lake had noted so exactly the date.

The ringing was now very loud in his head, but it had also
stopped growing; it had stopped growing sometime during
the night. The growing had been so gradual for so long that
he couldn't be certain it had stopped at all, but after some
hours he determined for himself that it was not growing anymore. The only time it grew was when he would walk toward
the gnarled twisted window of the oak and look down the
tracks westward into the fog off the river. That was when it
occurred to him. For a moment he indulged himself in believing it was the whistle of the train, but he knew that wasn't
it; he did not turn there in the cantina to ask if the innkeeper
heard the sound since he had, after all, always heard the
things others did not hear, like the music of fields, like the . . .

And then he knew what it was he now heard. Then he remembered the night he had heard it thirty years before. And
for a moment he was furious with himself, and then he remembered that he had, after all, spent half the lifetime since
he first heard this sound trying in vain to disprove it ever existed. And though he had never disproved it mathematically

and empirically, he realized he had disproved it to his heart: even in passionate pursuit of it, he would not believe it.

He watched down the track westward into the fog off the river and listened as he had listened, paralyzed, on another beach at the end of a train of footsteps. Then he went downstairs.

❧

When he stepped onto the tracks he faltered a moment; as he had done thirty years before, he was compelled to turn and go back the way he had come. But he did not turn. He did not doubt, on the sixth day of the sixth month in the sixth year of his sixth decade, that a dream destroys what is not fulfilled; what was rare was not that he had forgotten this dream, since he was born, after all, in a country that had forgotten the dream of which *it* was born: rare was that, once having forgotten it, he had come to remember it again. Rare was that, once having feared it, he had made himself brave. The porter ran along the platform in agitation. "Don't want to go down there, mister," he cried, "that train may come any time. Could come today. It's long overdue, could come in the hour. It won't slow down when it comes, you know that." Lake walked on down the track. The planks beneath him were sturdy but pliable from the wet air. Some thirty feet down the track he was tempted to turn and look at the huge oak coiling up through the clouds; he could still hear the porter and he thought he heard the innkeeper calling him as well, both of them shouting into the twilight they couldn't see. It was warm out on the tracks. When Lake reached the fog he continued walking, through the vapor and splattered sunlight, the spray and heat on his face. For a while he walked out of fog; the tracks curved gently; then he walked back into it. All the time he walked the ringing, which he now understood was not in his ears but somewhere down the tracks, became louder as he came closer to it. When he had gone three miles down the track he emerged from a swath of fog out over nothing but wide endless blue river, where there was only the track extending on into the clouds ahead and a figure kneeling in the distance before him. The sound suddenly stopped. He kept walking until he reached her.

❧

She hadn't changed so much. Older, of course. No longer the girl who had evaporated among the moors fifteen years earlier but a woman; there was a line or two around her brow, and the lips were not as deep red but a bit weathered in color. Yet her eyes were the same, incandescent and depthless, and her hair was a wilder swarm than ever; it glistened with the mist of the river. There was no telling how long she'd been kneeling here in the sun on the planks of the railway. She watched as he came to her. She did not pull away as he knelt down before her and, his hands shaking, shredded her dress down the middle. The dress fell on the tracks behind her and she fell too. His hands ran down her arms to her wrists, down the sides of her body to her hips, down her legs to her ankles. He hovered over her. Her hair hung across the edge of the tracks and blew in the wind. Above was the drained and livid sky and beyond was the long black rip of the monstrous oak; in her a weary clock still ticked. She shuddered with the bedlam of unsounded chimes. For a while neither of them seemed to breathe. Then she felt him exhale across her thighs and taste the red ribbon of her black curls; a new wetness exploded in her. The hot rail of the tracks ran against her face. His glasses fell from his eyes and bounded across the wood. He tried to bring her into focus, and when she grabbed his shirt and pulled him into her, he took in his hands her hair, splayed across the track behind her so as to fix on her eyes; he some-

how knew he could not look away. He somehow knew that in
the bond formed of their mutual vision he could not be the
one to break it: he sensed the doom of it. And then he
laughed at himself and she, perhaps misunderstanding,
laughed too. The sound of her laugh was foreign to her in the
way she had found foreign all the things in a country of face-
worship, where the visage is not the slave of the dream but
the dream is the slave of the visage. And released into this foreignness that had become her foreignness, joined to the
strangeness that had become her strangeness, she surged beneath him, ravening and abandoned, and pulled him wrath-
fully into her over and over, never severing the look between
them, so as to pull him into her new communion with foreignness: she had decided long before she would not be the
slave of those who aspired to be dreamers and then only
cowered before their dreams. She moaned in his ear. She did
not close her eyes. When he tore the virgin tissues of her she
bit down hard but did not wince. She stared into his face and
dared him to balk at his own vision. And then, for a moment,
he looked *and she wasn't there, brown and naked she was
gone before me, as though she had slipped through the
tracks into the black river far below, even as I felt her in my
hands, even as I felt her legs around me, even as I felt myself in her: I couldn't see her. I think I closed my eyes. No,
that isn't it: it wasn't that I closed my eyes: it was that I
had to turn away for just a moment. For just a moment. It
was too much to see that light; I turned from her just at
the moment I climaxed to see two blue moons the color of
the sky there on the tracks right beyond my reach, and I
was thinking, Now where have I seen these moons before?
and I was squinting to make them out, two blue moons.
And I emptied myself in her; and maybe, for just a moment, I even fell asleep.*

❧

"Lieutenant. Lieutenant?"

❧

And then there's the sound, the sound I followed out onto
these tracks: it's huge, the sound I can't bear to hear or disregard; huge, like the night of the shipwreck and the little
girl on the beach; huge, and close. And I have this funny
memory, of all things to remember; I have this memory of
Melody Lake sobbing in a mortuary. What a thing to
think. What a thing. And I say to myself, A memory, is it
only the dream of the wandering blind? And then it's there,
huge above me, the sound, coming from a light so sharp
and white that at first I think it's the sun until I realize the
sun's on the horizon; and then I think it's the train until I
realize the tracks are absolutely still but for the fading pan-
demonium of our bodies, and then I'm thinking it's her
eyes like the old man of the moors saw them the night of
the lighthouse until I realize the light's in her hand, loud
and white and sharp, in her hand as though to sear her fingers with it, as though to extinguish it: and then almost
faster than I can see it, it comes to me

❧

"There's someone out there."

❧

and it sings to me. It sings

ABOUT THE AUTHOR

Steve Erickson's first novel, *Days Between Stations*, was published in 1985; *Rubicon Beach*, his second, was named by the editors of *The New York Times Book Review* one of 1986's most notable works of fiction. Both books will appear in Europe beginning in 1988. In 1987 Erickson received a literary fellowship grant from the National Endowment for the Arts. He is at present finishing his third novel, *Tours of the Black Clock*.

V I N T A G E
C O N T E M P O R A R I E S

"Today's novels for the readers of today."— VANITY FAIR

"Real literature—originals and important reprints—in attractive, inexpensive paperbacks."— THE LOS ANGELES TIMES

"Prestigious."— THE CHICAGO TRIBUNE

"A very fine collection."— THE CHRISTIAN SCIENCE MONITOR

"Adventurous and worthy."— SATURDAY REVIEW

"If you want to know what's on the cutting edge of American fiction, then these are the books you should be reading."
                                        — UNITED PRESS INTERNATIONAL

On sale at bookstores everywhere, but if otherwise unavailable, may be ordered from us. You can use this coupon, or phone (800) 638-6460.

Please send me the Vintage Contemporaries books I have checked on the reverse. I am enclosing $ _____ (add $1.00 per copy to cover postage and handling). Send check or money order—no cash or CODs, please. Prices are subject to change without notice.

NAME _____

ADDRESS _____

CITY _____ STATE _____ ZIP _____

Send coupons to:
RANDOM HOUSE, INC., 400 Hahn Road, Westminster, MD 21157
ATTN: ORDER ENTRY DEPARTMENT
Allow at least 4 weeks for delivery.

005   38

CONTEMPORARIES

DATE

___ Love Always by Ann Beattie $5.95   74418-7
___ First Love and Other Sorrows by Harold Brodkey   970-6
___ The Debut by Anita Brookner   56-4
___ Cathe   1
___ Bop b
___ Danc
___ One to Count Ca
___ The Wrong Ca
___ The Last Ele
___ A Narrow
___ Days Betw
___ Rubicon Bea
___ A Fan's Notes by
___ A Piece of My Hea
___ The Sportswriter by
___ The Ultimate Good Lu
___ Fat City by Leonard Gardne
___ Within Normal Limits by To
___ Airships by Barry Hannah
___ Dancing in the Dark by Janet Ho
___ November by Janet Hobhouse
___ Fiskadoro by Denis Johnson
___ The Stars at Noon by Denis Johnson
___ Asa, as I Knew Him by Susanna Kaysen
___ A Handbook for Visitors From Outer Space
    by Kathryn Kramer
___ The Chosen Place, the Timeless People
    by Paule Marshall
___ Suttree by Cormac McCarthy
___ The Bushwhacked Piano by Thomas McGuane $
___ Nobody's Angel by Thomas McGuane $6.
___ Something to Be Desired by Thomas McGuane $4.95   5-5
___ To Skin a Cat by Thomas McGuane $5.95   21-9
___ Bright Lights, Big City by Jay McInerney $5.95   72641-3
___ Ransom by Jay McInerney $5.95   74118-8
___ River Dogs by Robert Olmstead $6.95   74684-8
___ Norwood by Charles Portis $5.95   72931-5
___ Clea & Zeus Divorce by Emily Prager $6.95   75591-X
___ A Visit From the Footbinder by Emily Prager $6.95   75592-8
___ Mohawk by Richard Russo $6.95   74409-8
___ Anywhere But Here by Mona Simpson $6.95   75559-6
___ Carnival for the Gods by Gladys Swan $6.95   74330-X
___ Myra Breckinridge and Myron by Gore Vidal $8.95   75444-1
___ The Car Thief by Theodore Weesner $6.95   74097-1
___ Taking Care by Joy Williams $5.95   72912-9